BOXWOOD

BOXWOOD

*(tales from a
Norfolk churchyard)*

Tony Warner

First published 2018
by WES
7 Abinger Way
Norwich
NR4 6NA

ISBN-13: 978-0-9931603-3-2

Typeset in Bembo by
Curran Publishing Services Ltd, Norwich, UK

Manufactured in the UK by Imprint Digital,

PROLOGUE

'Over there!' she said. 'The Roman fort, Venta Icenorum. Imagine Boudicca's men tearing out of there in their chariots to wipe out the invaders. What a magnificent sight it must have been!'

'Don't be so romantic,' grumbled her husband. 'Only the aristocrats would have had chariots. As usual the poor bloody infantry had nothing to ride on but Shanks's pony. Shit and blood everywhere. The smell would have been disgusting. Once the Iceni were all but wiped out by the Romans the Vikings swept up from the coast murdering and pillaging, killing off the rest.'

'Why is your imagination so grim? This is fertile land away from wars and invasions. People will have thrived here for a thousand years. Just look around you.'

They eased round a sweeping bend, met by the visual blast of a vibrant yellow rape field, the flowers fluttering like butterflies in the chill April breeze. He eased the car down the narrow country road, round the tight left hander and over the narrow hump backed bridge built two hundred years before for cowherds and shepherds, now barely wide enough for their elegant tourer. In the meadow stands of left-over flood water annoyed the cows, who lay down on dry hummocks, chewing angrily.

Swans drifted leisurely with the current, last year's young in camouflage brown as if touched by the late spring frosts. Slowly the road climbed from the wide river valley, past acres of meadow land. Mounds of resting sheep dotted the landscape like half-melted collapsed snowmen left over from the winter.

'This is it,' she cried. 'Pull in to the lay-by.' Awkwardly they changed shoes in the car, careful not to muddy their polished town shoes or to drop dirt from their walking boots inside. Folding puffer jackets around them they trudged off across the field, she exclaiming at the cowslips and early bluebells poking through at last; he exclaiming at the rough terrain and clinging clay.

By a shallow pond she halted, studying the map as he caught up, gesturing across the field to a stand of trees. 'There it is. See the top of the tower above the chestnut, strange rows of bricks above the flints.'

'Victorians,' he grumbled. 'Never knew when to leave well alone. Probably added it on to make it look more distinguished. There is some sort of track here. Better than tramping through this lot.'

Arm in arm they picked their way across the field to the gate and a 'Public pathway' sign. The way was blocked by stands of nettles, the gate itself firmly locked. Reluctantly, he forced his way through the vegetation, handing his wife over the gate, taking care to avoid the barbed wire fencing. Only a few metres now, crossing what might at one time have been a road. A sharp rise in the ground announced the church mound.

They scrambled up the path to the churchyard's gate-less entry porch. She stood back as far as she could, parting the low hanging branches of an ancient yew tree. 'Think of the generations of people buried here,' she said. 'All those stories, how they lived and died, fell in love, had children, worked and built a home, just like us.'

'Not at all,' her husband replied. 'They can't have been like us. They lived too long ago. This place must have been remote from anywhere interesting. The world probably passed it by. Look over where the village was, a few faint, ghostly lines of street markings. Besides, the church isn't very old. Victorian, I would say.'

'That's what Reverend Betts, the vicar, told us.' She fumbled in her handbag for her camera phone. 'But he also said the tower was much older than that, thirteenth century, probably. Can't you feel it here, all those centuries backing up behind you? He said there was a village and a church on this site even before the Conquest. It's mentioned in the Domesday Book. See, in the corner of the tower, a dedication stone. Scrape the moss off it. Gently now.'

He bent down gingerly, aggravating the pain in his joints, scraped at the stone with a tobacco stained fingernail. 'Not much to see. A 'W', perhaps. And a date, 1272. Nothing significant about that.'

'Of course there is. That is the year of the two kings, when one died and his son succeeded. We'll look it up when we get home. It may not be significant to you but it must have been a huge event in the lives of the people who lived here.'

'Well, whether it was or not, the local council archaeologists and Historic England don't seem to think so. They want to pull the whole thing down, just leave the tower standing. Not that it will last long up here, exposed to the wind and rain. Nobody except tourists like us ever come here any more. There can't be a congregation. Look around. A farm over there in the distance, Earlsford down the road with its own church. Why would anyone come here?'

'Someone must do. Look over on the south boundary. Two war graves with fresh flowers on them. And a grave next to us, covered in daffodils; 2006, it says on the stone. And there are several diggings around the north side.'

'I'm sorry, that is me. You shouldn't really have gone in there; it is much too dangerous.' She turned to see a thick set man, shod in mud caked wellingtons and wrapped warmly in two layers of frayed pullovers surmounted by a waterproof jacket. 'Henry Gedge, University of East Anglia archaeology department. The diocese has given us permission to dig here in the north part of the graveyard which is closed for burials.'

The husband turned away to wander round under the surrounding trees. His wife insisted on exploring her fascination with historical sites, one he did not share. 'Have you discovered anything interesting, any clues as to who lived here, what they did?'

Gedge shrugged. 'I heard what your husband was saying. In a way he was right, this village was cut off from the mainstream, out in a wild corner of the kingdom. But we have still found plenty to engage us. Finding out about kings and queens is easy. They had vast amounts of quality artefacts which lasted tens or hundreds of years. Ordinary people had almost nothing, little of which has survived. But those few things were essential to their lives. That's the sort of remains we are finding here and over there in the village.

'Look here, a robber trench beneath the foundations of the north wall, which means there must have been another church before, going back over a thousand years, to Anglo-Saxon times perhaps. These pottery fragments in my basket are medieval, a wine bowl for communion. My colleagues have dated some of the human remains to the twelfth century. I know generations of my own ancestors are buried here but their headstones have disappeared, if they ever had any. They are far more engaging to me than kings and queens who lived five days' travel away.'

'Are there many burials?'

'Quite a lot. We try not to disturb them too much. There is an interesting double burial between the north transept and the vestry and another we can't make out under the old yew tree over there. Looked completely ordinary at first sight. Then we dug underneath in case it was part of a plague pit or a later burial on top of an old one, which is quite common. Underneath was a heap of charred bones. My doctoral student has a theory that it is part of a pagan sacrifice. I think he is trying to make a name for himself. At first I thought it was the remains of an animal eaten at one of the festivals. All in all, it's what one would expect from a churchyard in this part of the world. Then we examined the bones more closely; they are definitely human, so he might be right after all.

'Judging by the name, the original site must have been around a copse or a spinney of box; typical of a pre-Christian pagan foundation, Viking, most likely. The inhabitants probably worshipped the spirits hidden in the sacred trees. Imagine them hanging holly boughs on them at mid winter, coloured ribbons in spring to welcome in the new growing season. Sometimes I can almost feel them standing behind me, commenting on what I am doing, telling this young Gedge he's nowhere as good as his forefathers.'

Impressed by his enthusiasm, the wife thanked him and wandered away to arrest her husband before making the short journey to visit Binham Priory and Walsingham Abbey. As he drove sedately along the winding country road she speculated on what living in Boxwood must have been like since those forgotten times when the Danes ruled this land. Had the people really lived exciting lives or was existence 'nasty, brutish and short' as Hobbes had insisted? One day she would search the county archives, see what she could discover.

852

FOUNDATION

'Brother, the mule is weary and so am I. We should stop for the night, pray for guidance.'

'Have strength, brother. The day is not yet done. Look around you, we cannot stop here in this wilderness where we are prey to robbers, devils and miasmas. How far we have yet to go we know not. Have strength, Wulfran, let the saint aid you.'

The pair ploughed on, their monks' habits wet and filthy from trailing through the mud and long grass. Today they had almost left the marshlands and salt lakes of the coastland behind. Ahead the land rose gently, promising easier going for a while before the forests began. Their old black mule, heavily laden with what looked like a four-foot post wrapped in sacking, plodded unwillingly onwards, head bent towards its knees. As the day wore on the biting east wind dropped steadily until now all was almost still.

The trio reached the shelter of the trees, pausing to survey the boggy land they had traversed during the day, sweating from their effort, shivering from the wind. The monk Wulfran unloaded and tethered the mule, hobbling its front legs as an added precaution, while his companion tore small branches from trees to make them a rough shelter, bunching mounds of dried leaves into a makeshift bed. Again they would need to huddle up together in the night to keep one another warm. Brother Edmund wished they could make a fire to warm themselves and keep away the wolves and other beings of the darkness. But a fire would attract men, the wild Norse men who raided and sometimes settled these parts, who would torture and kill them for the sheer joy of murdering monks, even when there was no spoil to be had.

'Edmund, this is the last of our bread. Tomorrow we will go hungry. The mule can browse on the grass, men cannot. Without succour we will be lost, the saint will find no resting place.'

'Brother, you are a man of little faith. Did not the Lord ordain we would find a fisherman at St. Malo who would ferry us across the dangerous waters? Did he not show us the field where this poor beast wandered alone and untended, his owner no doubt stricken down with illness or torn apart by the men of the north? Who are we to question his powers? We must journey onwards until he gives us a sign to stop, a place at which we and the saint can find our resting places. Let us pray, Wulfran, so the Lord can hear that our journey is at His command.'

The pair knelt and prayed together on the damp earth, crossing themselves from right to left in the old Orthodox manner, no longer approved by the Pope who is in Rome and the Emperor who is in the German lands. Their orisons completed they huddled together under their shelter, undisturbed by the hooting of owls and the rustling of foxes and badgers in the undergrowth, both of which caused the mule to twitch and moan in its sleep.

Morning broke calm and cold, a sharp sun smiling from the eastern horizon, a hint of sea in the far distance across the flat, unvarying landscape. Edmund destroyed their camp, leaving as little sign of their occupation as possible. Wulfran tied a cloth pannier to the mule's back, waiting for Edmund to finish before the two of them lifted the heavy sacking burden on top and secured it with more rope. He patted the mule gently before leading it on into the forest. Gloomy it might be but sheltered from the wind which had now veered round to the north, threatening snow and a hard day ahead.

At first going was slow, impeded by fallen branches, blocked by unexpected pools of stagnant water. As the land rolled higher the pools disappeared, the trackless waste now crossed by beaten runs which might be the making of foxes or of people. As the sun reached its zenith the mule increased its pace beyond its habitual dull trudge, forcing its way through a growth of thorny hawthorn to a wide trodden path beyond. The trio turned northwest, away from the coast, onwards towards what they hoped would be a welcoming habitation. Carts had been here before them, the traces of their narrow wheels still filled with rain water. 'We are the first today,' muttered Edmund. 'See, the dung from the horses is hard now from the cold last night. The feast is nearly upon us. These are farmers taking their goods to market. Follow them and we find the town, where we can stay and preach the good word.'

'And rest our weary bodies. Mayhap even eat a bite,' added Wulfran, his eyes searching ahead in the hope of spying a wayside cottage or even a poor inn. Cottages they did spy over the course of the day, tumbledown things of wattle and daub, but they were closed and shuttered, no smoke rising from their roofs. 'They have gone to the town, though they can have little to sell.'

'I see no livestock, brother Edmund. Can be they have deserted the land, given it up as infertile, or have heard rumours the Norsemen are coming and have fled?'

'It is a sign from God, brother, that we should move on. His purpose lies further inland where our destiny awaits us.'

Wulfran was not convinced. His legs hurt, his belly was empty; the mule plodded along slower as the day wore on. The short late winter day dragged to a close with no other humans in sight. Once more he complained to his companion, willing him to stop for the night.

'Have patience, brother. I see a light ahead. Tonight we may sleep under a roof, be it only a hovel or an old barn.'

Edmund's optimism was rewarded. Not just a barn or a cottage but a whole village, grouped around a spinney of box trees, on the branches of which hung shreds of coloured cloth. They approached carefully. In these troubled times not all strangers are welcome, all too often bringing with them death and disease. An old woman stood beneath the box trees, tying a red cloth to its branches, staring at the newcomers inquisitively, as old women will.

'Good woman, what place is this? Is there somewhere we can spend the night?'

'You are monks, sirs? From Frankia by the looks of you. We have little here, sirs. But a poor village, Boxwood is its name, after this stand of box, which has stood here from ancient times. Now is the feast of Eoster; we decorate the trees to placate the spirits, to ask them to give us a good harvest in the coming year. Tomorrow the young people will dance and sing, though there are precious few of them. You may have lodging, in return for a small service. I see you have a mule. I have no animal. I had a donkey, but it died from the cold in the winter. If you will plough my field for me you may have lodging for the night, maybe two, in my humble home.'

Edmund was unhappy. He was a man with a mission. Ploughing a field in return for a leaky roof and a mess of pottage did not accord with his devotion to the saint. For the last month he and Wulfran had carried his image across Brittany, dodging raiding parties, evading thieves and robbers, seeking a safe spot to establish their church under the saint's patronage, to bring half-heathen peoples back to the true faith. Their monastery lay behind them in ruins, the monks dead in their graves or scattered to the winds, blown before the power of the invaders who had brought with them their own gods: Thor, Woden, Freya and minor deities of wood and stream.

This old woman must be one such, seeking to propitiate the god of the woods with her pathetic rags, to dance around the spinney to celebrate the coming of spring. Edmund sighed. The great king Charles had pacified the west, made Frankia and the low countries bastions of Christianity, taken the word of Christ into the forests of Thuringia, fought off the moslem hordes in the south. Nearly two hundred years ago, Bede recorded, the Word had been brought to the island of the Britons, replacing the paganism of the Angles and the Saxons. But the Britons had backslid, forgetting the true word in an effort to curry favour with the Norsemen who ruled in these easternmost parts, their kings paying tribute, the peasants worshipping their gods.

"Your devotion to the cause does you credit, brother Edmund,' said Wulfran as the sun set, 'but we are mere men. We must eat, we must sleep. God has ordained it that men strive for their existence, must herd their cattle, dig their land. No longer do we have the monastery lands to till, we must earn our bread like any other. Only if we are strong and healthy can we survive to bring souls to God. Let us rest here, plough the old crone's fields, plough the fields of any others who ask, in return for food and shelter. When we rest with them to eat our meagre repast let us then make our efforts to bring them to true belief, to found our church upon the rock of our labour.'

'But we are devoted to Christ,' objected Edmund. 'It is our duty to praise him, to spend our time in prayer and devotion, not slaving for some ungrateful peasant.'

'You forget, our Lord himself was a carpenter, his followers fishermen. Like them we must be fishers of men. Even fishermen must eat, must sleep and rest. Let us remain here, cast our nets among these good folk, gather our strength for whatever greater task awaits us; a new monastery, perhaps, even the building of a great cathedral.'

Edmund grunted and turned over on his bed of straw. He was convinced Wulfran was a weakling, seeking only an easy path, his objective a quiet life sowing and reaping among these backward folk, perhaps even fathering children of his own. Goodwife Gudrun has given them food and shelter but man does not live by bread alone, nor does a man attain eternal life solely by faith but also by good works. Wulfran had faith but his spirit and body were weak, ready to give in to the temptations of an easy life. Too often on the journey had he wished to halt, to lie down, even to return to St. Malo and thence to Gandia to seek out the protection of the Frankish king. No, they will stay a few days, plough Gudrun's field, then move on to found their church as guided by the saint, the while preaching the gospel to the people.

Next morning, they awoke to a pale sun, frost on the ground reflecting the light into their eyes. In the woodland birds were beginning to make their nests for the summer. Gudrun eyed them speculatively; a pair of larks or a tasty blackbird would be the first meat she has tasted for several months. Now the spring was here there were enough young nettles and dandelions to combine into a soup with the last of her remaining onions, buried deep within a mound of river sand behind her shack. She could serve it to the monks. They could soak the stale bread in it to line their guts. Spring is a hard time, the heavy work of ploughing and sowing begins but the preserves of meat have been eaten over the winter. The gods will provide. She will pray to the old gods who live in the box trees and in the river, as well as to the new god, nailed to his tree.

Wulfran and Edmund harnessed the unwilling mule to Gudrun's crude wooden plough, struggling to keep it straight in the heavy ground, broken every few yards with sharp flints. These they removed, piling them along the border of her tiny plot of land to deter her neighbour making inroads into her property. By the time the sun was high they had ploughed only half the plot, their sandals caked in mud, their cassocks soaked to above their knees. The mule decided the issue, stopping by a tussock of young grass, which it grazed, refusing to move another step. 'We may finish this tomorrow,' declared Wulfran with unwonted determination. 'Today is a holy day, the celebration of Christ's crucifixion to rescue all our souls from sin. Surely there is a priest even in this backward place. Let us seek him out, confess our sins, celebrate the mass together.'

'We have so few sins to confess there is plenty of time for us to continue with this field.'

'You forget, brother, we spent last night under the same roof as a woman, in spite of our vows. We must do penance, cleanse our souls from the taint.'

Edmund reluctantly agreed. His back ached from bending over the plough, his feet were cold and numb. An afternoon devoted to prayer and penance would see him revived for the following day. Let them find the priest.

'There is no priest,' Gudrun told them. 'The last one was slaughtered by the invaders. Our church is not used, except for funerals, of which lately we have had too many. You are welcome to see it, sirs. It is open, there is no door. After it was broken down by the invaders old Alfred took it for firewood. See, there it is on the mound by the edge of the village. You will find it but a poor place.'

And poor it was, a wooden hut, no better than a barn. As they approached a young couple emerged, holding hands, looking embarrassed as they passed the monks. If no other confirmation were needed the imprint of their bodies was clear on a pile of hay in one corner of the church. Wulfran remembered the smell of fresh hay, the soft body of the girl beneath him, the hot summer sun on his back. That was many years ago, before his parents had hidden him away in the monastery at Fontenelle to avoid the ire of the girl's father. He still missed the girl, her shy smile, the touch of her hand upon his arm. But he must put such thoughts behind him. Life now was one of celibacy and asceticism. Even memory can be a sin and a drag upon his mission.

Edmund refused to be diverted by earthly concerns, consumed as he was by fury at the church's condition. A rough wooden barrier still remained before the east wall, a crude cross painted in red ochre upon the wall behind. Once a table must have stood here, the imprint of four legs clearly visible on the earth floor, the table itself long since appropriated by a peasant for his home or for winter firewood. At one time cows must have sheltered from the elements, eating the hay, leaving their smell and their droppings behind.

'What a sad place,' Edmund sighed. 'No priest to remind the people of their duty, no love of God in the people to keep His house in repair. We have fallen upon fallow ground, brother Wulfran. We can do nothing here. Tomorrow we finish the ploughing, as we have promised the goodwife. On Sunday we will celebrate the day of Christ's resurrection for all here who are willing to hear the news of man's redemption. Then we leave, look for a pulpit from which we can preach, convert the heathen, lead the populace from their false gods.'

Reluctantly Wulfran agreed. He was sick of wandering. Life at Fontenelle had been hard, a régime of prayer and work, following St Columba's instruction to consume nothing they had not grown or gathered for themselves. But life on the road was no life, begging, scrabbling for wild plants and berries. Even this pathetic village and its crumbling church was better than mere subsistence. No matter, Edmund was right, there was work to be done.

That evening the villagers gathered around the box spinney,

linking hands with their children, singing softly as they circled the trees. Those who had them wore shoes, girls had plaited ribbons in their hair, older women wore smocks with odd patches of half completed embroidery. 'A poor showing,' commented Edmund. 'See how few children there are. No-one has a leather jerkin or as much as a feather to wear in his cap. And it is not hymns they sing on this holy day but some ancient meaningless doggerel. Nor do we see a cross. See, an image of the green man tied to the tree. The fools believe he will bring the green harvest in the summer if they praise him now. Then in the winter they will light fires to fight away the evil spirits which beset them in the long dark nights. What a sad place!'

Next day the mule was brought out of his comfortable barn and harnessed once more to the wooden plough. Though the days were getting longer it was well dark by the time he had finished his day's labour, brought to a sudden halt by a huge stone lying at the extreme edge of the field as a marker left by neighbour or previous owner. 'Pray Gudrun does not feed us dandelion leaves again tonight,' groaned Wulfran. 'I am exhausted and cannot face being up all night pissing when I should be asleep, preparing for the day ahead.'

Another frosty dawn. Much remained to be done before the monks could be on their way. Gudrun insisted they should move the marker stone, for the neighbour had used it to steal some of her land. Wulfran argued moving the stone was not part of the bargain. 'We cannot in charity refuse,' Edmund replied. 'It is but the work of a few short minutes.'

They stared at the stone. Not one from this land of clay and flint, a solid nobbled thing, grey and hard. Immovable. Using old branches Edmund and Wulfran dug around its edges to release it from the land's grip. The more they dug, the more was revealed until a five-foot length lay before them, resisting their combined strength. 'Bring the mule,' Edmund instructed. 'We will harness it in; use it to raise the stone from the ground so we can push it over into the next field.'

The mule was duly positioned. The ropes with which they had tied their baggage were wrapped around its forequarters as they scrabbled in the mud, reaching round the stone. 'There is a hole in it here,' cried Wulfran. 'Pass me the rope so I can bind it through. Now pull.' Urged on by Edmund's shouts the mule heaved forward against the dumb weight behind. Slowly the stone rose, aided by Wulfran's wiry arms, until it stood a vertical block. Children and adults gathered round to view the excitement, pointing at the filthy block, now revealed as a Celtic cross, complete with halo.

'Look,' cried Edmund, 'Look, you backsliders. See how the Lord has risen on this, the day of the resurrection! He who has ascended to the heavens stands before you in His glory and His pain! Abandon your pagan ways, bow down before the risen Christ. See how your village has fallen upon hard times since you have turned away from the true religion. Your crops are few, your animals nothing but skin and bone, your children stunted and under fed, you yourselves tired and worn from constant labour. Turn, I say to you again, turn into the ways of the Lord. Bow down before the might of heaven.'

One by one the peasants knelt on the cold ground, still damp from the melted overnight frost, crossed themselves. 'The good saint Wandrene has led us here to rescue you from sin and heresy. Holy Father Wandrene, pray to God for us. Though our faith may be lacking in strength and our dedication to Christ of uncertain vigour, with boldness we raise our voices in thy praise on this day, praying for the grace to emulate the strength of thy virtue, O venerable father.' Leaving Gudrun to mind the mule, Edmund and Wulfran led the villagers over to the church to conduct an impromptu high mass with the last of Gudrun's hard mouldy bread and a flagon of weak beer, as the congregation looked on.

'We cannot move on yet,' observed Wulfran later. 'Should we do so, they will backslide once again with no priest to guard them from the temptations of the devil and no proper church to remind them of the glories of the life everlasting. At least let us put the church in order. When we reach the town we can find a priest to come and shepherd this lost flock.'

'What you say is true, brother Wulfran. Let us set to, clear the hay from the church, sweep away the filth of the years, find wooden nails to convert the old furniture into a strong door to keep out

straying animals and straying young people from the house of God.'
Although his speech was bold, still he doubled Wulfran's motives,
more concerned with another night or two of comfort beneath
Gudrun's roof than in finding a resting place for the saint.

For three days the pair toiled, converting the old wooden barrier
into a door strong enough to keep out all but the most determined
wolf or bear should any still be roaming these parts They mixed red
ochre to re-paint the cross on the east wall, swept out dirt and animal
droppings until the bare earth was solid and welcoming beneath
their sandals. A short hole was dug where the old table had stood
in which the stone cross was set, stones and earth solidly tamped
down around the base to keep it safe and steady. On the fourth day
they rose early, bundling their few belongings onto the mule's back.
'These ropes are well worn,' Wulfran muttered. 'They have been half
rubbed through by the cross when we lifted it. Never mind, they
will suffice. Let us lift the saint together, tie him on stronger then
usual to compensate for the age of the bindings.' So often had the
package been readied for a day's journey both monks and mule had
developed an easy familiarity with the process. Yet today all three felt
the weight heavier than they had ever felt it before.

'We have grown soft with easy living,' said Edmund. 'One should
not rest from one's task or one will become tired and flabby, easy
meat for whispering devils urging us to desist from our journey.
Let us move on with fresh enthusiasm, brother. The Word has been
embedded in this poor place. There are greater holy tasks for us to
conquer. But first we must pray, ask God's blessing upon us for the
coming days.'

Silently they made their way to the church, lightly tethered the
unprotesting mule through the hole in the door which awaited a
proper lock. What a contrast to their arrival! Village women had
swept down the cobwebs from the walls and ceiling, the cross on
the east wall caught the morning light, glowing like fresh blood.
A peasant had made two wicker barriers either side of the stone
cross. Now wiped clear of its mud the intricate carving on its face of
snakes and dragons eating their intertwined tails was clearly visible,
though defaced in places by runes and rough gougings. Edmund led

their prayers, emphasising the pair's meekness, humility and dedication as epitomised by the saint whose followers they were.

Slowly they rose to their feet, turned to what they thought were footsteps behind them. Instead of a person they beheld their mule, his chewed tether dangling from his neck. Furiously Edmund grabbed the beast's halter, trying to drag it from the building. No doubt caught by the lingering smell of hay the mule refused to move. Wulfran urged it from behind to no avail. 'Wait, I will fetch a stick,' he cried, rushing outside. Moments later he reappeared with goodwife Gudrun and several of her friends, raised from their slumbers by yet another burst of excitement which their visitors had initiated. Together they shouted and clapped their hands, stamped their feet in unison. Wulfran thrashed at the mule with a stick he had brought, until it broke.

"I will fetch the wise woman,' muttered Gudrun. 'She will know what to do.'

The wise woman must have been on her way to the disturbance for Gudrun reappeared with her only seconds later. Wise she might be, but also decrepit. Her head was bent towards her knees at an awkward angle, lines stretched across her face like the tracks of the autumn rains, her hands bent and crippled, twitched and fingered a brass charm in the shape of a goat's head. An incongruous circlet of fresh box twigs hung like a necklace on her worn and dirty smock. 'I have a charm which will move any animal,' she whispered in a voice as old as time itself. 'Mule, the gods of the boxwood and the forest will have you on your journey.' She began a piercing shrill chant, holding her charm above her head with one hand as she did so, clutching the box cuttings with the other.

'Cease!' cried Edmund, 'you defile the house of God with your mummery.' To no effect. The wailing continued unabated. The mule pawed at the ground, shrieked as in pain, shook itself as if to throw a devil from its back. At last it moved, turned to face the wise woman. Once more it shrieked, raised its head to stare the woman in the eyes; charged, knocking her to the ground, trampling her as it did so. Neighed in savage tones. Stood over the woman's body, looking down at her. Gudrun moved forward, tugged at the wise woman's clothes. The mule advanced menacingly, stood over its prey like a lion guarding its kill. A woman began keening. Another shouted at the monks, bringers of bad luck and death.

'We should move on,' cried Wulfran. 'They will raise the whole village against us.' He grabbed the mule's halter, dragging it ineffectually. In response the mule rose on its hind legs, shaking itself once more. Its legs hit the ground with a resounding thud, echoed by another as the ropes binding its load parted, sending the wrapped package crashing into the wooden walls of the church. The largest one flew over the low wooden hurdles, fetching up against the newly erected stone cross, bursting open as it did so. Wulfran struggled to keep his hold on the animal. Edmund rushed across to examine the precious package, now almost totally devoid of its wrapping. Carefully he stood it up, revealing the statue of the saint, portrayed as clad from head to foot in bright blue robes, a gold cross engraved into his monk's hood, the image of a church in yellow and ochre carved on his breast resting on his left arm, the other arm crossed to point to it.

'The blessed saint Wandrene the Abbot,' said Wulfran in awed wonder. 'He has come here to rest. This is where he must remain. The monks of our order will abide here, pray before his statue for strength and spiritual fire as they bring the flame of God to this benighted land.' The mule shook itself one more time, ambled out of the church, lay down on the ground and fell asleep.

'We cannot make a decision,' declared Edmund. 'Let us clear the church of these women and this dead devil, then we will pray upon the matter.' Between them the monks dragged the body from the church and buried it in a rough grave by the woods, ignoring pleas from Gudrun and her friends that it be interred in the sacred box grove. Brushing soil from their clothes they returned and prostrated themselves before the stone cross and the image of the saint. 'We pray to thee, Christ our God,' began Edmund, 'to aid us to be faithful to the end. We glorify thee, great father Wandrene, singing in praise of thee and ever seeking to follow thine example, and walking in the way of the Gospel of Truth for the salvation of our souls.' All night they prayed and into the next dawn before they both rose, groggy from their ordeal.

'The Lord has spoken to me,' Edmund announced. 'You will remain here, brother Wulfran, tired and weary as you are from our journey. You will be a father to your small flock. You will raise a shrine to our blessed saint, provide spiritual encouragement as well as bodily shelter to our brothers who will rest here on their pilgrimages. You will build an altar, construct an iconostasis to hold the holy icons which the faithful will bring. I salute you, brother. I leave you with the kiss of peace.' And with that Edmund picked up his bundle and set off into the woods and out of the village, to be seen there no more.

Wulfran looked around him at his new parish. Shivered. Wondered how he would finish the task of restoring and beautifying the church. His glance fell upon the box spinney, covered in the cloth offerings from the peasants. He strode off to borrow an axe for the love of God from wherever one might be found.

1069

POSSESSION

How I hate this miserable country. When it doesn't snow, it rains. The roads are just tracks between ponds; the beer tastes like it has been dredged out of ditches. The people are ugly, uncouth, irreligious and babble away in a barbarous tongue fit only for devils and horses. They do not know their place, invite foreign pagans to help them rebel against their lawful lord and master, burn castles, murder the king's dukes even in their own beds.

To punish them I trudge along this filthy track, leading my weary horse and exhausted men. Many are those who fled the city of York, home of traitors and oath breakers. Three times in the last year and a half has the king returned there to put down a rebellion. Each time the burghers and citizens swore fealty to him, promising to pay their due taxes, giving him gifts of gold and silver; for these strange people value silver over pure gold. The last time we showed them no mercy, burnt their houses to the ground, including their precious minster, all at the orders of William the Bastard, now the bastard king of this bastard country.

Behind me, growling curses under his breath, walks my own bastard son, Robert fitz Auban, fruit of my younger loins. His mother was a wild thing, a dweller of the woods, unconstrained by church or lord. As my son would be now, anxious to rule his own lands, to shrug off my tutelage, sack towns and cities, rape and pillage

19

unconstrainedly. Already he has begun, mistaking suppression for anarchy. In his baggage is hidden a golden cross, studded with jewels, ripped from the high altar of the minster in York. By rights it is the king's property, or the Pope's. He will give it to neither, nor will he devote it to any church. In time it will be broken up, the jewels sold or bestowed upon some doxy for her favours. The gold he will have melted down for the purchase of land in our beloved Normandy or a wife of royal blood.

For the moment he sweats and stinks like the rest of us. Perhaps shivers, too. We know the enemy is near. They have broken down the bridges and patrol the other bank of the river, determined to deny us crossing. Any ford will be guarded, the river rushing by to wash us away, the enemy on the far bank fully armed and armoured as we struggle across, weighed down by our equipment. My Robert will not shrink, he will be there in the vanguard, glory even more precious to him than land or gold. Should he survive King William will reward him royally.

Once more the rains come on bringing the twilight early. Our scouts are returning two by two with news of river, routes and settlements. There is a ford ahead, they say, but with an English encampment nearby. To attempt a crossing now would be suicide. After three years of constant war and suppression we do not have the men to lose. Robert is furious at this, calling the scouts cowards, shouting that pusillanimous leaders are losing us the kingdom, leaving the north to Swein Estrithson of Denmark, to Malcolm and his wild Scots.

I lead Robert aside to a quiet glade, out of earshot of the men. 'You are no longer some mewling, puking child but a grown man, a leader of soldiers. You utter treason against your elders and betters, you accuse your soldiers who have seen much and bourn much of incompetence and treason. One will lead you to the block, the other will see you deserted and alone. Speak your mind only in counsel, and then with moderation. If you do not have anything to say which will further the cause, keep your mouth shut. When you do speak, keep your voice low for your enemies may be listening. Think first. Plan. Test your ideas against those with more experience than yourself. In such a way you will learn and grow strong. Now, what have you to say.'

'Father, I have spoken out of turn, in anger and in frustration. These English lead us a merry chase. They will neither fight nor run. We advance, they disappear. Even the Danes have tucked themselves away on their ships at the river mouth or snuggled up beside the nuns in Ely. Where is the glory? Where is the reward?'

'You forget how much reward is already in your luggage.' Already red with anger, Robert turns an even brighter shade at this sally. 'Now is the time to think, to give me advice, suggest what I may have overlooked in my caution.'

Robert shuffles his feet, turns over leaves on the forest floor, rolls his head from side to side. Since he was a child this rolling of the head has been a sign he was considering his options. Admittedly as a child he usually followed the wrong course. At least it was always the result of contemplation, not some wild instinct inherited from his mother. 'I have a plan,' he says at last. 'It is not without danger but safer than an all out assault across the river, less tiring than yet another long march to find an easier crossing. There are mutterings among the men. Should we wander thus aimlessly for long we will find fewer and fewer soldiers at our backs. Many will leave for the warmth of their hearths and the heat of their wives.'

On this he showed much insight. Even the nobles are demanding to return to more clement climes, from Rouen to Le Mans, where the cows grow fat and there is good wine to be drunk, far from marauding Danes and perfidious English.

'The crossing of the river is not a problem, as long as we have a bridgehead on the other side. How do we secure the bridgehead without showing ourselves to their archers like targets at the butts? Tonight I will take six men, cross the river in silence and secure our landing. We will wear nothing but our hose, blacken our faces and bodies with river mud. Mail would make too much noise; jerkins weigh us down in the river. Each will carry a knife, enough to silence any sentry or unwary man who comes to the river for a piss. Do you lead the rest of our party across at first light, as fast and as quietly as you may. We seven will hold back the English archers as long as we can until your vanguard can relieve us. Pray be fast for there will not be much time.'

I refuse, calling the whole plan crazy and ill thought out, demanding why he wishes to commit suicide in such a manner. Robert remains firm. Our discussion moves onto practicalities, such as using archers to support the crossing and the men on the other bank, which men should make the first crossing, how quickly we can get the whole party across.

Robert chooses his own men. They spend a long while sharpening their knives. As the gibbous moon sets they strip, covering themselves with mud, sliding down the river bank above the ford, allowing the current to carry them to the shallower water. We hear nothing. For all we know they could have been carried away down to the Humber's mouth and the wide German Sea. An hour before dawn we rise, clad ourselves in leather jerkins and bright chain mail, creep one by one to the ford, the archers closing in behind us. The first line of men slips into the water, which comes well above their waists, slowing their progress to a crawl; the second and third line follows. A man falls on the greasy surface, disappearing under the water with a shout. Vaguely we see sentries rush towards us from the enemy camp.

Robert and his men rise like ghosts from the undergrowth, taking them unawares. Several of them fall, their swords wrenched from their hands. 'Faster!' I cry to the men in the water, 'Faster, or we are all doomed!'

Loud shouts now from the camp before us as more pour forth, alerted by the sentries. I see Robert retreating before the press, his companions fighting with knife and captured sword. Our archers pour bolt after bolt into the milling crowd around the bivouacs. The English longbow men have a greater rate of fire but our crossbows are murderous at any distance. Momentarily safe, Robert rests on his sword, turning to watch our vanguard splashing through the shallows and on to shore, rushing to stand behind him. Line after line follows, surging past him into the enemy camp, slashing at men still groggy from their night's sleep. Unnerved by our assault they break and run, pursued by our wilder elements, leaving the rest of us to loot the camp, finish off the English wounded and care for our own.

A day's rest. Now we can turn back towards York, sweep up the last of the English resistance, relieve the defenders in the castle who have been besieged by the citizens of the town backed by Danes and the followers of the old Thanes of Yorkshire. First we will pause at Ripon, allow ourselves the luxury of a soft bed, good food and a roof over our heads.

Ripon is in the middle of a trackless waste, the people grim and unfriendly, unwilling to provide food or shelter. If they will not give, we will take. There are fights in the taverns, curses hurled at us in the streets. The bishop, fat lazy and ugly, only celebrates communion for us at the point of my sword. Mindful of the massacre at Durham last year I commandeer several houses next to one another, sending away the occupants. This is our temporary fortress, sentries posted and doors barred against murderers in the night. All is quiet. Next day the king's messenger arrives from York, entrusted with finding the king's men wherever they may be. He bears news. The king has relieved the garrison in York and is rebuilding the castle which the Danes destroyed earlier in the year. He is furious. Men who have pledged their obedience to him time and time again have once more rebelled, now throwing themselves yet again on his mercy. William shows none. When he returns to Westminster or Rouen they will rise once more against him, joining the men of Yorkshire with Durham and Northumberland. The pretender is still at large, Godwinson's brothers have followers and are not to be trusted. Marauding Danes go where they will, living off the land, taking us from the rear, fomenting mischief.

At the market cross the messenger reads the king's proclamation. 'I command that all crops and herds, chattels and food of every kind should be brought together and burned to ashes with consuming fire so the whole region north of the Humber might be stripped of all means of sustenance.' Such cruelty. So many will die, starved in winter and summer alike. Robert is cock-a-hoop. Now he is free to pillage and destroy as he wishes, venting his frustration on the population he so despises.

He begins with the town of Ripon itself.

I divide my command into five groups. One remains behind as a reserve. The other four take a quarter of the town each. One by one they search the houses, removing any valuables and all food. Soon we are overwhelmed with live pigs and chickens, preserves, barrels of ale. I order all but one of the barrels staved in. The men must have something to drink but there must not be so much that they over-indulge and leave themselves open to attack. Robert has herded all the women in his quarter into one of the houses so he can decide which ones he will have for himself. The rest he turns over to his soldiers for their enjoyment. When finished he fires the house, pushing back any woman who tries to escape into the flames. A small child rushes up, crying for its mother. 'Go join your blasted mother!' Robert shouts, picking up the child by one leg and flinging it onto the flames of the collapsing roof.

I watch aghast. Depriving these people of food and chattels is bad enough, but to burn women and children to death is depraved. My own child to do such things! Every house in the town is burnt to the ground except for the six we occupy. Never have we eaten so well, full of chicken and pork, bread and ale. The few cows are slaughtered and burnt, their bones thrown into the river. Whatever flesh we cannot eat is dumped into the privies and fouled by our own excrement. When we leave the town we burn the last houses behind us, leaving the town a smoking wreck with not a bird, animal or human in sight. We ignore the few fleeting figures we spy in the forests. They will starve to death soon enough without our help.

Methodically we travel from village to village, destroying all before us. Other bands are doing the same, harrying the whole of Yorkshire into a wasteland, broken only by the castles of our Norman lords, now secure in their property, ruling over a supine and starved population. Yorkshire and the English resistance is no more. Our job is over; we may return to Westminster to receive our reward for a job well done.

William the Bastard is no voluptuary. His court is austere, dress is simple. There are no loose women here. Instead there are bishops and abbots, bewailing the fallen state of the English church, a lair of simoniacs and home of carnal incontinence. Even archbishops have wives and children, as well as governing several bishoprics besides their own. There will be a cleansing as Christ cleansed the money changers from the synagogue. First to go will be Aethelmar, the married bishop of East Anglia, as soon as the king can find a suitable replacement. Aethelmar does not know this; he is left in ignorance to enjoy his temporary pomp.

Austere the court may be but it is full of young men fresh from glorious and inglorious deeds in the north, their tempers high, their patience short. To while away the time, they practice their swordplay in the courtyards, ride their horses in the new chases the king has decreed, frequent the drinking houses in the town, spend their money and their seed on the prostitutes the court has attracted and on the willing wenches of the countryside.

Yet the days are long now there is no fighting to be done. For me, it is a relief. I spend my time in attendance upon the king, ordering the building of castles, sending out patrols to put down minor uprisings and civil riots. The king is busy pulling land and wealth to himself. Those who fought against him at Pevensey and Hastings have been deprived of all their land. In his haste the king distributed it wholesale. Now he has little left for minor loyal followers such as me. Like a housewife slicing sausage he cuts off shreds of land to reward those who have destroyed the north. I wait my turn patiently. Robert waits his turn in anger and desperation, as young men will. At night he drinks and gambles with others of his ilk. The abbots and bishops do not approve, regarding it as a symptom of English laxity which is infecting our youth.

Tonight he and his friends sit at a table on one of the balconies inside the great hall. They are rowdier than ever, shouting and banging on the table with their jugs and flagons. Each roll of the dice produces great shouts and thumping of boots upon the boards of the balcony. 'You are too rowdy,' shouts an abbot from below. 'Have some decorum in the king's house. Cease your noise and irreligious ways.'

'For Christ's sake,' shouts Robert in return, 'listen to the old crow who has nothing in his head but prayers. A eunuch and a parasite upon poor soldiers such as us.' His companions shout in agreement, turn back to their dice. Robert winks at them. Surreptitiously he pours a jug of water in the gap between the boards onto the heads of the clerics below. They look around, puzzled. More water follows. At length they realise from whence it has come. As one man they rise, shouting at the company above in their anger, calling for the guards.

It was not only the guards who come, but the king himself. 'Who dares insult holy church insults me,' he cries above the tumult. 'Have these miscreants brought before me on the morrow. I will deal with them as they deserve.'

Threes years ago I stood at the bottom of the hill as Harold Godwinson's army charged down upon us as one man. This year a berserk Viking threw himself at me, battle-axe raised. As we crossed the river to attack Ripon arrows rained above my head. At no time was I more frightened than this morning, staring into the flaming eyes of Duke William of Normandy, king of England, destroyer of the north, conqueror of the English. A man might melt under his gaze. He held out his hand. I knelt before him, kissed the amethyst ring upon his finger. Stigand, the Archbishop of Canterbury stood beside the king's throne, regarding me with disdain.

'Auban,' began the king. 'You have done us much service. We know your greatest desire is to retire to your lands in the Maine, to retire from this life of struggle. Yet we need men like you to keep our kingdom safe. Swein of Denmark still harbours designs upon us, raiding the east coast almost at will, terrifying our people and robbing them of their goods. A lord who cannot protect those who depend upon him is no lord at all. You may not return to Maine or to Normandy for we have too much need of you here.'

'Whatever your majesty requires,' I reply, though with little enthusiasm.

'We see, Auban, you are disappointed. Further, we shall require more service and duty from you in the coming years, as will those who come after me, for the task I assign to you will not be easily fulfilled. I gift to you all of the land between the river Humber and the city of Lincoln, from the sea to the city. In extent nearly a thousand hides of land. You will be a great lord in your own right. For which I will demand knight service. For every hide of land, you will provide one knight, horsed and armed cap-a-pied. In lieu of a knight you are to provide two men at arms or two bowmen, not armoured but well shod and ready to march. You are responsible for collecting the king's taxes and assembling the levies when required. What rents you charge and how they are collected fall upon your head.'

So I am to be a great lord in this barbarous land, where I know not the language nor the customs of my people. Perhaps I may thrive if the Danes leave me alone. My wife may even consent to join me when she learns how high I have risen. And my children, the eldest of whom stands behind me at this moment.

'Robert fitz Auban, we have words for you also. You have been valiant in our service. You have fought well against Danes and English alike. You have been zealous in the harrying of Yorkshire, though my lord archbishop here regards you as having been over-zealous in many of your actions there. For your temporal service to us you will be well rewarded. However, you have repeatedly committed adultery. In this very house you have blasphemed, taking the Lord's name in vain, insulted members of the clergy. These are spiritual crimes which are to be punished under canon law, to be judged before the archbishop himself or his deputy. For the meanwhile those crimes remain in abeyance, to be dealt with by Archbishop Stigand when I have completed my temporal judgement.'

'As of your father, I have need of you on our east coast. While he guards the lands of Lindsey in Lincoln, you will guard our city in Norfolk. We grant to you a gift of land, some four hundred hides in extent to the east of the city of Norwich, which you are directed to protect from marauding Danes and disaffected English rebels. Like your father you will also give me knight service when called upon. To show your appreciation you may donate to our treasury one of those gold chalices you took from the cathedral at Ripon when you sacked the town.'

Robert and I bow our way out of the royal presence, both of

us satisfied with our increase in status though bowed down by our new responsibilities. Archbishop Stigand follows us into an adjoining courtyard. 'His majesty has once more made wise, just and merciful provisions for his followers. The church could not be less merciful than he, as the almighty Judge watches over high and low alike; a just avenger who will punish wrongdoing, as the eternal law makes clear to all men.' Stigand stares straight into Robert's eyes as he proclaims this dominance of divine law over the laws of man. 'Bishop Aethelmar will accompany you to your new feodum, where you will be judged before a canon tribunal. The new abbots of Crowland and Thorney will accompany you, to act as jury before your judgement. I bid you both a good day.' The archbishop made the sign of the cross over our heads, strode pompously away.'

'Horrid old man,' snarls Robert, 'and an Englishman to boot. They say the king will have him replaced, and none too soon. God rot such clerics.'

'Be careful, my son. These clerics will decide your fate. For blasphemy or adultery, you can be sent to the block or imprisoned for ever in London's new fortress. They say the dungeons are below the water line, cold, damp and infested with rats. Those who disappear into them do not live long. It is an unpleasant way to die. Keep on the right side of the bishop and his abbots or you may not live to enjoy your new land wealth.'

In good conditions and on dry roads a man alone may make the journey into the depths of East Anglia in five days. With monks riding on mules and a bishop in his carriage it takes us nearer ten. The coming is as cruel as the arrival. Four hundred hides of land there might be; more than half of it is marsh and breckland, poor soil producing poor crops and poor rents. Here we are in the village of Boxwood, struggling to support its eighty or so inhabitants. They are not starving but have little in the form of moveable wealth. Robert will need to fight hard to squeeze a decent income from these churls.

Bishop Aethelfrith is similarly unimpressed with the village church, a wooden box with ageing thatched roof, not a place he would deign to enter if it were not part of his own diocese. He and the two new abbots enter it as if they expect cow manure to accumulate on their shoes. Robert and I follow them, nearly falling over the monks as we enter. They have prostrated themselves on the earth floor, chanting in unison: 'O father Wandrene, shepherd of souls and glory of Fontenelle; ever pray for us, that emulating thy true piety; we may find salvation.'

'What is this nonsense?' demands Robert of the bishop. 'Surely such demonstrations are excessive?'

'Young man, you need to learn more of your feodum. This is the church of Saint Wandrene; you see before you the statue of the saint who bears in his arms the carving of his abbey at Fontenelle. They say the statue contains many relics of the saint himself and can work wonders, but few come this way in this time of trial and turbulence. As you see, the church is rarely visited. These worthy monks, soon to be abbots of the holy Edward's abbeys, are from the monastery of St. Wandrene in Normandy. No wonder they fall down in ecstasy before the image of their sainted founder.'

Robert merely shrugs. He has little patience for saints or clerics of whatever persuasion, however much my wife and I have tried to instil some Christian values into his young soul.

The bishop has not finished. 'We have an important matter to decide, Robert fitz Auban. You have charges to answer before these good men who will decide your fate alongside me. On our journey we have given much thought to the matter. As for adultery, your incontinence cannot be denied. You are young and unmarried and your actions were those of a soldier high in his wrath. Blasphemy is not so easily dismissed, especially in the king's halls, among many holy men and in the course of drink and gaming. We have decided to exact from you a fine, or rather an indulgence, upon the payment of which you may be forgiven for those egregious sins. In return for you feodum the king has requested you donate a gold chalice you removed from the cathedral in Ripon. I believe you have two more, made of solid silver. For your sins you will donate one to the abbey of Thornham and one to the abbey of Crowland.'

Robert made as if to protest. I slapped him on the back. 'Well done, my son. Such donations to holy causes will weigh heavily upon your soul on the day of judgement. As well as rising high in the king's esteem you are also rising high in the love of the eternal judge.'

'There are a couple of other matters,' continued the bishop. 'Most pressing is the matter of the Penitential Ordinance.'

I bow my head, for it is a matter which weighs heavily upon me. King William has decreed that the killing of men, even of enemies and pagans, is against God's law and must be expiated. For every man I have killed I must do one year's penance or penance one day a week for the rest of my life. There are not enough days in the week or years left in my life to expunge the stain of slaughter. Robert's burning of houses and villages, many with their occupants still inside, has placed him in a similar position, despite his youth. He may not have much patience with clerics but he still wishes to save his eternal soul.

'You are both men of blood,' continues the bishop, 'who must spend the rest of your lives in severe penance. Both church and king regard such a life as impossible unless one were to take the tonsure and retire to a monastery. We may gain many devout monks but the king would lose his best fighting men and the bulwarks of his kingdom. There is a third course which I offer to you in the name of King William and Archbishop Stigand. To wash away the blood guilt, you may build or endow a church. Auban, the bishop of Lincoln will discuss the matter with you when you claim your lands. Robert fitz Auban, since this is the centre of your own land, you will rebuild this church in flint and stone, glorify it with a solid tower from which will hang a bell cast by the master craftsmen of Rouen. The statue of the saint will be mounted in its own alcove, repainted in blue and gold.'

My arm is around Robert's shoulders. I dig my nails firmly into his flesh. 'Great bishop,' he begins. 'I do not know how properly to express my gratitude for your provision of a path to forgiveness in this life and a pathway to eternal bliss hereafter. I can only regret I have no knowledge of building, of the craftsmen involved or the materials. I do not know where to begin and I am wary of wasting my wealth and energy in futile attempts, deceived by evil and cunning men.'

'Do not fear, my son.' The bishop is all unctuous smiles. 'Only the best and most knowledgeable craftsmen are employed by the diocese. My canons will oversee the building of your new church, the digging of flints from the ground, the best stone brought up river from Rouen. You will not have a cathedral, which is, after all, the prerogative of a bishop, but you will have a handsome church of which you may be proud. And it will cost you nothing.'

Robert stares at the bishop disbelievingly. Quite rightly.

'However, a cathedral has need of decoration to the glory of God. To date it has little. They say that York, which boasted a mere minster, once had a jewelled golden cross. My cathedral would welcome such a one if it could be found. Its discovery would expedite the building of both your church and your pathway to heaven.

'Your grace is excessively kind,' I say. 'We will search to discover where one such can be found.' My nails in Robert's shoulder must by now be drawing blood.

'I did say there were two matters,' continues the bishop. A groan escapes Robert's lips. 'I have a ward, the daughter of one who has died in battle She is a girl of some fourteen years, dignified and reserved, serious and modest, affectionate, generous and honest. She is also heir to her father's lands, some ten hides of good grazing land to the south of here, contiguous with your own land. An important man such as yourself has need of a wife, especially one who brings with her a large dowry. She is of good stock and will bring forth many fine sons when allied to a strong and powerful husband.'

For a change it is Robert who responds. 'My lord bishop, you have fulfilled all of my worldly desires as well as my heavenly aspirations. Would you be so gracious as to officiate at the marriage?'

1272

ABSOLUTION

"Marry first, love will come later." For William love was not a problem. He was totally overwhelmed with love for his Eleanor. Of all the women in the world she remained the one he would have chosen for his wife; the most beautiful, most intelligent, most desirable woman he had ever encountered. Other men, especially priests, tell him how inferior women are to men, to be commanded rather than obeyed, good only for bearing children and harrying servants. She had not brought him great wealth, a bare twenty acres, mostly forest land and scrub, fit only for running pigs or cutting for the boat builders. But still he loved her, lusted after her like no other.

Boat builders there are aplenty here on the Suffolk coast in this major port. Dunwich, one of the Cinque ports, defends the land of the new Plantagenet kings from the predations of the French. William's father told him of how the old king, John Lackland, had been overthrown by the French king, who entered London to the acclaim of the barons. King Henry will have none of that. William and his ilk will defend the ports to their last gasp or they will find themselves minus a head on Tower green. Eleanor's father was a builder of boats, rich in money but poor in land. William's father was accounted a noble for his large landholding which brought in but little income despite its size. Eleanor's wealth and William's status made an ideal combination, the two fathers decided. Their offspring would have titles and sufficient money to support their status, even should William remain merely the governor of Dunwich, never attaining the wardenship of all five Cinque ports. Even in this minor post he is a rich man, receiving the princely sum of a hundred pounds every year from the king.

Betrothed at twelve, married at fifteen, they had been the town's golden couple, never seen apart, even on official occasions, their eventual wedding the sensation of the year. Eleanor dressed in the latest fashions. William never tired of showing off his elegant wife to the local populace. In her turn she was loved and admired: a devout woman who gave freely to the church for the support of local fisher families deprived of the head of the household by the cruel sea. At the assize she pleaded the cause of orphans and beggars forced into theft and prostitution by their poverty and destitution. Yet she was fierce on heretics, those who did not pay their duty to God or ate meat on Fridays and holy days of obligation.

To all appearances a happy marriage, unlike many among both high and low alike. How Eleanor burned to be rid of it as strongly as William burned with lust for her, the love of his life. But who could love this shrunken gnome, a barely literate provincial who spoke English instead of French, who parroted the Latin of the mass with no understanding, crude in his manners, inelegant in his dress, cruel in his treatment of servants and workmen? As a girl she had spent her time at her father's boatyard, admiring the certainty of the men as they sawed and hammered, drove in wooden pegs, shaved down masts and planking. In time she became their mascot, a good luck charm. They swore there were fewer accidents when she was around, that the work went faster. Their skill and their spare muscled bodies fascinated her. She fantasised about becoming the wife of this or that young workman long before she had any appreciation of the physical and erotic attractions of the married state, for which she had no taste or inclination.

Dunwich had no market square. The best houses looked out onto the quayside where the ships lay in wait for the mackerel to migrate or for the French to invade. Every day William left the house early to inspect the channel, ordering the labourers to clear any silt brought down by the river, checking that the neighbouring cliffs had not been further eroded by wind or storm to threaten the town itself. He faced a continuous battle but not one which would be lost until long after his death, his house and all four town churches drowned beneath the waters. Eleanor organised her servants to strew fresh rushes on the floor, wash clothes, gut fish for the evening meal before putting on her finery in anticipation of her husband's return. For he may come with the mayor, the skipper of one of the king's ships or a member of the clergy making the week long voyage to London from Hull or delayed by contrary winds en route to the Low Countries. Dinner was a formal meal, even when the couple were alone, an opportunity to show off silver tableware before visitors and servants alike, to impress all around with their status and importance.

As usual after the meal Eleanor left matters to her steward, following her maid to her room behind a real wax candle. Already the maid had turned down the bed. Now she unfastened her mistress's gown, took the pins from her hair, which she brushed first then attacked with the thin comb to remove any nits or lice which may have found their way across from some less fastidious person. The while Eleanor stared at the empty cradle in the corner of the room. The child had caused her much pain, from early one morning until late into the next. And had not survived the next. Just enough time for her to love it, to miss its pathetic wailing cry, its clutching hands at her breast. 'There will be others,' said her maid, catching her gaze. Eleanor bent her head, ushered the girl from her room.

She shook her hair, luxuriating in its ghostly warmth upon her shoulders. She would miss it. The shutters were still slightly open; she pulled them tight closed to keep out the cold night air and the sirens who haunted the shore at night to lure unsuspecting sailors to their doom. One day, William had declared, they will have enough money to fit real glass in the windows to keep them warm and snug in the winter. She locked her door and retired to bed, waiting for the nightly rattle at the handle which would announce William's demand to be admitted. Once he had gone she would be able to relax and sleep until dawn when she could begin her domestic tasks once again.

Nowadays William was a bear at breakfast time. He attacked his porridge with ferocity, swallowed his mug of small ale almost at a gulp, drummed his fingers on the table. 'Wife,' he proclaimed, 'once again your door is locked against me. Am I not a husband to you? Does not the church teach that a woman should do her duty by her husband, that it is the first aim of the marriage state to produce good Christian children for God's greater glory?'

'Husband. No wife in all of Dunwich is as devout or knowledgeable of holy writ as I. Holy church does not permit us to have carnal relations, for I am not yet churched after the birth. I am unclean. Today is my fortieth day, when I shall be blessed and anointed again, made pure like the holy Virgin Mary, purged before the altar. From today we may sit together in the same pew in the church and take communion together.'

'And our full life together will be resumed,' continued William. 'I have need of sons to follow after me and continue my name, to care for me in my old age. We are yet young; there will be many children to follow.'

'Husband, I have much to do this morning. All have been invited to celebrate the ceremony. There is food to be cooked, wine and ale to be purchased. You will excuse me to go about my duties.' She left hurriedly, leaving William to pour another flagon of ale for himself. He missed his wife, her soft body, her yielding lips, her beautiful face close to his. For six months he had been denied her bed once she had discovered she was with child. The forty days before her churching had felt like an eternity. The priest said celibacy during this time was not required by canon law but the old women of the town declared it was demanded by custom and to give the woman time to heal. After today's ceremony she would no longer lock her door to him and he would no longer need to drown his lust in flagons of strong ale.

The ceremony itself was mercifully short. A quick blessing, followed by the administration of the sacrament, William following and providing responses by rote, though he understood none of the ponderous Latin. He had fortified himself for the ordeal with much of the strong ale Eleanor had ordered in for the celebration afterwards and was longing to relieve himself. By contrast Eleanor listened attentively, feeling the word of God flow into her alongside the blood and body of Christ. With it came the trembling she had felt so often before at the altar, this time as an avalanche, a determination of her vocation. She blessed herself once, twice, three times before turning away to kneel in her pew, praying for guidance.

William waited patiently, helped her rise to her feet. 'We are once more man and wife,' he whispered in her ear. 'I look forward eagerly to visiting your bed once again.'

'My dear husband, you have always treated me well. I have nothing to complain of in you but I am determined henceforth to live a life of chastity, to devote myself to God.'

'Woman, we are man and wife. A state of perpetual chastity can never be. You are mine to honour and to obey. We will beget many children and live together until our old age, God willing.' His rising voice attracted both congregation and priest to the pew, shocked the couple should be arguing over such matters on holy ground.

Eleanor was adamant. 'If you will not consent to us living together as brother and sister I will plead before the archbishop to annul our marriage and allow me to enter a convent as a bride of Christ.'

'A bigamous marriage indeed!' cried William. The onlookers gasped in shock at his blasphemy, turning to the priest for guidance.

'My son.' The old man stepped forward, arms outstretched, 'you forget yourself. Your wife is a pious woman. The discomfort of childbirth and the pain of the child's death has disturbed her mind. Let her be, allow her time so she may arrange her thoughts, to decide she can both honour the Lord above and her lord on earth. Time will bring her to you once again.'

'I have no more time. I have been banished for nigh on a year. Do I not deserve reward for my forbearance? I shall have her. This very night, whatever she may say.'

Eleanor pushed her way out of the pew, aiming for the safety of the priest and the gathering of her friends. William staggered after her, grabbed her by a sleeve, pulling her towards him. She tried to shrug him off, held on to the back of the pew to keep her balance.

Infuriated, William reached out once more, tangling his fingers in her veil, pulling the pins from her hair as he did so and losing his footing, saved from falling only by the bench. 'Leave me off!' Eleanor screamed, now white with fury.

William persisted, twisted his hands in her hair, swung her head from side to side.

'Villain, let me go. Christ save me. Christ help me.'

The priest rushed forward. Too late. William's fist smashed into Eleanor's mouth; she felt her teeth rattling in her head. Still holding her hair, he hit her again and again until she slumped unconscious, pivoting on her captured hair, crashing her forehead into the corner of the pew so hard splinters flew from the aged wood. She hung in mid-air, held aloft by her hair grasped in William's hand. He stood staring at her body as if he had only now seen it for the first time. Gazed at the priest as he untangled Eleanor's hair. Laid her gently on the ground.

'She is dead,' the priest whispered. 'You have murdered her.'

The congregation surged forward as one, shouting threats and waving fists. 'To the gallows,' shouted one man, a hefty boat builder. Others took up the cry. William stood with a puzzled look on his face. He looked down once more at his wife's blood-stained head, shuddered, screamed, finally came to himself, moved faster than he had ever done in his life before. With one leap he vaulted over the front of the pew, raced towards the altar. Before anyone could stop him, another leap took him over the communion rail to the very altar itself. He wrapped his hands around the gold cross like a drowning man clinging to floating wreckage.

'Sanctuary! I claim sanctuary!' he cried. 'Before God and the king, I claim sanctuary.'

The crowd advanced, led by the hefty boatbuilder, intent on tearing William from his life raft; ready to rend life from him, with their bare hands if necessary.

'Hold off!' The priest thrust himself forward to stand on the altar steps. 'You may not touch a man who has claimed sanctuary. For such a crime you would be excommunicate, you would die without absolution, descend into hell for all eternity. Go to your homes.

Tomorrow we will bury this unfortunate woman. Her murderer will remain here until the Bishop comes. He will decide his fate before man and God. Go home and pray for this poor woman's soul and for your own.'

The church emptied. The priest locked the door, leaving William to an uncomfortable night lying drenched in tears beside the body of his dead wife. Next day men arrived to fetch her for burial. Servants brought William bread and water but neither meat nor ale. For four days he lingered, slept upon the cold flags of the church floor, waited for the Bishop and his judgement.

Bishop Stephen was known to be severe but fair. He listened to the accounts of priest and congregation; sat patiently as William professed his utter love and devotion for his wife and explained how she had deserted him, left his bed for almost a year and refused to return to it. He had hit her in anger. 'A man may beat his wife,' argued William, 'as long as he does not use a stick thicker than his thumb.'

'But not his fists,' continued the Bishop, 'and not upon holy ground. You were in drink?'

'Yes my Lord Bishop, I confess I was. It was meant to be a day of celebration.'

'You are known to be often in drink, which itself is no excuse. You have killed your wife, and in a church. These good people have testified that there was no premeditation. You struck her in anger but it was the fall which killed her. I cannot forgive you, nor may I offer you absolution until you have expiated your crime. Should you have done this in your home the king's law would have you swinging from the gallows this very minute, the crows pecking out your eyes, the worms and maggots devouring your flesh. In this place you are subject to canon law. Since you have committed a crime of the flesh, not one of heresy or blasphemy, I may not order your death. But you must be severely punished as far as the Church allows.'

'You can not remain here, although you may return to the town once you have done penance. Tomorrow you will set out on your journey to the shrine of Our Lady in Walsingham. You will walk clad only in a penitent's gown, begging your food as you go. To eat you shall have only bread: neither meat nor fowl. To drink, only water. On your return journey Our Lady will direct you to an act of great penitence and restitution. Only when you have undertaken your penance may you return to this town, cast off your penitent's sheet and receive absolution for your great sin. Spend the night in prayer. Ask Our Lady to have mercy upon you.'

The Bishop swept out of the door accompanied by the parish priest, who locked the door behind him. William puzzled at the words, trying to conceive what act of penitence it was in him to perform. The sixty mile walk on rough roads was not an enticing prospect, though far better than swinging in the sea breeze on the town gallows.

By the end of the week he was weary and sore, his belly crying out for more than the odd crust of dry bread, his feet broken and blistered. The closer he came to Walsingham and its famous shrine the more pilgrims he met upon the way. Few were willing to admit to the gestation of their journey or to the length of their penitence. At the edge of the village, hard by the abbey wall, where the sellers of indulgences had their stalls, William sank to his knees on the earth and stones of the road. Painfully he hobbled the few hundred yards to the shrine itself, telling his beads as he did so. A monk demanded a groat for entrance to the shrine, which he willingly paid, though it was the only one in his purse, kept for exactly this purpose. Once inside he prostrated himself before the altar, praying aloud for the Virgin to forgive his sins, for her to manifest to him the great penance he was to undertake.

As night closed in at the end of the day another monk ushered all of the pilgrims from the premises. They were surrounded by the sellers of relics and medals by which to attest to their attendance at the holy site. With no money in his purse William was of no interest to the hucksters, who left him to continue upon his painful way, once more upon his knees, to the edge of the abbey precincts. He lay the night beneath a hedge; even the monks would demand payment for a night's lodging. Still no call had come to his soul. How could he return without expiating his crime?

Returning was far harder than the journey from Dunwich. Then he had been fresh and well fed. Now he was tired, half starved and devoid of hope. Our Lady had not appeared to him. He was a sinner cast out for ever from church and man. Besides, he lost his way, taking the wrong turn on some trackless heath, forced to detour around a large and dirty town, where he would have been arrested and scourged as a homeless beggar.

Asking his way of a stranger, he was directed to the coast road, much frequented by carts and horses bringing in fish and taking out cloth for the merchants in the low countries. Half the way home and still no sign. He must rest before tiredness and despondency overwhelmed him. Around a long winding bend, upon his left hand a village came into view, low lying thatched houses huddling close to the ground. Populous it seemed, perhaps as many as a hundred souls, but poor and mean, its church badly in need of repair, thatch missing, stones crumbling from its tower, mortar flaking from between its flint work. William paused before the church, surveyed it with distaste. 'You have come for the festival?' enquired a peasant, trudging homewards with hoe and pick over his shoulder. 'I am Julian of this parish. On the eve of a happy day it is a holy thing to give our hospitality to the wandering pilgrim. Come.'

William slept well that night. The air was warm and he had a thin blanket to take off the chill of the dawn air. 'We take no food nor drink,' announced Julian as they both rose, long after the sun had risen,' for we must fast before communion. Then we may feast and be merry.'

'What day is it?' asked William. 'I have lost time in my wanderings.

'Today is the twenty-second of July, a day upon which we do no work either for ourselves or for our lord.'

"The feast of the blessed saint, Mary Magdalene. I had forgotten. But why do you celebrate her. Is your church dedicated to the Magdalene?'

'No, sir. Today is also the day of the blessed Saint Wandrene, whose image adorns our humble church. Saint Wandrene was a great lord who helped the poor and the needy, assisted a carter stuck in the mud even though he spoiled his clothes, appearing before the mighty king splattered with dirt until the angel of the Lord cleansed him miraculously. He gave up his wealth and his finery to serve God and protect the humble ones such as us. Which is why we revere him so, a poor man's saint.'

William remained unconvinced. 'He does not appear to have done much for your village, goodman Julian. There are few cattle, no houses of note and your church is badly in need of repair.'

'Alas, sir, the depredations of the mighty in the land are worse than those of the men from the north who our grandsires told of. King Henry taxes us heavily to pay for his French wars. Our tithes are collected by the Bishop for the good of the whole diocese but much of it is spent on new copes and vestments for the clergy and repairs to his cathedral. None of it has been spent on our poor church in many a year. We live in hope and expectation. God will provide.'

Unconvinced, William wrapped his blanket round his shoulders before taking a stool outside to gather more warmth from sitting in the morning sun. The village was already awake, smoke from fires rising from the thatched roofs, women returning from the fields clutching warm jugs from the morning milking, youngsters running about chasing one another, scolded by their elders for making such a din on the saint's day. Towards mid morning a ragged priest appeared at the church door, clapping together two flat slabs of wood like a small boy trying to scare the crows from a newly sowed field.

'The call to mass,' Julian announced. 'We have a bell, but the old tower is not strong enough to bear its weight. We make do with what we have.'

Silently the peasants filed into the church, standing in family groups in the bare interior. No reredos or pews in this pathetic crumbling pile, long neglected. All that remained was a wooden cross upon the altar, another in red ochre painted above on the east wall. Beside it stood a statue of a figure in the blue robes of a monk, holding a carving of a church beneath his left arm. The congregation parted as Julian led William to the front, where he knelt, head down, in his penitent's robe. The priest offered him his blessing, which William refused. 'I have not yet expiated my crime, though I am truly repentant of it. I may not be blessed or receive the host until I have done what is required of me.'

The priest bowed his head, then lifted it again to the congregation. 'Today is a holy day of celebration, twice over, for on it we celebrate the life of the holy abbot Saint Wandrene and Saint Mary Magdalene, companion of Christ, spiritual sister of the Virgin herself. Man's laws teach us a woman is inferior to a man, that a wife must obey her husband in all things. Mary Magdalene and the Virgin Mary remind us that in woman the spirit dwells, the goodness and truth shows us a higher life, an image of the life eternal. Where a man may lead in temporal matters his wife's goodness will show him the path to paradise. To the women of this parish I say, lead your men forward in their lives. Show them yourselves as examples of virtue, fidelity and piety. Be true helpmeets to them in your homes and fields, obey them in all temporal matters but support them in their faith, be a staff to them when the stumble, forgive them if they stray, lead them away from idleness and drunkenness.'

'To you men, I say this. Scripture tells us a virtuous woman is a jewel beyond price. For a virtuous woman will save your eternal soul, will lead you into the paths of righteousness. Cherish her as a helpmeet, be kind to her in difficult times. Remember the pain and difficulties of childbirth which may lead her to repine and withdraw her favours. Recall, you and your wife are equals before God. In the final balance your souls will weigh the same should you have been equals in piety and devotion. A man who does not love and respect his wife does not love and respect God. May the blessings of the Saint Mary Magdalene, the love of the Virgin Mary and the life of our Saint Wandrene teach you all to see heavenly treasure as the summit of you both in your strivings in the vale of pain below.'

William now lay stretched upon the floor, his arms to each side. Tears flowed from his eyes for his sin rose like a mist before him. He lifted his face to the altar, to the wooden cross and the painted cross behind it. And to the carved figure in the monk's blue robes, who also had tears streaming from his face, landing on the carved church on his left arm. Priest and congregation sank to their knees. William rose, took two steps to the altar and embraced the statue.

The rebuilding of the church took several months, stone quarried from the remains of the nearby pagan fortress, wood cut from William's land in Dunwich. Come the sixteenth of November, the very day the old king died, the work was complete, roof re-thatched, the bell hung on the newly repaired and strengthened tower. A stone was carved to commemorate William's restoration of the church and tower. By the end of the year he was dead, of disappointment and apathy said the old scolds, leaving a large sum of money for masses to be said in perpetuity for the souls of himself and Eleanor. And the amount of one hundred and sixty silver pennies to the nunnery of the Carmelites as a propitiatory offering to Saint Mary Magdalene.

1349

Pestilence

'Oh help me. Please help me. Will nobody help me?'

The woman writhed on her bed, throwing off the cover, threshing with her feet, riding up her coarse gown above her swollen belly. Tears flowed from her eyes mingling with the sweat in her wet, matted hair.

'She cannot be dying,' thought her husband, 'I saw her and her baby last night in a dream. Both of them were brown as we are on earth, not white as they are in heaven or red as they are in hell. Besides, the lice cling to her yet. All know that lice leave a dead or dying body, seeking for fresh meat to feed upon.'

'Help me,' cried the woman once more. 'I am dying. The pains are too great; I will split myself in half. Help me. Now.'

The husband hesitated, fixed like Balaam's ass between two possible destinations. If her life were to be saved it was to the wise woman he must turn. If she were to die she must not do so unshriven, so the priest must be called. Still irresolute but unable to bear the woman's shrieks for any longer he pushed his way out through the cow skin which served as a door to their hovel. Before him rose the church tower, the symbol of safety in a world of sin, gateway to the blessed life beyond. He will go there first, roust out the lazy priest, force him to attend his duty.

Stumbling in his haste on the rough path the husband kept the tower ever in view, his wife's cries receding behind him. To his dismay the church door was closed and locked as it should be each night, though this was broad day. Groaning, the man hurried round behind the church, heading for the wattle and daub shack behind it. A human voice, hummed tunelessly, from beside a nearby hedge.

Brother Erwin had not shaved for several days, not since celebrating mass the previous Sunday, his tonsure overgrown with wispy white hair, cassock coated in mud and leaves from the hedgerows. He swayed slightly as he edged a bee skep onto a shelf made from rough cut boughs. 'Do not disturb me, child,' he murmured. 'This is a delicate operation. Stand back or you will be stung. This is a wild swarm from out the box grove. I took them this morning before dawn when they were still asleep. Once I have them in place they will live here and multiply and I will have honey for the winter to keep my stomach warm.'

'And mead to keep your head confused,' added the husband to himself, despising the old man's failings.

''We may not tarry,' he cried, 'my wife is like to die and must receive absolution. Your duty and your cloth command you to attend to a human soul. The wild bees may wait; they have neither bodies nor souls.'

With one final push the priest eased the skep onto the shelf, testing both skep and shelf for solidity. 'I come. Return to your wife. I will bring ease and holy water to her. Return to her, be with her in her final moments.' He turned towards his shack, waddling uncertainly, leaving the husband standing. Perhaps he only took a few moments but they were long enough for the husband to lose patience. Instead of returning to his wife he struck off for the outskirts of the village, well past the pond and a sparse patch of communal grazing, almost as far as the woods that covered the mound. Here, they said, lay the bones of kings of old, giants who had fought one another and died, leaving only the puny men of the present days to inherit the land. None from the village gathered sticks from the wood or allowed their livestock to graze within it, for fear of contagion and curses from the bad spirits within.

The wise woman took no notice of the villagers' fears. Her pigs roamed and snuffled around the oaks and ash trees while she gleaned their fallen branches for her fire. Snuggled in the lee of the mound her hovel was no better or worse than those in the village, though warmer and less draughty. Fences of hazel hurdles protected beds of herbs and sweet vegetables: sorrel, beet, parsley, sage, turnips, beans, borage and others few recognised. For she could cure anything, or at least make its symptoms less painful. Poultices for the gout, mouthwashes for the quinsy, salves for an aching back, spells to dispel curses, love potions for the heart sick and desperate.

As this man was desperate. She knew him, had delivered him and his brother both, tended his mother in her last moments. His wife, she remembered, was with child. Spring, a strange time to be delivering, no doubt the product of a roll during the warm summer haymaking instead of the autumn babies conceived in the long, cold dismal nights of a hard winter. 'Your need is plain. Come with me, I must gather some herbs. Camomile, as much as you can find and carry. I have lavender dried from last summer, the smell to keep away the insects that creep and bite all year long. It will sooth your lady from her travails. See, I have dried marigolds also, should she take the fever. Hurry, but do not fret. Without his tools the carpenter cannot work his wood. Without my tools I cannot tend the sick.'

'She is not sick, she is dying.'

'If she is dying, that is God's will. But we must test whether that be God's will or a deceit of the devil. Our herbs will keep the devil at bay, deliver one more soul to fulfil God's purpose here on earth, one more soul to make its way to paradise and eternal life.'

The man shook his head in disbelief. One cannot thwart God's dispositions, however old or wise one might be. Nor can one hurry the old. He tried to run, his arms full of bundles of cut camomile, only to be held back by the crone's grasp. 'Do not crush them, they must keep their goodness. There will be time for haste later.'

Slowly they wended their way through the village, where women made the sign against the evil eye as they passed, spitting on the ground at their feet. 'They revile me now,' spat the old woman 'but when they are ill or their cows run dry they will creep up to me in the dead of night, offer me a hen or a rabbit in return for a magic cure. As long as their neighbours do not know what they have done or who has effected the cure.'

A woman's cries could still be heard from inside their hovel. Words no longer; shrieks of pain, inhuman, like those of a cow or a horse being crudely slaughtered. The husband halted, looked around as if for a hiding place, like a rabbit confronted by fox or stoat. 'Come, goodman Hennidge,' urged the wise woman. 'You must be strong, determined. Without you I cannot help your wife. Give me the herbs. Fetch me a bucket from the well. Clean water, no sand or dirt. Do it now.' She pushed him hard, towards the village well. The pond was nearer but its scummy water was only for the beasts to drink from. Knowing village women did not even use it for washing their few clothes.

The wise woman walked awkwardly to the entrance to the hovel, encumbered by her bundles of camomile and pouches of lavender. She paused, set down her load, crossed herself three times, repeating a Hail Mary between each, the Latin badly mangled in her ignorance, knowing only that the words were an appeal for aid to the mother of Christ.

'Why do you tarry? My wife is dying.' Hennidge staggered under the weight of a leather bucket full to the brim with bright water.

'I do what I can but without the aid of the Virgin all my skills are useless.' She gathered up her bundles once more, pushed her way inside. The priest was warming himself beside the fire, his jar of holy water and bronze crucifix beside the woman's bed. 'You have made yourself comfortable, already, priest. Fires on earth will warm your outside; only the fires of hell will melt away your idle fat. A fat shepherd and a thin flock, they say. We are all poor here while you grow fatter by the year.'

47

'And the Bible says: suffer not a witch to live. One day I will see you burned, not in hell but among the tombstones before the cathedral, you and your idolatrous spells. As for you, Goodman Hennidge, you have done ill to summon that crone to your wife's bedside, to undo the good work that I have performed this day. Your wife has repented of her sins. She could not tell them, the pains from the devils sitting upon her too great, but she was able to nod her head when asked if she repented, and kissed the crucifix when I held it to her lips. You owe me money for this service, but I will not bother you now. You may pay me when you pay for my further orisons at the funeral. I wish you a good day. May God go with you.'

'Fat pig,' spat the wise woman as he left. 'He knows neither men's souls nor men's bodies. Help me now, we have little time. Put water on to boil. As much as you can, we will need it to distil the herbs and to wash the child afterwards. Spread camomile around the bed. Trample upon it. The odour will calm your wife and attract the child to the world outside, instead of tarrying in the womb. Find me a bowl. Wait while I crush these elder leaves. Crushing allows the goodness to flow from them. Elder is what the disciples spread on Christ's wounds. From those wounds the healing of Christ and his miracles spread into the elder tree so its berries ward against noxious fumes and its leaves spread a soft peace wherever they touch. See how the forester is calm as he goes about his business, soothed by the smell and touch of the elder. Now, hot water over the leaves. More, fill up the bowl. Do you have soap?'

'Only from the fat of the pig.'

'That will do. The potion is efficacious on its own but the strength is multiplied with soap, which allows may hands to spread its balm across the afflicted parts.' The old woman washed her hands in the bowl before crossing herself once more, allowing the water from her hands and arms to drip upon the earthen floor.

'We will see to you, mistress,' she assured the writhing figure on the bed. 'You will be delivered safely. Scream as much as you wish, it will do you good to exhale the bad humours shrouding your soul. Goodman, fetch me a knife. Make sure it is sharp.'

'You will not cut her. I will not allow it. If you cut her she will die, even if the child is alive.'

'Fool, do as you are told. I will need a knife to cut the cord. Unless you want to do it with your teeth, like a dog?'

She washed her hands in the elder water once more, crossed herself whilst looking in imprecation towards heaven, parted the woman's legs. 'As I thought, the child is misarranged. Goodman, you should look away.' Gently she forced her hand and arm into the woman's vagina. Here is a shoulder, an arm, a soft part which might be a bottom. Limbs in place but lying awkwardly, refusing to allow the child egress, a refusal which will destroy both mother and child, already weakened by nearly a day of ineffective labour. Manoeuvre the child, push the bottom away, ease shoulders across. Take the head, gently; ease it forwards into the birth canal.

'Push, goodwife, push. Shout. Louder, so the Virgin in heaven can hear you and come to your aid. Push again, and again. Hennidge, the knife. See, I cut the cord, tie it off. Wait. The afterbirth will come. There. Take it now and bury it deep, somewhere the pigs will not find it. Put a rock on top should there be a large one to hand. Then come and boil me some more water. Your wife and child are to be washed.'

Guzzling at the breast the baby protests against being disturbed by rag and water. Goodwife Hennidge does not stir, exhausted by her ordeal and brush with death. 'The priest will not be pleased,' says the old woman. 'He is paid less for a christening than for a funeral. Do you know, he takes half the grave digger's fee? I do not need your money but I am old and feeble. My field needs ploughing. A strong man can plough and sow it within a day. Boil more water, mash camomile leaves and comfrey into it to give to your wife when she wakes. They will sooth her both inside and out. Make sure the water has boiled, for only then will the calmness of the camomile be revealed. Only let her take small ale after a day or two, it excites bile which is bad for nursing mothers.'

The old woman hobbled out, leaving the husband bewildered. He had seen the wise woman making magic spells in his wife's womb, the while muttering charms under her breath. She had drawn forth the child, waving a sharp knife above its head to make it hard, able to fight off the assaults of the world. Now the screaming is done, now the world is calm and his wife and child asleep in one another's arms, his thoughts turn to cleansing them of the magic, turning once more to the ways of the church. He will go immediately to the priest to organise the christening of the babe. Who knows for how long it will live? The sooner it is baptised to rid itself of the sins of Adam and Eve and pave its way to paradise the better.

The small congregation stands, watching their priest as he performs the rites of the mass. Jealously they gaze at him as he partakes of real wheaten bread which is miraculously changed into the body of Christ. From a silver flagon, the gift of some ancient pilgrim, he pours himself a generous portion of red wine, allowing it to flow through the air between flagon and cup, to remind all this is now the blood of Christ, transformed by the mass. All bow their heads in grateful prayer, disturbed only by the crying of a newly born babe. The priest is unhappy to be so disturbed, rushing through the baptismal service in confusion, unnerved by the child's continual crying. 'That is what comes of being delivered by a witch,' he says to a pair of women as they leave. 'The child shrinks before the holy water, the devils already within him. He will grow to be a scourge of the village; you mark my words.'

The women bow their heads respectfully, as is due to God's representative on earth, each dropping a farthing into the bag he holds before him. Neither believe his prediction, knowing Goodman Hennidge and his wife to be upstanding people who would never let their children run riot. Not like some. 'And where are the Daynes boys?' asks one, looking around her. 'There is free food and drink to be had to celebrate the child. It is not like them to be absent when there is beer to be had.'

'They are out upon the road,' declares the other, 'Pointing their arrows at any traveller who dares to stop by the village on his way. We want no strangers bringing the sickness here. Those fleeing from it in London have spread the poison throughout the land. We will have none such in this village. Daynes and his sons will keep us pure and free from harm.'

The other shrugs. 'I have heard that half of London has died, the other half on the road. We do well to pray hard and keep strangers at bay. We want none of them Londoners or odd folk from Ipswich either. My St. Christopher medal will protect me and mine. I will pray to him for my protection this night, as well as to the Virgin.'

There is another who is missing: simple John Black who earns his living as a pot boy in the village tavern. He has been sweating heavily all night, tossing and turning so his wife has had little sleep and has grown fractious with the children. John is in pain; his limbs have begun to ache in every joint. For a short while his wife has left him in order to attend mass and bring back a few of the oat cakes the mother of goodwife Hennidge has baked for the christening. Food is scarce this time of year, little as yet showing above the ground after the winter.

By the time she returns with the children John knows he is dying. 'Fetch the priest,' he whispers, 'I have much to repent before I die.' He thinks of the times he has given short change to customers too drunk to notice the difference, the fumblings with merry women at weddings and harvest time, the number of times he lay with his wife before they were married. Those sins must be washed away before the fires of hell close over him.

The priest is not happy. He has already conducted two services in the day and he has not yet taken his lunch or nibbled at Hennidge's oat cakes which he secreted in his cassock. But death abides for no man's pleasures and absolution is well rewarded on earth as it is in heaven. He makes his way to Black's hovel, meaner and more dirty than the rest, scratching himself in advance from the flea bites he knows he is about to receive.

The dying man moans and coughs. His wife wipes his head with a cloth soaked in vinegar and water. Against the mud wall three children sit, eyes huge in their half starved faces, silenced by the incomprehensible scene before them. Moving from the bed the wife gestures towards her husband, wraps a thin shawl tightly around her shoulders and sagging breasts. Once again the man coughs, deciding the priest there is no point in offering bread or wine. A detailed confession is out of the question. 'Do you truly repent of your sins

51

and ask forgiveness in the name of our Lord Jesus Christ, your saviour?'

Another racking cough. 'I do so repent,' whispers the man. He reaches out, clutches the priest's wrist, drags the crucifix to his lips, kisses it humbly. The priest backs away, gabbling his offices rapidly in Latin, leaving the wife to return to her post at the bedside, her husband visibly much weaker for the effort he has made. She bends forward to wipe his brow once more. He coughs. Huge gouts of blood fly from his mouth, spattering her face, shawl and blouse in black gobbets. She screams, lunges backwards. The man coughs once more. Dies.

She turns towards the priest. "He has killed me; I am covered in his poison. What will become of my children? I am dead.'

'Not so,' says the priest. 'This is the white sickness. I have seen it much before in the city. Like a mouse behind the wall it lurks in secret, doing its worst, eating a man from the inside. Some carry it for years, others for only months. Your husband must have been suffering for some time, afraid to discomfort you. Calm yourself. You have many more years to live, to look after your children and bring them up in godly ways.'

Despite his calm confidence the priest leaves as hurriedly as he can, though not without taking a whole penny as his fee. The wise woman, returning from the copse with boughs of box wood for the coming Easter festival sneers as he passes by. 'Creeping slug, squeezing the last drops from the poor to line his belly. The grave digger will be busy this season. See how he hurries to seek him out. We will have mourning on the morrow.'

For once she is wrong. The grave is dug, awaiting only the body and the mourning widow, neither of which have appeared. She sneaks down behind the hovels, peeking to see what has transpired with the dead man's family. Young Graves, known only by his occupation, stands staring at the cowhide door. A small crowd has gathered. He shouts, urging the widow to come forth. There is no reply. Gingerly he edges forward, pushes aside the hide, peers inside, jerks back. 'What is it?' cries a woman. 'What do you see?'

'Come no closer,' orders Graves. 'They are dead, all five of them, their bodies already putrefying. I must tell the priest.' As he rushes off the spectators coagulate into discrete groups, gossiping and telling their beads. The wise woman shrinks away, she knows this can be no sudden onset of the white sickness. On the walls of the cathedral she has seen the painting of Death mounted on his horse, not at a trot but at a gallop. Soon he will turn the whole village into a graveyard.

Graves arrives leading a scabby horse pulling a small cart. He has wrapped a scarf around his nose and head so that only his eyes show. Crossing himself he enters the cottage, re-emerging with a man's body. A woman's next. Two children, and a third. They are piled promiscuously onto the cart which he leads off back towards the church. Unnerved, the spectators retreat to the safety of their homes, bar their doors against their neighbours and prowling Death.

At the church, Graves finds the door barred against him, the priest nowhere to be seen. He hammers on the solid oak. 'Father!' he cries,' what shall I do with the bodies?'

'Bury them, for Christ's sake. Bury them quick and deep.'

'Will you not say the service for them?'

'No. Let them go. Come not near me. Dig more graves, bury who you can.'

Graves does as he is told, only to be prostrate the next morning, great buboes rising in his groin and armpits. His wife flees in terror, taking to the woods and leaving him and their children behind. All day the children wander through the village, shouting for assistance, for a priest to administer the last rites to their father. Every door is shut against them. They sit sobbing against their cottage wall until the wise woman takes them by the hand and leads them to the shelter of her shack, where she feeds them on a thin pottage.

The Daynes boys do not return. For the next months they live in the woods, shunning all human contact. Fewer and fewer fires rise from the dwellings in the village. Some like the Daynes boys have fled, others are no longer seen, the stink of decay and dissolution rising from their homes. Some call it the stink of hell, for the occupants have died unshriven, the church still firmly locked. From there, too, rises the now familiar smell. At the Hennidge cottage fires burn. A thin wail rises intermittently through the rough walls.

The wise woman, conducting her entourage, grown now to four small children, pauses. She has enough to do, enough mouths to feed, neither money nor time to ease the burden. Well she knows what she will find inside: dirt, blood and death. The child may well carry the disease, which could be conveyed to the brood behind her. But this is a child she has so recently delivered herself after much travail. Could all her work and the pain of the mother be so easily wasted? 'Wait here,' she tells the accompanying children, wraps her shawl across her face, enters as quickly as her ulcerous old legs will allow. The baby lies next to its dead mother, blindly seeking for a breast upon which to suck, oblivious to the mother's immobility and growing stink. The wise woman makes the sign of the cross above the mother before sweeping the child up in her arms and exiting as rapidly as she is able.

By the end of the summer the pestilence has passed. Two monks from the cathedral arrive, breaking open the door of the church and removing the rotting body of the priest, prising a skeletal hand from the statue of the saint. At night the wise woman comes with her tiny brood, strewing sweet smelling herbs throughout the nave. Joyously, the children trample upon them to release their odours, waking the few remaining inhabitants of the village before making their way back to their new home. 'Old witch,' mutter offended sleepers. 'Pity the pestilence did not carry her off as well. The devil looks after his own.' They turn back to their dreams, making the sign against the evil eye once more as they do so.

1485

Recruitment

The sun shone, a light breeze blew across the fields. Children were gay, adults were content, harvests were abundant. This was the longest period of continuous peace in human memory.

Rose was as happy as any. Her new dress, which she had sewn herself, fitted perfectly, hiding the worn condition of her shoes. Mother and father did not fight any more and seemed closer than ever, their nightly grapplings more frequent than Rose could remember. Now over forty, her mother was confident there could be no consequences to the love making she had always enjoyed, none of the ensuing childbirths she had feared.

The children were all loved but eight of them were too many, alongside of the pain of the five interred in the graveyard. Rose held little Dicken's hand as they skirted the field towards the church, lifting her face to the bright warmth of the sun.

'Do we have to stay for the sermon?' Dicken asked. 'The sermon is so boring.'

'You are a big boy now, nearly five. If you listen carefully to the sermon you will learn how to behave when you are grown up.'

'But the priest uses such big words. I don't understand big words. Will his sermon teach me how to look after the lord's cows, sister? Or when to sow the wheat in the spring or reap it in the autumn?'

'That is not all there is to life. You must learn how to behave with other people. How to treat your parents and your lovely big sister. How to deal with the men you work with. Your rights and duties to your wife.'

'I don't have a wife.' Dicken swiped at a stray nettle with a stick he had detached from the hedgerow. 'I'm never going to marry. Not like you. Father says you should have been married long since. Why are you not married?'

'I'm not married because I have not found someone to suit.'

'Father says you will die an old maid.'

'I'm hardly an old maid, at sixteen.'

'Mother says you do not look after yourself properly, always smelling of hay and cow shit.'

'Cow shit smells very sweet when it is fresh. And what does she expect? All morning and all evening I sit in the lord's byre, milking his herd.' The happiest times of her life, she thought. Head hard against a cow's welcoming flank, strong fingers squeezing the teats while the cow panted in relief. She knew them all by name, their quirks and foibles, the ones she had to encourage, those who could turn on her at the least provocation. The milking shed was her personal universe, neither lord nor cowman daring to gainsay her decisions or deny her expertise.

'Father says you do not have a husband because you sleep all day. If you do not sleep you are as grumpy as a cow which has lost its calf.'

'I am grumpy and tired because I have done a day's work before a little lazybones like Dicken has even got out of bed.' Long before dawn she was up and across the fields to milk the cows before they were released at dawn. Even in winter the walk was magical. She was a wild animal like stoat and fox, badger and owl, far from the concerns of man, one with the stars and the wind. Evening found her once again in the byre, fighting the cows made frisky by a day's diet of delicious fresh grass, resentful at being disturbed by calf or milkmaid.

Dicken took another swipe at a cow parsley nearly as tall as him, releasing a couple of angry bees from their breakfast.

'Let us hurry along,' urged Rose. 'At this pace we will be late for the service. Besides, we should get as far from those bees as we can.

You don't want to be stung again.' Dicken had an unfortunate habit of attracting bee and wasp stings, which blew up on his delicate skin like mole hills.

'We are almost there. No need to hurry. You look very pretty in your new dress. Perhaps that will find you a husband. And you have put your hair up nicely. You need some flowers. Wait a minute.'

Before Rose could stop him Dicken had raced ahead into the churchyard, where a rose climbed and rambled around a sturdy Norfolk pine. She watched him go on his chubby legs, always ready to help, always ready for mischief. All her brothers and sisters were adorable but she had to admit Dicken was her favourite, as little as she tried not to show it to the others.

He tramped back, like a knight returning to his lady, presenting her with a nosegay of white roses, their prickly stems wrapped in pulls of grass. 'Sit down, now.'

'I'll get my dress dirty.'

'Bend over, then.' Which she did, smiling as Dicken wove other roses in her hair.

'I'm not sure the priest will approve,' she said when he had finished.

'The lord's ladies wear bonnets in church with pearls and jewels on them. We do not have pearls or jewels but we have the jewels God has given us.'

'Dicken, you are a sly one. You have been listening to the priest's sermons after all!'

Many were the envious eyes in the church. Women's eyes; their men more appreciative of a well-built English rose in her clean new dress and white roses woven in her hair.

'Brazen hussy,' said one.

'Blasphemous heretic,' muttered another.

'Richard's whore,' swore a third; much the most dangerous.

Rose remained oblivious of men and women alike, twirling the nosegay in her hands, thinking how much she loved little Dicken and how she would bring him a pot of warm milk for his breakfast on Monday.

While she dreamed through the sermon and little Dicken slept on her lap others followed their own dreams.

Few had seen Rose drift through the early morning dew on her way to the milking shed, especially on the short white nights. Many a morning had Hal watched her in secret from out of elder grove or curled up next to an unshorn sheep. Since early spring he had spent every night in the fields waiting to aid any pregnant ewe having trouble giving birth. No point trying to sleep at home in the lambing season. Ewes have a magical ability to detect when a man has at last fallen fast asleep, to be aroused for a difficult birth of singleton or twins.

A woman who can rouse herself at four to do a day's work makes a perfect match for a shepherd. Besides, she is handsome and, they say, clever as well as handy. If he were honest with himself, he would forget all else. She is a beauty far beyond the confines of this miserable village, to be loved and courted for that alone. He does not care that she smells of cows; with luck she will not care that he smells of sheep. Their children will be well fed at least!

He has danced with her at the May festival, helped her father in his fields when hard pressed, introduced little Dicken to the new born lambs. What else can a poor man do?

More sophisticated eyes rest upon the back of Rose's neck. Eyes which belong to a pale face, unburned by summer or winter sun, dark beard closely clipped in the pointed fashion of aristocratic society. Abel is not an aristocrat, much as he gives himself airs. He is a mere house servant; but a house servant to a Duke. My Lord of Norfolk is visiting relatives, drumming up support for the embattled king concerned by the possibility of a French invasion before the summer is out. The Duke takes his devotions to the cathedral in the city, as befits his station. Abel and the house servants trail through the dusty lanes to the village church.

Martha nudges Lucy. 'Look at him. There he goes again. Any piece of skirt will do. No care she smells of hay and shit as long as he can nuzzle up under her skirts. Still, we in the household are aware of his little ways.'

'So he goes hunting village girls in the highways and byways,' adds

Lucy. 'The cook gave him such a beating January last for leaving the little pastry cook with child.'

'Quite right. Best pastry cook we ever had. I'm taking care of the new one. He'll not have his way with her while I'm around. Don't know why the Duke puts up with him.'

'The Duke knows nothing about what goes on below stairs. He is more interested in what goes on in the king's council. As long as his meals are well cooked and on time, his jerkin clean and his horses properly exercised, Abel can knock up every female in the household as far as the Duke cares.'

'Do we warn the lass?'

'None of our business. She seems old enough to look after herself. Already has one brat by the looks of it. No shrinking violet; ready to take on any man around for a groat or two, no doubt.'

Left to his own devices Abel might have come to the same conclusion, but like a good servant he has learnt to keep his ears open and his mouth shut. Service with Norfolk demands the above stairs servants be invisible, gliding around palace or grounds like wraiths or bogles, only assuming corporeal form when called upon.

Rose, he knows from the village gossips, is free and unsullied. White roses in her hair bespeak a virgin of whom nothing can be alleged. Only village manners and her reputation allow her to walk to church without a female relative while her parents visit other relatives in Earlsford. Listening to the Duke pontificating at table in his cups, Abel knows to make a thorough reconnaissance before undertaking an attack. Next Sunday will be soon enough.

Consequently, the following week he wears his best jerkin, decorated with white roses to show the Duke's allegiance to the Plantagenet kings, so important as rebellion lurks once again. A nosegay of white roses appears almost by magic on Rose's pew, as it does for the next three Sundays.

Rose knows she is being courted but is not wise enough in the ways of these things to understand by whom. Not by the black-smith's lad, he is far too young. Rob the miller is far too old and has seen two wives in the grave already. Hal the shepherd is the right age but he smells of sheep, which are filthy animals. By all appearances he is strong and healthy, well able to please his wife and capable of earning a good living for her and her children. But he is not handsome, with a face which looks like it has been puddled out of river clay, foot marks still embedded in it. Nor is he forward or sharp witted, much too slow to think of leaving a maid a bunch of white wild roses.

Nor would she put it past Dicken himself to take a lover's part in jest, make her think there was a special someone who desired her. He denied it, of course, but he would, wouldn't he?

'Who would you like it to be?' he asked her on the way to church on the third day. 'What do you want? Looks? Beauty? Fine clothes? A gentleman, perhaps? There is a gentleman who positions himself in the pew so he has a good view of you, whichever way you turn.'

'I hadn't noticed,' declared Rose, turning red.

'You haven't noticed the fine gentleman in the jerkin with the white roses who leaves his own white roses for you every Sunday?'

'Of course not. I have no interest in men, especially fine gentlemen.' Today she looked around her slyly. Seductively, said some. Hal was looking at her, as was the smith's son from time to time. Certainly the fine gentleman had positioned himself with a clear view of her, such that she could not study him without turning her head. Old Gudrun had done her duty, shone the brass candlesticks to a mirror surface in which his face and figure were reflected. Abel found it naïve and touching that the girl felt he was not aware of her watching him.

What can a girl do? Even a country wench is not free enough to approach an admirer without either an introduction or the presence of a female relative. She could linger at the top of the lane, stop to pick flowers in the hedgerow, find fault with her shoes (worn only on a Sunday). The miller was warned off by a raised voice, calling to Dicken to desist from his search for birds' eggs. The smith's son merited only a sharp frown.

'Boxwood is my favourite village in the whole world; it has such a delectable collection of wondrous wild flowers.'

'Particularly white roses, no doubt.'

Hal laughed. Here was a pert one, sharp enough to make the game worth the play. 'I prefer my roses without thorns.'

'Then you had best find another village, Framlingham or Ely, where the Duke may have had all the thorns removed or where his followers may have performed that duty for him. Should you essay to pick roses in Boxwood you may well find your white roses stained Tudor red.'

'Be careful of what you say, girl. Such comments may be construed as treason, if rumours prove true.' He looked around as if seeking for one of the spies King Richard had in every town and hamlet in the realm. 'I am sure any man who plucked the sweetest rose in Boxwood would find himself rosily anointed.'

'Such a lucky man who had that pleasure, would need to change the sheets on his bed on his wedding night. My mother would proudly display the sheets on the washing line next morning. My father would take his club and seek the despoiler should there be no stains. A loving husband would beat his wife thoroughly, throw her over, despatch her to brothel or nunnery.'

'Unless he were the despoiler himself.'

'No sensible woman trusts a man's word until she has the ring on her finger and the priest's words in her ears. 'Men were deceivers ever' goes the song.'

' 'Trust not a kind word or a pretty face', says another. There are as many deceived husbands as deceived wives. Which is why we must get to know one another better; to assure ourselves we are to one another's liking, that we can put our full trust into the other's hands.' His eyes strayed downwards to her breasts.

'My trust is as much as you are likely to have in your hands, sir. I bid you good day.'

'A milkmaid with all the airs of a lady,' mused Abel as Rose strode away. 'This rabbit is not to be caught with one arrow. A snare is required. Or a terrier.'

The conversation had not gone unnoticed. Martha and Lucy nodded wisely at one another. Rob the miller sighed and looked forward to another lonely winter before his fire. Hal made his own plans.

Purely by chance next morning several ewes and their lambs managed to stray into the cow pasture. Hal's dog seemed incapable of rounding them up despite all his shouting and whistling. Seduced by the sight of furry bundles tottering along on their matchstick legs, Rose only noticed the now silent Hal once she was upon him. 'You are lost in thought, mistress.'

'I was thinking what a wondrous morning it be. Another glorious day to ripen the crops. The butter churns are busy, the cheese ripens in the cellars, even your disgusting sheep are content, ruining the grass which ought to lie long for the autumn cutting.'

'Sheep do well to keep down the weeds, follow after the cattle and the mowers, allow the land to rest.'

'Sheep and cows cannot abide in one field; the odour of the sheep is too strong and disturbs the cattle.'

'Only money has no smell, mistress. It has merely the stink of bribery and dishonesty, not of honest labour such as ours.'

'I would fain have the money without the labour. But you are right. No money is honestly gained which is not by the sweat of man's brow. The miller does well, though they say five stone of wheat goes in and a mere stone of flour comes out.'

'We must not believe all the stories gossips tell, mistress, or we would count no man honest. Nor woman either. Many have flowers in their hair who merely wear a lover's favours without granting any favours of their own. They say you be one such.'

'I have no lover, as you well know. If I find nosegays on my pew it is none of my doing or encouragement.'

'Glad am I to hear it, for a hard working shepherd such as I has need of a beautiful and sensible wife whose head cannot be turned by a pretty face and a smart jerkin.'

Rose ground her feet into the soft grass, looked into the distance towards the Phillipot's mansion. 'A man who works indoors for a great lord has much to offer. His smells are only of powders and pomades, his hands are soft and smooth, his manners gentle and polite. Nor is he tied to the land but can go wherever he wist.'

'Pooh!' cried the shepherd. 'He is but a slave. Look at us. I see my lord once a year, at shearing. 'Have we a good harvest, Hal?' he asks.

'Yes, my lord,' I reply. 'Better than last year; the fleece will fetch a good price in Antwerp. For every ten ewes this year we have eight live lambs. Your flocks are increasing.' 'Well done,' says the lord and leaves me alone for another year. I tend my sheep and no man bothers me. I have a patch of land which none can touch, a cottage warm and dry, sufficient for my mother and me and a wife were I so minded.

'What does an indoor servant have? He is no-one, the servant of the lord's servant. Every move is watched. 'Why is there a stain on the lord's shirt?' asks one. 'Clear these dirty plates immediately,' says another. The lord comes to Boxwood; the servant comes with him. Tomorrow he may be in London, or in Yorkshire should the rumours prove true. Tonight he serves at table, tomorrow he empties the lord's night soil. True, he wears a smart jerkin and black hose. They are not his, they are the lord's. He possesses nothing: neither clothes on his back nor roof over his head. When the lord has no use for him he will be turned onto the street with nothing. Dukes are not known for their generosity.'

'Just like a husband. A wife has no house, no land, no clothes of her own. She can be beaten or turned out at a moment's notice, reviled, traduced.'

'Loved, cherished, spoiled, if she chooses the right man.'

'Hardly likely the right man will come along in a smock, holding a crook. As soon whistle for a wife as you whistle for your dog. He'll round one up for you.'

And she flounced off across the pasture, swinging her hips as she went, leaving Hal not one bit dismayed or disappointed. A good wife is like a good dog: needs some spirit before she can be tamed.

'All the men are to parade upon the common,' said Martha to Lucy. 'Phillipon is required to deliver ten archers to the Duke's levy. They must all have stout shoes and a leather jerkin.'

'And be fit enough to pull a bowstring,' added Lucy. 'My lord will be hard pressed to find ten such in Boxwood. Why do they take our men from the land where they do good instead of all them popinjays of the Duke's, prancing around in their finery? Good working men sent off to be butchered, while the lord's servants lounge in luxury and lie with our lasses.'

Rob the miller and John the smith's lad are of the same opinion. John is a mere thirteen but strong for his age, already built up from years pumping the bellows for his father. One look at the muscles of his arms and the Whiffler will whip him into line. 'Where do we go?' he asks the miller. 'Be it to London?'

In his youth Rob had fought for King Edward in the Duke's armies, imbibing vast amounts of military wisdom which he was delighted to deliver to all and sundry, whether they wished it or no. 'Richmond has landed in Wales, from where he hopes to raise the north. King Richard's lands are in York where he will raise his northern armies. Even if he does, Richmond stands between them and the London army so they cannot unite. He will fight one, then the other if he is successful. That way he fights two smaller armies instead of one large one. Much depends upon the speed of his march.'

'And what are we to do?' asks John, not wishing to fight in any army, large or small.

'We do what we always do. Stand about and obey orders. With luck Richmond's army will melt away. The Duke will bring two thousand men, Lord Stanley as many, Northumberland thousands more. Richard of York will have the largest army ever seen in England: ten, maybe twenty thousand men.'

John cannot comprehend such numbers, larger even than the amount of sheep in the whole of Norfolk. 'There will be much slaughter,' he observes.

'Do not fear, lad. When Richmond spies our army before him he will quake at its sheer size. Welshmen are not up for a fight and his French mercenaries will do what they always do, take their money and run. We will stand at the back of the mêlée, wait for it all to be over and boast about it later to our children and grandchildren.'

The Whiffler has a hard task finding ten fit men of the right age in Boxwood. To fulfil his quota, he is reduced to recruiting two old men of forty as well as thirteen year old John. Others are rejected for their crooked legs and bent backs, leaving only five as well as Hal and Rob to be called to the colours.

'Who is to tend the sheep?' asks Hal.

'The harvest is upon us; who is to mill the grain?' demands Rob.

All the answer is a surly summons for them to parade before Lord Phillipon's mansion the day after tomorrow, armed with their longbows. 'Any man who does not appear shall be hung from the gallows, where the crows will peck out his eyes and the wolves and foxes tear his carcass to shreds. Get ye gone. Prepare food for yourselves, enough for a three-day march.'

Already a platoon, the ten repair to the village inn to drown their sorrows and learn from Rob the ways of an army on the march.

Next morning Rose is late returning from the milking. She has been talking to the cook, who has heard crazy stories from a scullery maid in the Duke's household. 'They say the French take milk from sheep, cows not being able to thrive in their upland winters. Once churned they leave the cheese in caves and cellars covered in mouldy bread. Of course it rots and turns green. Though it smells to high heaven they still eat it and it is considered a delicacy.'

Rose does not believe the story. Even the French are not weird enough to eat rotten cheese, though they say the French are so poor and uncivilized they eat anything, like frogs and snails. If Richmond's army is on the march with its thousands of King Charles's French mercenaries, pray they do not come this far.

'You are lost in thought, pretty maid.' Abel once more out upon the fields, now clad in leather gaiters taken from the steward's peg before he can awake, and armed with a well polished longbow, one of a pile stacked ready for the coming campaign.

'I think upon country matters, sir. The milking of animals, the making of cheese and the such.'

'Surely you contemplate the beauties of the morning, how the sun sparkle on the leaves, the birds singing to praise the Lord for giving us one more glorious August morning. Or is it love which so occupies your thoughts? Or fine dresses, or rich food.'

'There is food enough at home, as well as my other dress.'

'Yes, the one you sport so wonderfully of a Sunday. Should you wish, I can show you even finer ones. The Duchess has ordered hers to be cleaned ahead of King Richard's triumphal banquet.'

'Why, is the pretender finally defeated?'

'The outcome is not in doubt. Who can stand against the might of King Richard and the leadership of the Duke of Norfolk? There are special dishes being prepared for tonight to celebrate the Duke's departure. Swans made of sugar, larks stuffed into partridges, into chickens, into geese. Special possets and cheeses such as have never been seen here before.'

'Ones green with mould?'

'Those, too. You may taste them if you wish. For a milkmaid the smell should not be too strong.'

Though offended by the reference to her own lingering odour Rose was anxious to see both the finery of the rich and the disgusting depths to which French cuisine had sunk. 'I will come if you will give me that fine fat coney which swings from your belt.'

'Of course, I have little use for it. All my food is provided for me in my lord's kitchens. Is it not a fine coney? I shot it myself earlier as it ran across the meadow.'

Rose remarked the burn mark across the rabbit's neck where it had strangled itself in some peasant's illegal trap. To bring down a rabbit with a bow as it scampered across an open field she knew to be an impossible feat.

Abel insinuated his arm around her waist as they crossed the pasture, forcing her to move away and place a greater distance between them. 'I have no need of your assistance in crossing a simple field.'

'Nor of mounting this style?'

'Certainly not. Look to your own fine feet. Where cows have grazed is no place for indoor men with fine shoes.'

Abel wiped the edge of his shoe against a tussock of grass. Hardly a 'fine shoe', but sturdy enough and well made; the best he had. He made no further attempt to touch the girl, leading her round behind the mansion to the servants' quarters at the rear. Rose had often visited the kitchens but this brighter abode of seamstresses, maids and house servants was new to her. Instead of pewter bowls and wooden trenchers' prepared cold dishes stood on silver salvers or in decorated bowls waiting to be carried up later in the day to the banqueting hall.

Her eye was immediately drawn to the multitude of cheeses on a round wooden platter: the flat soft cheese she made herself in the spring, the hard cheese built to withstand a long winter, a peculiar white cheese, smelling of wool and at last a cheese threaded through with veins of green, trembling in a thin pool of whey. Delicately she picked out a tiny piece with her thumb nail; tasted it. 'Smells like sheep's urine and tastes of sour turds,' she said, turning from it in loathing. 'How can anybody who isn't starving to death eat such nauseating manure?'

'I can assure you the Duke is not starving. Walk through here and I will show you such richness as you cannot comprehend.'

Rose followed him along a narrow passage worn smooth by generations of servants and seamstresses. 'When her ladyship's gowns have been cleaned they are left here to dry gently. Take a look.' He opened a slatted door to a small chamber, no larger than two yards in each direction, a faint shaft of light penetrating from an opening high on the outside wall.

Her eyes adjusted but slowly to the gloom of the room. Slowly the glories within revealed themselves to her. Rich silks, which must have come overland all the way from China, the finest of Flemish wools, lace from the low countries, thin knitted stockings and delicate leather shoes covered with finely decorated cloth. And the jewels! Even without full light they sparkled and shone: a dark green amethyst circled in gold wire, three crosses formed by strings of pearls on each sleeve, mother of pearl formed into rose petals, a diamond standing in the centre of each.

Gently she stroked the fabrics, running her hands over the jewels and along the fine gold thread. 'You could try one of them on,' suggested Abel, close behind her. 'You and the duchess are a similar size. Let me help you with this.' She felt him bend, begin to lift the hem of her dress. It had reached the level of her thighs before she had time to respond. She span round, pushing vigorously at his hands, backing away into the safety of the silks and lace behind her.

'Down here is very quiet,' he growled, leering at her face. 'None will be here until the robing begins. We are quite alone, my pretty.'

Hal struggled beneath the weight of a dead lamb, impeded by the mother bleating piteously around his legs. Why lambs died suddenly he never understood. Perhaps it was the drying up of the mother's milk or some inborn weakness such as happened with human children. Tempting as it was to hide the death and procure the food for his own table, the risk of discovery was too great. With luck he might escape the noose only to find himself slowly dwindling away in some foul prison, neglected by family and gaolers alike.

Deep in his meditations he was late in spying Rose running like a hare across the adjacent field. Dropping the lamb, he raced across towards her, easily fording the ditch between, now dry in this scorching August. To slow her wild career, he grabbed at the sleeve of her dress, already torn and tattered. Diverted, Rose beat at him with her fists, sobbing and spitting. Hal waited as her fury subsided, pulling her close and stroking her hair like a child awoken from a nightmare.

At last she pulled away, wrapping her torn and disordered dress around her. 'He locked me in a cupboard,' she snarled. 'Tried to have his way with me. I bit him and scratched him so deep he had to let go. Not such a pretty face any more. Then I ran away. Is he chasing me?'

'He dare not. His type operate in the darkness when none are about but devils. You have nothing to fear now, but you must let me escort you to the milking this evening. Though you may not see me, I shall be there like your guardian angel, keeping you safe from harm. Let me wrap my blanket around you, preserve your modesty. Then I have a lamb to deliver to the manor house if the crows and foxes have not already devoured it.'

The sun was already high in the sky when Hal wended his way back to Boxwood from the manor house, contemplating how he might wreak vengeance for the assaulted Rose. By the graveyard he was accosted by Rob the miller, a determined look on his puffy face. 'You are my last hope,' he declared, throwing his arm over Hal's shoulder. 'I am need of a small loan, just until the harvest is gathered. I have an urgent expense which cannot be delayed. You know I am good for the money; my mill is the only one for miles.'

'How much,' demanded Hal. 'Why and what for?'

'Only two silver shillings,' replied the miller with a shrug. 'A mere trifle.'

'A trifle it may be for you, but for me it is all the money I have in the world. Why would a rich man like yourself require such an amount so urgently? Have you been playing at dice?'

'No. You know I never gamble. Do you know Swineson, from over Earlsford way? He has seven children, the eldest a strapping lad of fifteen. How do you keep nine people on a pig man's wage? So, he has need of money and I have need of a substitute. For five shillings the lad will take my place before the Whiffler tomorrow, but I am two shillings short.'

'What if the lad is killed?'

'If he is killed, Swineson has one less mouth to feed and five shillings with which to feed them. If the lad lives, they are still five shillings better off.'

'Brother miller, I like not your plan. However, I have a proposition of my own regarding the terms of the loan. We should discuss this over a mug or two of ale, which you will be kind enough to pay for. While you order yourself comfortably in the ale house I will find the smith's lad, who will himself require a mug or to quench the thirst from the brazier's heat.'

Well refreshed, the three men found themselves comfortable resting places beneath the hedges bordering the manor house and waited for the sun to begin to set and Rose to arrive for the evening milking.

Following direct orders from the Duke himself, the Whiffler arrived bright and early on the field before the Phillipot mansion, armed with a tally stick on which he had scribed the number of foot soldiers he was anticipating delivering to King Richard's growing army. Ten notches were inscribed upon his stick and to his surprise ten there were lounging and lying on the dry grass, longbows at their sides. He could have sworn only one of them yesterday had been a youth, but this other appeared strong enough to draw a bow or wield a pike. A substitute, no doubt, but it was no part of the Whiffler's duty to identify every recruit. All he cared for was that the numbers tallied.

All the men rose as the Whiffler approached, save for one huddled in a shepherd's smock, groaning and whimpering while his three friends looked on in sympathy. 'He was long in drink last night,' explained one of them, a muscled youth clutching his own longbow. 'We had some difficulty persuading him to answer the summons, but we explained it is better to march to war than swing your heels at the end of a rope.'

'It is not true,' cried the recumbent man. 'They have beaten me, captured me. I should not be here. I am one of the Duke's men.'

'You certainly are,' said the Whiffler. 'Move your fat arse before I kick you to your feet. Get in line over there, shepherd. Get moving you lot. You are all the Duke's men now. Shout hurrah!'

A feeble shout as the line moved off, the shepherd prodded forward at the end of a dirk held by the smith's son.

Who reappeared some two weeks later, tired and ragged, with many a tale to tell. Swineson's lad accompanied him, his wounded arm roughly bandaged and strapped across his chest. They were all of the ten, the others lying on Bosworth field alongside the body of the Duke and the ill-treated corpse of the late King Richard.

Rob the miller stood witness for Hal on the day he married Rose a week before harvest festival. Her youngest brother Dicken had woven flowers into her hair, plaiting together the finest nosegay he could find from among the late roses in the hedgerows. Red roses, for white roses were no longer in fashion, even among country folk.

1525

DECORATION

'Yet another brat! You go on dropping them like a sow drops a litter. Six is quite enough. If you continue to produce them at one end, we must dispose of them at the other. Train the girls when they are old enough. They can go into service. The boy Richard, pass him off to the church. Already the priest has taught him his letters and he writes a fair hand for his age. I will arrange matters.'

'But husband, the child is only seven. And he is our only son. Let us wait a while, until Beth is ready to go out. She is a strong child and knows her way around the kitchen.'

'Wife, we cannot wait that long. The boy eats like a man and is help neither to you nor to me. For such as he the church is a fine prospect. His uncle, my brother, is already rising within the clergy. One day he may become a bishop or even a cardinal like Lord Wolsey. With a powerful man to sponsor him and help him rise' Richard will be an asset to our family. Let him go, it will be the making of him.'

And go he did, hanging his head in fear, clutching at his mother's skirts, holding the hand of his mentor, the vicar of All Saints church. Used as he was to the parish church, the city cathedral looked like the very vaults of heaven, the stained glass on the windows reaching up to the imperium. And what colours! A lapis blue he had seen only on the brightest of summer's days, a yellow sharper than the ripe corn, greens like the grasses in the water meadow, a vermillion he had never seen in life before.

For six days he sat in the kitchens, turning spits in fireplaces larger than his father's whole cottage, stealing more scraps of meat to eat in one day than he had eaten in a year at home, receiving in return more buffets and insults than he had heard hurled at the most refractory of beasts. On the seventh day he rested, lounging in the nave of the cathedral as priests intoned their way through the mass and the bishop thundered forth his imprecations against recusants and Lollards who had strayed from the ways of the true church.

'There is our Lord ascending into heaven,' whispered the monk next to him, pointing at the east window. 'See how he grasps his cross with one hand, reaching out to God his father with the other. Lady Mary, his mother, stands to his right, her dress the colour of the sky. And to the left the sainted Lord Phillipon who gave so generously of his wealth that this great cathedral might be built.'

Richard was confused. He knew of Lord Phillipon, aged to his young eyes but surely not old enough to have overseen this edifice that must have taken hundreds of years to complete. 'That is the first Lord Phillipon,' whispered the monk, 'who came here with the Conqueror. His descendants own all the lands around here, every village is his feoff. The present lord claims to be the tenth in the line.' Richard understood. His father rented his smallholding and his cottage from the lord, farmed the lord's land for ten days every year, even when he would have preferred to work upon his own to prevent approaching rains from ruining his harvest. No wonder his father cursed Phillipon for an arrogant and grasping parasite.

Sundays came and went, with them the stories from the windows: John the Baptist standing with Christ in the water, Saint Christopher with the Christ child on his back, Lazarus rising from the dead, and his favourite, a rueful looking Saint Sebastian gazing at his body bristling with arrows. Days in the kitchen became fewer, days in the classroom and the scriptorium longer and more interesting until his final release and the award of a white cowl as a postulant within the cathedral abbey. By now he could not only read the Bible and holy works in Latin but could also translate them for the less learned into the vernacular English, although this was frowned upon by his superiors. There were rumours that a man called Tyndall had translated the Bible in its entirety. For now, it existed only in handwritten versions but it was said that printers were interested in making copies on their new-fangled machines.

Richard did not care. He worked happily in the scriptorium, helping monks make their own copies of holy works and books by the physician Galen and the philosopher Aristotle which had travelled west after the fall of Byzantium. His writing was competent and confident enough for normal purposes, recording events for the Cathedral journal or minor legal documents but insufficiently fine or beautiful for expensive copying onto vellum. Instead he was set to colouring, imitating the glories of the cathedral windows. And then on to drawing: decorative plants and flowers, small figures, illuminated initial letters. At last full-page gospel paintings: Saint Matthew with his angel; St. John, an eagle at his feet; Saint Mark's lion floating above his open eyes and Saint Luke's winged bull. Others came to stare at his work, the drawing sharper than his peers, the colours shining at the church windows with the morning light behind them. As the eyesight of his elders faded, Richard was regarded as the leading master within the scriptorium, despite his age.

'There is excitement of the morrow,' one of the younger monks told him. 'A Lollard has been taken. He has been put to the torture but refuses to recant. He is to be burned. Fancy, the pernicious heresy of the man, denying the primacy of the Pope who is God's representative on earth! Then, all goods to be held in common, no lords, no king. Some even hold their wives in common, fornicating with whomsoever they wish. Theft, adultery, lust, the overturn of the whole order. No wonder he is to be burned, before he can turn this realm into a hell on earth.'

Richard inclined to the idea of holding all goods in common, of despoiling the lords in their huge mansions to give to the toiling poor like his father, forced to pay rent on the spot even when he had not enough to feed his large family. His father still quoted the rhyme from the Peasants' Revolt, deeply etched in the common memory:

When Adam delved and Eve span
Who was then the gentleman?

Perhaps his own father was a Lollard at heart? Nevertheless, he will join his comrades the next day, as his superiors expected. It was not every day that a man was burned among the ancient tombs on the green before the Cathedral gates.

A stake was erected on the green, surrounded by piles of dried wood as high as a man's waist, enough to heat a poor family through a cold December. Overnight the timber was soaked in bucketfuls of water. 'Are his friends hoping it will not light?' Richard asked an old monk. 'That the mayor will give up and turn the man free?'

'Not at all,' replied the monk, scratching at the flea bites beneath his habit. 'They want the fire to catch, but badly. There will be much smoke. It will envelop the heretic, fill his lungs, perhaps kill him outright. If not, it will destroy his senses, render him unconscious so he does not feel the heat of the fire. Either way he dies, but avoids the agony of his flesh melting away and his innards bursting. The punishment will be for naught. He will have to wait until he arrives in hell for the bite of the flames everlasting.'

More wood was brought, mixed in with the sodden boughs, the authorities determined to produce more heat than smoke. An armed guard was placed on the green overnight to prevent further interference. Next morning dawned dull and overcast. 'The heretics have been praying to the Green Man for rain,' muttered the brother infirmarian, ' but they have not prayed long enough. See, the wind rises from the east, it will blow the rain away. We will have a dry day yet. Make haste, brothers, for we must accompany the procession on its way.'

Richard joined his fellows, all fingering their wooden crucifixes. A Sacristan led the way, holding aloft the Cathedral's own gold and bejewelled crucifix, the bishop next, followed by the deans in their best robes. To a gasp from the assembled townspeople the sheriff's men trudged along behind carrying a chair tied to four long poles, to which an ashen faced man was bound with strong ropes. 'He has been tortured so bad he cannot walk,' commented the infirmarian. 'I was called to him this morning to urge him to his feet. They have stretched him so far his legs no longer attach to his body. See how his arms swing loose from the shoulder. It is a cruel thing, even for a heretic. Fire may burn away his guilt but pain will not cleanse his soul.'

The younger monks and postulants brought up the end of the procession, singing the psalm ordered for the day as they came, forming a crescent around the pyre. Facing them the townspeople stood silent, shuffling their feet anxiously, a bunch of apprentice boys in leather jerkins muttering at the back. Richard looked up as the prisoner was lifted from his chair and carried to the stake, his arms pinioned redundantly to his side. 'Tie him in tight, boys,' cried one of the sheriff's men, 'we don't want him flopping about and spoiling the spectacle for these godly people.' A growl rose from the apprentice boys, ignored by the officials. A dean detached himself from the crescent, addressed himself to the condemned man. A monk followed him, a bag in his hand tied loosely with rope to leave a noose at the top.

'Do you repent your heresies, throw yourself upon the mercy of mother church, embrace the power of his holiness the Pope and our sovereign lord King Henry?' As he spoke he offered up a crucifix for the man to kiss.

'Take away your graven images and your flummeries. There is no power but God and Jesus Christ his son. We are all one in the eyes of the Creator. Get you gone, you black robed crow. Though you torture and burn me I die with my soul intact. He who conquers shall not be hurt by the second death.'

'Well said, brother,' cried a voice from the crowd. 'Keep the word of patient endurance. Neither Pope nor King.'

The crowd stirred irresolutely. To cry up the slogan was to commit treason; many secretly relished the thought of the twin burden removed from their backs. Only the apprentices shouted and jeered at the sheriff's men as they moved forward, lighted torches in hand, the monk and dean retreating as they did so.

'That is his last chance for a painless death,' whispered the infirmarian. 'See that bag? It is full of gunpowder, to be hung round the prisoner's neck. Once the flames touch the gunpowder it will explode, killing him instantly. Now he has refused to recant they will just let him burn. And we must watch, for not to do so would be sure sign that we are heretics ourselves.'

Flames licked at the wood around the condemned man's feet. Sweat stood out on his brow; he gasped for air, suppressing a scream. "Our father who art in Heaven,' he began, the crowd joining with him in the only prayer they knew in English. The choir master signalled to the assembled clergy, urged them into a reprise of their psalm. 'Louder,' he cried, 'louder.' Not the soft sound that echoed around the cathedral of a Sunday but a masculine roar, trying to drown out the prayers of the watchers on the other side of the graveyard. Prayers which grew the louder as the Lollard blackened, before boiling blood burst through the disintegrating flesh.

By now the new wood had generated enough heat to set fire to the drenched wood beneath. The Lollard's screams ceased. Unable to take fresh air into his lungs he hung forward on his stake, poisoned at last by the smoke and fumes which had put him out of his agony. Richard pinched himself hard to avoid the fate of two monks who had collapsed, overwhelmed by the scene they had witnessed. The crowd began to disperse, leaving only a handful of their number behind and a gang of apprentice boys who continued to chant the Lord's prayer.

'Be gone!' shouted the bishop. 'The Lord's will has been done. Heresy has been extirpated. Return to your homes and meditate upon God's mercy and the rule of church and king. Follow the paths of righteousness or you, too, will meet the same fate as this poor wretch.'

The apprentices stood their ground. A hunk of broken gravestone hurtled through the air, narrowly missing the bishop. He turned with as much grace as he could muster, gesturing to his entourage to follow. Almost as if this were a sign, lumps of gravestone, cobbles and clods of earth rained down upon the assembled clergy, forced to remain before following their betters in correct sequence. A couple of the younger monks bent down, gathering up missiles and returning them at their aggressors. Richard hesitated. Young enough to relish a good fight, old enough to fear the consequences should he be seen by his elders. Caught in two minds, he looked up, to be struck a heavy blow on the forehead by a flying flint.

It was dark, silent. He could neither see nor hear anything. 'Perhaps I am blind,' he thought, 'Or dead.' He reached out, felt his body was still intact, fingered the rough sheet that covered him. Not a shroud, surely? Slowly his eyes became accustomed to the dark, the thinnest of moonlights creeping in from somewhere. His head hurt. He put a hand to his forehead, found it covered with a thick bandage, damp above the left eye. Gingerly he levered himself up to a sitting position, tried to stand. Fell back again. From somewhere came the sound of footsteps, the faint light of a tallow candle.

'You stay right where you are, brother. That's a nasty gash you have on your head. Rest and quiet is what you need. We will pray for your speedy recovery.' The infirmarian gently eased Richard back onto his cot. 'Tomorrow I will replace your bandage. Most of the bleeding has ceased. The wound cannot be stitched for it is too close to the bone. You will carry a jagged scar for the rest of your life. Not to worry. Being in orders you have no need to attract a wife to your pretty face.'

Richard did not care. Soon he would be back in the scriptorium, pouring over his beloved pictures, illustrating the gospels with green and gold. Till then, he would do as the infirmarian ordered, the sooner to escape his captivity.

Three days were sufficient. On the fourth he sat, brush in hand, lightly brushing a grey wash across the figure of Death. While it dried he drew in the lineaments of a horse, trying to capture it in full flight. He was certain the standard representation, with forelegs and hind legs extended in opposition to one another, was incorrect yet he could not envisage exactly how it was that a galloping horse moved its legs. Never mind, the grey had dried. Automatically he reached for his tiniest brush, a mere four hairs, dipped it in a dish of light red paint, drew the main veins through the figure, an edge to Death's scythe. A vision of the Lollard rose to his mind, the man tied to the stake, screaming as the blood bubbled from his legs.

'You are not well, brother.' The infirmarian once more, removing a gag from Richard's mouth. 'You have returned to your tasks too soon, as I warned you.' Richard looked around him at his fellow scribes, nudging and pushing one another to get a better view. His last memory was of dipping his brush in the paint. All since had vanished from his mind. Helped by the infirmarian he stood, staggered, almost fell. The scribes stepped back in fear and consternation. 'He is disordered by his wound,' said the infirmarian in a sharp voice. 'I will take the best care of him. Return to your tasks. In silence! What you have seen is not an occasion for gossip.'

That Sunday Richard collapsed once more, just as the host was being raised at the climax of the mass. In his agony he bit one of his fellows who had gone to his aid. For days he lay on his bed, unable to raise enough energy to get to his feet. His return to the scriptorium brought murmurs from the scribes, quickly silenced by the scriptorium master. The day echoed his mood, dark and damp, bullets of hail spattering against the meagre glass set high upon the walls, enough to allow in extra light, sufficiently high to provide no distracting view for the industrious monks below.

For what seemed an eternity he stared at the lightly sketched scene before him: Saint Jerome seated exactly as he was, pen in hand, about to begin work upon a parchment, a lazy lion staring up at him in wonder. Richard reached for his brush to add ochre to the saint's face. The brush slipped of its own accord, spreading paint across the page. He dabbed at it with a cloth, erasing the marks as best he could, revisited the half inch of face upon the page, only to find his brush skidding down the parchment once more. Again he wiped it clean. Again applied the merest hint of paint, steadying his right hand with his left. The brush yet again wandered of its own accord. 'You are not yet well enough to return, brother,' spat the scriptorium master at his elbow, attracted by Richard's feverish activity. "We will discuss the matter at a later occasion.'

Richard half rose from his seat, only to find himself once more upon a pallet in the infirmary. 'He is touched by the devil,' the scriptorium master was saying. 'Let him remain and he will infect his brothers. Surely the devil has escaped from the Lollard as he was burned and entered into the body of our poor brother.'

'No, that is not so. Many a time have I seen the falling sickness.

It comes upon some poor souls unannounced when the world has overcome their delicate natures. God intervenes to protect them from the ills of the world, erects a barrier through which evil may not pass and enter their souls. Sadly, they never recover from their delicacy, though their malady may lessen as their lives become more secure. Our brother's safest place is here, with us.'

'Brother infirmarian, you have made this place a haven of safety and healing for those who suffer the ills of the body. But our brother, Richard, has neither an illness of the body nor a disorder of the mind. His presence among us brings a disturbance to the life of the cathedral community which I cannot countenance.' The abbot's face assumed the determined scowl of the nearest gargoyle on the south face of the cathedral spire. 'I have discussed the matter several times with the bishop, the boy's uncle. He will return to Boxwood, the village from whence he came. There he may assist the incumbent, one Brother Stephen, with his duties. Since the boy is in minor orders he may assist with confessions and burials, even serve at the mass. His sickness will be no handicap and the Bishop will grant him a small stipend for life. Thus he will carry forward the work of the church while preserving himself from the evils of the world.'

'While I would prefer him to remain here, as the safest of all places,' replied the infirmarian, 'if you, brother Abbot and the Bishop himself insist that he be expelled from our community, then I agree that a subsidiary post in his home village of Boxwood would be the safest place for him.'

Richard could see the scriptorium master nodding his agreement. An illuminator who could not control his limbs was of no use within his empire, nor would Richard wish to stay somewhere within sight of paint and brushes which he could not hold. He will bury himself back in the country, where he can do Christ's will for however long the good Lord might grant to him.

At the month's end he set off on the lonely trail back to Boxwood, mounted on a donkey. 'Like Christ entering Jerusalem,' he thought to himself, appalled and amused at the blasphemy. In one small bag he carried his worldly possessions: a breviary, a handwritten copy of the New Testament in the tiniest of scripts in order to save on valuable parchment on which remained the odd word of some old text long damaged and erased by time, the merest trace of a palimpsest, a single change of under garments and a few coppers kindly donated by the infirmarian as a parting gift. The other bag was lighter and less bulky. Inside lay bones crumbled to fragments by the heat of the fire, further ground down by the abbot's fanatical sandal. "Take these and bury them deep,' the Abbot had ordered him. 'Bury them where no Lollard or reformer will find them to use as relics for their cause. Plant the yew sapling that I give you on top, that no-one will think to disturb nor cattle ruminate upon.'

Although he thought little of the Abbot's reasoning, Richard was determined to carry out his task. Surely the reformers, strong in their vilification of idols and ancient relics, would not set up martyrs and idols of their own? But he was young and would be guided by his elders. The bones and ashes he would bury to the north of the village church, among the beggars and vagrants, the poisonous yew tree kept away from cattle by the churchyard hedges.

"See him in his pride,' whispered the village gossip to her neighbour. 'Thinks he is the risen Christ when he is just another of the witch's children.'

'His mother is no witch,' objected the other. 'I know her, she is a good woman, though she may have been the one to re-populate the earth after Noah's flood she has so many brats. She may be fertile but she is no witch.'

'Listen, neighbour. Have you not heard of the witch of Boxwood who in the olden days had fifty children, though there was no man who would touch her fearful carcass? Each of those children was let loose upon the world to open the door for the devil: this boy's father, now the lord's steward, grinding us into poverty; his brother, the new Bishop, grabbing gold to ornament his palace. And their uncle, calling himself a banker, lending money upon interest to the king and his improvident nobles just like some ringleted Jew. Some say the lord of the manor himself is one of the witch's children, though I know that cannot be true, for it is his wife who descends from the witch. It is she who will not let us comb the fields for the gleanings after the harvest, but brings in her own servants to gather what has been our right from the time of Moses and Adam. You will see what evil this one brings with him, posturing little clerk with his ink stained fingers.'

In a village of fifty houses such tales take less than a day to circulate. Not all believed them. Of those who did, a few felt it advantageous to curry favour of one who could do great harm to their souls, offering the new arrival a bowl of pottage of a barn in which to spend the night, the priest declaring that his modest home was too small for two. For the priest had heard the rumours and wished to keep his purity unsullied and his small ale unshared. Nevertheless, the boy was put to use granting absolution to those careless enough to die in the middle of the night or to hear the confession of old women with their imaginary sins, even to teach the unruly village children, many of them Richard's own brothers and sisters, a few elementary prayers or tell them cautionary tales from the Bible.

Removed from the pressures of cathedral and scriptorium Richard felt more confident within himself, his fits became less frequent and less severe. More importantly, they came not as a lightening strike but like a cat stalking an unwary mouse. By the time one was upon him he was able to take shelter in the church, away from preying eyes and gossiping tongues. There was still talk, of course, but most of it was kindly, incidents of the falling sickness being frequent among the inbred villagers. Only a few regarded it as a legacy inherited by the witch's children.

His main problem was boredom, for there was little enough for a priest on his own to do in such a tiny hamlet, never mind for two. They tilled their joint vegetable garden, looked after a couple of skeps of bees with minimal success and kept the church itself clean. On one of these days the priest complained that pilgrims no longer came to the village, either to view its relics or on their way through to the shrine of the Virgin in Walsingham. 'We are not attractive,' moaned the priest, 'there are so many wonders in this modern world to be seen. The rich make pilgrimage to Rancon Rouen or Rome; the poor trudge to the holy St. Thomas in Canterbury. But there are new marvels to behold even in our tiny community. An angel came to me in a dream and vouchsafed to me that this Easter the venerable Saint Wandrene will be among us. This year the church will be so full many will be left without.'

Richard remained unconvinced. He had little faith in dreams and earthly wonders. All that was wonderful resided in the book of the New Testament, God's word revealed to man. He looked around him at the church, at the statue of the saint, its colours faded into the palest blue, all traces of gold fallen, or scraped, from his costume. The walls were no better, decorated with scenes from the life of St. Wandrene: his presentation at court, helping the old peasant with his wagon, his dirty clothes miraculously cleansed as he stood mud spattered before the irate king; parting from his wife to take the tonsure; his years as a hermit; the abbey he had founded above the stream of Fontenelle, crowded around by all three hundred of his monks. Very laudable, but hardly enough to set the soul racing towards redemption or to turn the errant from sin and temptation.

'I will paint the walls!' he cried aloud. 'They will become one of the wonders of the whole of East Anglia. They will draw in the hundreds of pilgrims who once made their way here. At Easter we will have miracles, sinners shall repent, the rich will put aside their wealth and turn again to God in holy poverty. The blessed shall rejoice!' He felt it come upon him. He lay down, put the rope belt from his cassock between his teeth and gave himself up to the convulsions that the holy spirit laid upon him.

As so often nowadays after he had given himself up to his illness rather than fighting it, his recovery was swift. The first Monday in Lent saw him clad only in a pair of flopping drawers slopping a light lime wash across every available surface, erasing the old paintings, creating another palimpsest on which to inscribe God's word. The priest had suggested miracles from the Bible as a subject, ones which Richard had immediately rejected. What did these inland folks know of whales, or farmers know of fiery furnaces? Lazarus rising was any old man heaving himself up from his bed. Besides, these were stories that he could tell the children himself. What was needed was a call to arms, an expression of the faith united, of the destruction of false prophets and devils, the pain and tortures of heretics and unbelievers. Most important, the ultimate triumph, the resurrection of the faithful into eternal life within the New Jerusalem. All will be wonders and revelations!

Richard set to serious work on Ash Wednesday, much to the ire of the local gossip. 'A desecration of the day,' she grumbled to her neighbour. 'On this of all days we should be humble, keep our heads down in the hope and expectation of God's grace.' Richard did not hear or did not care. He began on the wall opposite the church entrance, so all could see the power that dwelt within, a picture of Christ with white hair. The brush in his hand would not restrain itself. As he strove for detail the brush thrust itself upwards, reaching for grandeur. 'This is no mere book page,' it scolded him, 'but an extravagance, a clarion call to the faithful.' Now the figure was twice life size, eyes of fire, feet shining like burnished bronze, echoing the sun of his face. A huge sword floated from the face, daring the viewer to withstand the potent vision before him, to deny its power. Long into the late winter night Richard slaved away at his image, returning the next day to add detail and subtlety. 'But there is no subtlety, no detail,' his brush told him. "work on, work on!'

And he painted a white horse, and a red horse, and a black horse, a balance in the rider's hand and a pale horse, all galloping upon the bodies of screaming folk beneath. Not only peasants but lords and kings and bishops who had thrown away their mitres or been found in the midst of their lusts. Faster they galloped into a land of earthquakes and fire in which trees and men dissolved in flames. Cities fell in flames while prophets sat upon rocks, frogs spouting from their mouths, as a horde of locusts descended, crowns on their heads, teeth like a lion's, women's hair streaming behind them. On the tenth day of Lent Richard began work on the north wall against the altar. A woman in scarlet and purple, her clothes covered with gold and jewels sat on a beast no-one had ever seen before, a scaly animal with seven heads and ten horns upon which he expended all of his skill, making each head more fearsome than the last, covering the animal's scaly body with paint the colour of a rotting carcass, so lifelike the priest declared he could taste the smell of putrefaction.

Entering the third week of Lent Richard began on the opposite wall. Facing the scarlet woman, he painted an elegant angel, a huge key dangling from the chain around its waist. Beneath the angel's elegant sandals, a scarlet devil, horns tipped with gold, fell, arms flailing, into a huge stone cauldron. By the angel's side, taking up the remaining space to the entry porch, a walled city descended from the clouds, its walls studded with every colour of precious stone that Richard could contrive: gold, vibrant green, cornelian, purple, light and dark blue so that the whole shone like the morning sun in summer. From the city flowed a river, watering the fruit trees below: apple, pear, greengage, plum, the rare quinces that Richard had seen only in the Bishop's garden, medlars, figs, pomegranates and others purely found in his imagination. Reaching up towards them figures rose from the earth, faces beaming in anticipation; the figures of the dead, diadems faintly outlined behind their heads.

On the Monday of the last week of Lent Richard sat immobile all day staring at the space above the altar, broken only by a simple wooden cross and the statue of the saint staring mournfully from his corner. The following day he spent adding yet another coat of lime wash to the wall, full knowing it would take some days to dry. Notwithstanding the mess, he incised into the still wet wash a figure seated on a throne, a shadowy figure as if seen through a cloud. A rainbow curved like a palanquin above the throne, a rainbow exaggeratedly green and gold. Faces gathered around the throne, holding up their arms in joyful veneration. Symmetrically around the figures Richard painted in the symbols he knew so well from his days in the scriptorium: lion, ox, bull, angel.

Beneath the throne, hiding the feet of the figure seated upon it, he painted in elegant detail, as if he was once more working upon a tiny parchment rather than a three yard high wall, a lamb staring out at the congregation, its body covered with seven gold crosses. From out of the lamb's mouth rose a sparkling river which wound its way downwards to irrigate a flourishing young tree onto which Richard nailed the old wooden cross which had hung at the east end of the church for so many centuries. Meticulously he cleaned his brushes, washed out the leather cups from his paint, left the church, leaving the key with the priest on his way back to the pile of hay that was his bed. For the first time in many months his head was clear of voices and images, leaving him to sleep the sleep of the angels.

On Maundy Thursday the church remained locked, on the priest's insistence, despite a thin gathering of pilgrims around the church-yard. At the manor house the poor of the village, the vast majority, gathered for their Easter dole while those better off stayed at home and sewed the rents in their best clothes ahead of the Easter service the next day. Richard wandered around the village, showering blessings on all he came across, pilgrim and villager alike. Towards afternoon he filled a bucket from the village pond to water the yew tree he had planted not so long before which was now thriving on the human ashes upon which it fed. "Nothing is wasted,' he thought. 'God makes use of all; see how new life flourishes upon the bones of a dead heretic.'

Good Friday, he stood beside the priest at the altar, gently swinging a censer as he chanted a hymn in his melodious voice. The congregation entered in small groups: families, pilgrim friends, neighbours. Each stood in amazement as they entered, gazing around at horsemen, angels, a city descending from the clouds, God in majesty, the old wooden cross growing from a painted tree. Half frightened, half amazed, the congregation buzzed like a disturbed beehive, exchanging comments on the wonders before them, much to the disquiet and frustration of the priest. He began his homily, describing Christ's entry into Jerusalem, his betrayal by Judas, Peter's denials, His judgement before Pontius Pilate and condemnation by the Pharisees. Lowering his voice, the priest described in detail the ascent of the Mount of Golgotha and the crucifixion between two thieves. 'The whole world weeps for the death of the son of God!' declaimed the priest, brushing past the now silent acolyte, throwing one arm around the shoulders of the ancient statue of St Wandrene.

Richard swayed as the priest passed. He could feel his senses drifting on the waves of incense, making the angel's sword shine the brighter, the hydra-headed monster seem to open and close its multiple mouths. Faintly he was aware his illness was creeping upon him. 'I cannot be overcome,' he thought, 'not at this moment of Our

Lord's triumph. Begone, foul darkness. You may have me when the mass is over.' But still the threat hovered around him, despite his determination.

"See,' cried the priest, 'even the saint weeps for the sacrifice of Christ upon the cross!"

The crowd gasped as four bright red tears trickled down the cheeks of the saint, dropping onto the earthen floor. Richard watched the tears soak away before collapsing on top of them, frothing and twitching. All his previous fits had been dark and mysterious, leaving a gap in his life wider than that of any sleep. Not so now. He heard himself apologise to God and the angels for failing to keep his promise to ward off its onset until the end of mass. A shooting pain pierced his skull, leaving blood in his eyes. 'The mark of the blessed,' said a soft voice. As it said so the scarlet woman and her monster dissolved before his eyes. The horsemen: white, red, pale and black, turned and fled. Towns and villages that he knew dissolved before him, to be replaced by a glorious bejewelled city, larger than he could contemplate, which descended upon him.

Richard was buried in the north part of the graveyard, beside the yew tree and the remains of the Lollard, alongside robbers and beggars. 'One of the devil's brood,' opined the gossip. 'If not for his uncle he should not be buried in consecrated ground at all. Look upon those monsters he has wished upon our poor church. The priest says they are all there in the Bible but I never heard of the like. Never a birth in a stable nor a good crucifixion. He can tell us anything, poor folk who cannot read or mouthe the Latin, but we know what we know. This Richard was an unholy fellow, like all of the witch's children. We are well to see the back of him.'

1648

DISSOLUTION

 Going on the soft sand of the brecks was hard for the horses. Though the men were half starved their weapons and bivouac gear weighed heavy, driving the horses' hooves to their fetlocks in the shifting sandy soil, especially where sheep had grazed away the soft grass, leaving escaped rabbits to take advantage of easy digging. The men, too, were weary and ill tempered having spent dreary days and nights before the walls of Colchester waiting to pounce upon human rabbits incautious enough to poke their noses out of their burrows.

'Those men had surrendered,' grumbled the oldest of the riders, a grim faced man sporting a bushy untrimmed beard. 'They should never have been executed. It is against the rules of war.'

'Brother Gabriel, you should know the rules of war have been suspended in this conflict where we fight against the devil himself. Those three were chosen by lot from the five leaders. Obviously it was God's will those three should die. We must not criticise God's choice.'

'But it was not God's will to have them chosen by lot in the first place. General Fairfax made that decision. It is Fairfax I criticise, not God.'

'Almost the same thing,' sniggered the third of the small party, a bulky man mounted on a huge Suffolk Punch. 'When Fairfax says we attack, we attack. When he says we retreat, we retreat. The town paid the generals an indemnity to keep us at bay but it is a soldier's right to sack and pillage a town that has held out for so long against a siege. Royalists and papists are to be punished, not allowed to walk free, off to their homes with silver in their pockets. Do not worry yourselves about dead aristocrats, there are plenty better poor men lying dead in ditches because of them. We should have sacked the town to teach them a lesson.'

'We are men of discipline, John Bagehot. We follow General Fairfax and his orders as the Israelites followed Moses out of Egypt.'

'And get fed just as badly, except there is no manna from heaven for us. We must take what we can find, where we can find it. A fallen city is a better place than most to feed the belly and put a roof over our heads.'

'You don't need a roof, John Bagehot,' Gabriel snorted. 'When it rains all you need do is to shelter beneath the belly of that huge monster you call a horse.'

'This is the finest horse in the world. She may be slow at times and not much use for foraging, but in a battle she is fearsome. If you had been at Naseby, you would have seen Charles Stuart's infantry turn in terror and run for their mothers' aprons when we charged upon them. Besides, she will pull a plough across any land you care to name: clay, rocks, flint, gravel and even this Breckland sand. When we come upon that traitor Phillipon she will trample him underfoot. No need for fire or axe for that one.'

'At this speed, John, he will have fled as far as Scotland by now, never mind Boxwood.'

'Trust me,' growled on the worthy John with a tilt of his head. 'Those Royalists always run home to mother, whether it be their own mothers or mother church. He will flee to Boxwood; you may be sure.'

The other two remained silent. They had little faith in their mission's outcome but were nevertheless happy to be free of army discipline and the hunger and squalor of the camp outside Colchester's walls. Breckland might be bleak and hard going for the horses, but there was food to be had from a countryside relatively untouched by war. All day they plodded their weary way north-wards, past the ruins of Thetford Abbey, finding shelter further on among a welcoming band of gospel people in the village of Attle-borough.

Next morning, refreshed by food and prayer they struck out determinedly for their destination. 'We should avoid the city,' coun-selled Gabriel. 'Sickness lingers there still among the rats and the sewers, and the churchmen of the cathedral carry no love for such as us, Arminians and mummers that they are. Wren was the bishop there before he was carried off to Ely. Not one of the godly would he admit to hold land within his domains. They praise him there still, despite the efforts of our brethren fighting the swarms of foreign priests and Jesuits that Charles Stuart has encouraged to worm their way into the country, the grim wolf of Rome insinuating its privy paw into the skin of our commonwealth.'

'Truly you are right, brother Gabriel,' spoke up Walter, the youngest of the trio. 'We should avoid any taint of Rome or bishop. They are naught but the panders of the whore of Babylon and instruments of the devil. Look at how they suck the tithes from the poor, tearing their puny mite like wolves tearing the sinews of the slaughtered lamb. Let us lose no time in securing this papist Phillipon and returning him to the tower for trial and execution.'

'What if the court were to find him innocent, Walter?' John asked.

'How can he be innocent? He is a self-declared papist and traitor, having fought in Charles Stuart's army. We are not murderers. There will be a trial and he will be found guilty and executed, or the army will ask why not!' His companions appeared content with this explanation and for a while they rode on in silence, passing round the city by some five miles. By which time they had become lost.

'Prime your pistols!' cried Gabriel at last. 'There are fortifications ahead. Walter do you go ahead and enquire of what sort of place that may be, whether the occupiers be for us or opposed. Take care in case of ambush.'

'Brother, I shall take care but I shall also commend myself to the Lord,' answered Walter with unwonted solemnity before urging his horse forward. His companions hid themselves in the shadow of a group of willows while their horses waded into the cool river for a well earned drink. No sound carried to them beyond the lowing of a cow in some nearby pasture and the buzzing of insects around their heads.

At last Walter returned, a smile upon his face. "Tis neither friend nor foe. The ramparts are empty and deserted and have been so these centuries past. All that live inside now are flocks of sheep. Mayhap it is a castle built in some bygone age by a race of giants that inhabited these parts.'

'Walter!' cried Gabriel, 'you blaspheme. Where is it in the Bible that God created a race of giants? All that were created walk upon this earth now, no more, no less. If those walls were built, they were built by men like ourselves.'

'But the learned men of Cambridge tell us of giants like Gog and Magog who inhabited the earth before mankind. They tell of tales of great heroes who fought many battles among themselves.'

'Believe not these so called learned men. Learned men will lead us into pernicious error. All we need know is in the Bible. All else is the devil's deceit; this learning is nothing but the idolatry of the mind, an adversary to God's truth and spirit.'

"You speak true,' added John. 'I have heard even churchmen from the universities tell of gods who change form to degrade young women and maidens, though they claim these are merely legends. I say they are put about to corrupt our youth and lead them into godless ways.' His companions nodded in agreement.

'Pleasant as it is to stand by this stream and discuss the ways of the world,' spoke Gabriel at last, 'but we have our mission to accomplish and our destination to discover. If there be sheep and cattle in the neighbourhood there must be people as well. Let them direct us on our path.'

At the confluence of the river with a small stream they found a group of houses huddled around a communal barn, now in August piled high with sodden wheat and straw after the wettest season any could remember. "They will rot and stink before winter sets in,' opined Walter. 'Many cattle will starve for want of fodder this winter, and poor folks alongside them.' An old woman was busy feeding her chickens, calling each one by name as she hobbled across the yard. 'Take care of your fowls, old dame,' cried Walter jocularly, 'there be hawks around ready to plunder your flock.'

'That be no hawk,' spat the old woman, 'that be a heron. I may be ancient but when the wind is in the right direction I can tell a hawk from a hansa. What do you be about in these lands? We have no troubles here since the king's men were subdued five year since, we be all godly folk.'

'Right glad am I to hear so, beldam. We are travellers on our way to the village of Boxwood but we have mistook the path. It would be an act of charity to direct us.'

'It would be a greater act of charity, sirs, to turn you from your way. Boxwood is not for the likes of you. They are all the witch's children, they worship monsters, harlots and devils. You should see their church, sirs, full of idolatrous images. And, too, they have a reliquary which is said to weep tears of blood every Easter. 'Tis a papist trick no doubt but the gullible still flock to see it on their way to worship the Virgin's milk at Walsingham. No wonder them at Boxwood all have six fingers, even he that calls himself a lord. Phillipon. What sort of name is that? Foreign and Jesuitical, I'll be bound. Go not to them, sirs, for the good of your souls.'

'Our souls are safe, good woman, but our bodies are in dire need. Boil us a half dozen of those fresh eggs to eat upon the road. We will pay you well and shower you with our blessings.'

'I thank you, sir. I could well do with both your coin and your blessings. While the water boils I will give you your directions since you insist upon your destination.'

Another meal is being taken only a few miles away in the darkened dining room of the manor at Boxwood. Removed from the village it stands back from the road on a rise to the west, dominating church and village. Grown to some fifty hearths the hamlet has increased its population but not its income, now shared even thinner than before. War has reduced the passage of pilgrims to a mere trickle, while the lord of the manor has steadily assumed ever more land to his personal control. The manor house itself is a grand structure in deep red brick, brought all of a hundred miles from the works at Bedford, surmounted by twisted chimney pieces, tall and thin to refuse entrance to the sharp north wind that blows down from Scandinavia of a winter. The mullioned windows proudly display acres of glass, brought up from the Suffolk coast at vast expense. So confident are the owners, the house has neither battlement nor moat, relying on fear and the king's favour to keep them from harm.

No longer may they be so confident. A dishevelled figure eased around the manor, entering by the rear door used only by servants. His fur lined cloak was torn, his doublet stained with grease and black blood, boots caked with mud. By appearance a soldier, he carried neither sword nor pistol, moving in a furtive manner far from a soldier's rigidity. Cooks and kitchen maids turned their heads away as he passed through, like a man negotiating a forest he has heard about but has never frequented. A narrow staircase wound upwards, wide enough only for a servant carrying a tureen to pass, emptying itself discretely in the far corner of an ornate room decorated with heavy oak furniture carved in the best Tudor manner.

A woman stood by the window, staring out at the village. Despite the summer weather she shivered inside her long woollen gown, which she wrapped around her heavy black dress. 'What do you do here? I gave orders not to be disturbed. I wish only for news, news of my son, who I desire to be here, far from the clash of arms.'

'You could not more desire me to be here at home, more than I desire to be here.'

She turned, her face joyful, held out her arms, surrendered to a torrent of tears. 'My dear child, I have prayed for you, waited for you. They said you had died fighting outside the walls of Colchester, weak from starvation. This cruel war has taken your father from me. God's grace and your own bravery has restored you.'

'But not for long, mother. They have slaughtered Lucas and Lisle in cold blood. The same will come to me unless I escape. But I could not leave without seeing you, assuring you I am safe. Tomorrow I must leave for Lynn, take ship for France to join Prince William and Her Majesty. You will be safer here without me. Once it is known that I have flown, the roundheads will turn their ire elsewhere.'

'And you will be safe, but oh! so far away. And so lean and wan as you are now. Let me ring for food for you and a fast horse to speed you on your journey. Tell the servants to heat water so you may bathe. My maid will set out clean clothes for you.'

'Nothing fancy, mother, I beg of you. Tomorrow I must be a simple countryman travelling to town to pay his taxes or to sell the wool from his sheep's' backs. Imagine me, as lumpy farmer Rudd, all small ale and red cheeks!'

'My darling, how I wish your cheeks were round and red like a farmer's or as an apple in autumn. Sit you down and tell me the tales of the wars. Tell me of Prince Rupert and how you met the King himself.'

Night caught the riders upon the open road, still short of their destination, having accidentally taken a detour to avoid the marshy banks of a swollen river. 'We bivouac here,' said Gabriel, 'on this mound under the shelter of the trees. We can see any riders approaching and with God's grace the night will be dry and warm for once. The horses may forage on the grass, ready for the morrow. They must be fresh, should we need to give chase, not that John Bagehot's monster will be of much use.'

'My mount will yet prove its worth to you doubting Thomases. But he and I are both weary. Let us dismount, prepare ourselves for the night, spend time in prayer to beg for success upon tomorrow's duty. Even the elect should cleanse their souls of sin whenever the cares of the world allow.'

Despite a covering of cloud, the night remained dry in answer to the soldiers' prayers. Five of the clock found them riding before the dawn along a well used track heading towards the city. 'The old woman told us that once we sighted the cathedral spire in the distance we would be within a half hour's ride of Boxwood,' Walter reminded his companions. 'This pestiferous mist rising from the river brings forth all manner of miasmas but I swear I see a spire rising in the distance.'

'Do not swear on any matter, Walter,' chided Gabriel. 'But you are right. See there, beyond that rise in the land. And before it there is not mist but a thin ribbon of wood smoke from village fires. Let us haste along to catch our bird before it has fled.' Even John's mighty steed burst into the semblance of a trot at its master's urging, skirting the side of the higher ground to come unexpectedly upon a squalid village. Shacks a-plenty, though many of them seemed to be unused and falling into decay, populated solely by gaunt women, with ragged children clinging fearfully to their skirts.

'What village is this?' demanded Walter of one of the women.

'This be Boxwood, sirs,' muttered the woman. 'We are but poor people, sirs, as you may see. We were never rich but now our menfolk have gone to the wars to serve with the Lord Cromwell and the Maiden's Troop we have none to do the heavy work. Harvests be poor, hardly enough to supply the grain for the next year, though the Phillipons still demand their share as if the sun had shone all year, and the Arminians demand their tithes, though our poor priest sees little benefit of them.'

'It is a cruel time, sister. Now the war is over we shall rid ourselves of kings and bishops. Your men will return to plough for the winter sowing. God will provide and all manner of things shall be well. No longer will the Phillipons ride upon your backs like the devil upon that of a sinful man. But first, conduct us to your church, that we may pray with your priest before concluding our mission.'

'He is but a poor body, sirs, much worn down as we all are by poverty and the demands of those in power. What he has done, he has done to retain his benefice. Do not punish him, sirs, for he has been forever good to us, his flock, and has suffered with us, doing what he can for our body and our souls.'

'This is ominous,' remarked John Bagehot to his companions. 'The old woman warned us of irregular practices in this village. Let us pray inwardly that our souls be strong to withstand the wiles of the devil. Beware of the women here. This territory is rife with witches, twenty have been burned in the county this year alone. 'The witch's children' the old woman called these villagers. Let God manifest to us that which he wishes us to prosecute.' They found the priest by the village well, staggering under a wooden bucket full of water, his black gown, rent and tattered in places, sharp cheekbones highlighted by the morning sun.

'Good morrow, sirs,' cried the priest. 'Come you here as pilgrims to worship at the shrine of our Lady at Walsingham or to witness the miracles of our own Saint Wandrene? It is long since such as you passed this way, most pressed to the wars or taken ship to France or the American colonies. I wished to do so once myself, to spread the gospel among the heathen but times have been hard here, the Word much in demand. See, even those two houses, the best in the village, now crumble from disuse.' He pointed at a couple of sturdy buildings faced with flint, healthy by contrast to the flaking wattle and daub of others around them. Strong the walls might be, but the wood around the window openings sagged above, splintered with rot below. Wild winds had blown thatch from the roofs in plenty, leaving them deserted even by rats and nesting birds.

'I see dissolution in this village,' remarked Gabriel. 'Pray lead us to the church. We have much to do there.'

'Your prayers would be welcome, sirs, as would any contribution to its upkeep you may wish to make. The Lord of the Manor is fierce in his collection of the tithe but neither he nor the bishop is forthcoming with pennies for the upkeep of the building or the sustenance of its poor servant. All the bishop sends us is witch finders. This after the Phillipons gained all the holdings in the area of the monasteries of Thetford and Ely when the great king Henry dissolved them. Nothing have they put back into the village save further destruction. See there, the house of the wise woman. Many a babe has she brought into this world, cured us of our ailments though she could do nothing for her own. Wicked voices slandered her, said she poisoned the well, brought pestilence to those she hated, chose which mothers, which children, should die and which would live, brought forth idiots from sound parents. Sound parents, indeed! Such as were cousins married to cousins over many generations. 'Six fingered Boxwood' they call us. It is not true, none in this village have six fingers. But people here are slow witted, their brains drained by generations of in-breeding, understanding enough solely to follow the plough with the same understanding as the ox that drags it along. None could comprehend that the wise woman's falling sickness was sent by God through her parents and her parents' parents. The gossips slandered her that it was the sign of possession by the devil and her familiars. They are God fearing folk, sirs but their fear surpasses their understanding.'

Gabriel remained unimpressed. 'It is the duty of the village priest to guide his flock in the paths of righteousness and comprehension of God's word. Where the flock strays it is the shepherds job to lead them to their true home, a home where they may commune with their souls in peace.'

'Our church has always been conducted in the manner laid down by king and archbishop, sirs. You will find nothing amiss with our arrangements, poor though we be.'

John, Walter and Gabriel looked at one another dubiously, unconvinced by the priest's protestations or by the stumpy grey flint church with its impressive square tower. 'We do not have time for this,' complained John Bagehot. 'We have an urgent task before us. We are wasting our time.'

'Time spent in prayer is never wasted,' chided Gabriel, dismounting and securing his horse's reins to the branch of a spreading yew tree. Together the three entered the church.

The manor house was all abustle, servants running in every direction under the orders of their mistress. Her son stood, hands behind his back, staring out of the long-room windows at the village beyond. 'Soldiers were seen in Caistor yesterday, asking directions to Boxwood. Only the river being in unseasonable flood may have delayed them. I fear they are seeking for you. My darling, you must flee these wicked men, make haste to Lynn as fast as you may.'

'Mother, I fear to leave you alone to face them but I must save myself in order to serve my king. Do you order up the steward, your cook and his wife. They say she is a mighty woman. Her strength may preserve me.' The young man turned with a smile on his face. 'I am not pretty Prince William to escape as a girl but a woman's disguise may yet suffice. Make haste! I have tarried too long and led them here when I should have ridden directly to the coast. But I could not forbear to see you once more, mother, before I began my exile.'

Both cook and his wife were truly mighty figures, due no doubt to hefty consumption of ale to counteract the constant heat of the manor kitchens, their fires banked high day and night. By contrast, the steward was a lean and hungry man, sharp in his movements and in his wits. 'Have all the horses led out into the woods,' commanded the young man, 'keep them safe from the marauders who will come seeking me. Have the fastest saddled and kept somewhat apart from the rest, in the glade where we surprised the poacher the winter before last. As for you, mistress, I have need of the smallest gown that you posses.'

Unused to dealing with her superiors, the cook's wife turned scarlet with embarrassment, her fat calloused fingers fumbling with her voluminous skirts. 'I have but one other gown, master, which awaits the weekly wash. It is not fit to be seen outside of the kitchen, your honour.'

'Never mind, bring it to me. And a bonnet, one which I can tie on against the wind and the rain.'

Muttering and with a cursory and inelegant bow, she dragged her husband off to the more familiar architecture below stairs. Lady Phillipon waited for their steps to recede before turning to her steward. 'There is a metal box hidden away. You know where. Bring it to me.' As he turned, she grasped at a bunch of keys dangling from a chain around her waist, choosing the smallest and least conspic-uous. Turned to her son: 'I have a few jewels that can be sold should I have need. Rudd will bring what little we have left in coin. You will have need of it for your journey and for lodgings in France. Once the rents are in I will send you more to wherever you command. I know you will not live riotously but you must live according to your station so as not to disgrace the Phillipon name. Take the key; keep it safe. Here comes that ball of lard from the kitchens. Let me help you on with her greasy attire. Burn it as soon as you may. My prayers go with you, my son. When the king is on his throne again you will be among the greatest in the land.'

The son left by the back doorway through which he had entered the day before, a casket under his arm, petticoats swirling around his ankles. Dry eyed, he turned to wave to his mother at an upstairs window. She clutched a velvet curtain to prevent her from falling as she waved with her free hand.

Stowing his bucket of water by the nave wall the priest struggled to open the heavy oak door of the church, leading the three soldiers inside, dipping his fingers into the stoop as he did so. 'Forgive me, sirs. It is an old man's habit. I was brought up by my grandmother; she could never be cured of crossing herself on entering a church however many times she was punished.' He looked askance at Gabriel's clipped and disfigured ears, sure sign of a zealot ready to condemn all that displeased him. He was not mistaken.

'What Popery is here! A tabernacle for the devil! Look, a font housed about with graven images. See, what an insult to God, an image of Christ our Lord, as if any man could contemplate his goodness and glory.' Holding Walter's arm, he launched his muddy boot at the font, shifting it from its mounting. A second kick toppled the heavy stone to the floor, breaking off the head of Christ and the raised arm of John the Baptist. 'And the avenging angel of the Lord with his sword of righteousness. Here, the whore of Babylon seated upon the many headed beast. What blasphemy!'

'It is a warning to the faithful, sirs,' quavered the priest. 'They can see the horrors of the devil, the riders of war, plague and death from which they will be delivered at the resurrection, transfigured into the new Jerusalem.'

'Devil worship! Backslider! Men need nothing but the Word and the certainties of their own conscience. All else is mere clutter, obscuring the word of God, a temptation to the worshipping of idols. Parliament has delivered us from the spiritual plague of Egyptian darkness which heretofore has covered the light of the gospel shining upon the nation. And what do you have there? Tombs of dead Phillipons, icons to the glory of man placed for the ignorant to admire and worship when they should be at prayer. Where is the altar? Hidden behind those rails, closing off the people from the act of communion. Tear them down, John Bagehot. Take them out and burn them. No. Break them up, use the wood to smash down the plaster from the walls, relieve us of this pagan sensuality.'

Gabriel strode up to the altar rails themselves, lashing out with his boots as he did so. 'And what else do you have hidden there, priest, papish heretic that you are? Remove that thing from the wall.'

'That, sir? The crucifix? What is a church without a crucifix?'

'We do not worship two bits of stick nor attempt to bind God by making an image. Why do you stand there? What are you hiding?'

'Nothing, sir. It is merely the statue of the saint.'

'I know of this,' sneered Walter. 'A piece of idolatry left over from the reforms of the blessed King Henry who removed us from the yoke of Rome. The credulous say that at Easter time it sheds tears of real blood in sympathy for Christ's passion. Who can believe such nonsense! To have the image of man within a place of worship is an insult to God.' Walter strode forward, grasped the priest by his shoulder, sent him spinning across the floor. The statue, slightly smaller than life size, was nevertheless carved from solid yew so even the sinewy Walter found it difficult to move. In his fury he grasped the statue's head, pulling with all his might. For a moment it seemed his effort had been in vain, but slowly the trunk toppled, hitting the floor of the nave with a crash like thunder heard in the distance. As it hit, a chunk of the back of the head flew off, spinning in the air.

Walter recovered his equilibrium, helped to his feet by John, who stared into the vacant space in the cranium. 'Would you believe this monkish nonsense! See, here is a leathern pouch, stained red, connected to the image's eyes by a wooden tube. When the priest squeezes the pouch the red liquid inside will ooze from the statue's eye sockets. A miracle indeed!'

'Burn the thing!' commanded Walter. 'Throw it on a fire in the churchyard along with what is left of the railings. Bring the altar back into the centre of the nave where it belongs. As for you, sir,' turning to the priest, 'remove your gown, retire to the woods and pray for redemption. In the name of God, go!'

At first the villagers were fearful of the flames, images of saints and angels charring before their eyes, images which had informed their worship for generations disappearing to the heavens. Gradually all gravitated towards the scene. Small boys wrapped birds they had trapped in their snares in coffins of mud before edging them into the ashes. Old women eased their ancient bones in the unwonted heat, others dried their mud smeared clothes, filthy from a series of wet summers which had allowed no time for any attempt at cleanliness. Before long the fire had become a festival, a celebration of the new regime, reviving memories of the days of Wat Tyler and the great revolt.

Gabriel hunched his shoulders, cleared his throat, stepped forward towards the throng. 'No, brother Gabriel,' cried Walter, clutching at his arm. 'Now is not the moment for sermon or prophesy. Well as we have worked this morning there is still a task to be fulfilled, the rabbit to be tracked to its burrow. Phillipon could be escaping even as we stand glorying in burning pagan images as the Israelites burned the god Dagan of the Philistines. Now we destroy tyranny, set free the poor of this land from under the boot of the rich and powerful, bring about the kingdom of Christ where all distinctions of men, of bishops, priests, kings, magistrates, lords will disappear and all will labour together, each according to his talents.'

'Well said, brother Walter.' commended John Bagehot, already reaching for the reins of his vast steed. 'Let us make haste to catch our rabbit, for the blessings of the Lord and the commendations of our general.' Using a low yew branch he swung himself into the saddle, ambling off ahead of his companions whose lither horses caught him before he could leave the confines of the village.

'John, you and I will ride to the front of the house. Walter, your horse is the faster and your arm the younger. Tack off around the copse to our right and come at the house by the rear. Prevent anyone from leaving be they male or female. Our quarry may be in disguise so do not be deceived by a servant's clothing. Get what information you may from the female servants. Women are always ready to gossip and show themselves to be wiser than others. Let us all three prime our pistols; a shot fired by one will be heard by all. We take our man alive if God wills it, though a dead body is sufficient for our purposes.'

No servants responded to Gabriel's hammering on the door or his shouting in the courtyard. The door proved to be unlocked, allowing him and John to enter unopposed. Five years before they would have stood in awe and amazement in such luxurious and commodious accommodation, but years of war had led them into even grander buildings in search of supporters of the one they termed 'Charles Stuart, that man of blood'. Now they were confident enough to make their way to where they supposed the main hall might be, leaving trails of mud behind them on the polished wooden floors, flinging open oak doors, calling raucously for any Phillipon still in residence.

They found Lady Phillipon in the main hall, standing with her back to the window, staring at them ferociously. 'What do you here, trespassing upon my property, trampling the dirt and filth of the byways upon my hearth?'

'If the byways are filthy, woman, it is because the Lady of the manor has not fulfilled her duty to maintain them but has lined her pockets with gold, that she may live among luxury and debauchery with her spouse and her renegade son. The earth was made for us as much as you; we have ventured our lives, paid our dues, tilled the earth to reveal its richness.'

'My earth,' hissed the woman in a grating tone. 'My earth that my ancestors have bequeathed to me.'

'Conquerors who set themselves to rule on the thrones of tyranny, crushing the conquered and making of them slaves. The earth was made for all men, not for a pampered few. The Lord will unseat you from your jewelled thrones and exalt the lowly.'

'Enough of your rant, good Gabriel,' interjected John Bagehot. 'We have come not to preach but to avenge our brothers murdered by lead shot and poisoned bullets before the walls of Colchester. Tell us, woman, where be your son, that we may take him into lawful custody to be tried before a panel of his peers.'

'They are no peers but low-bred oafs who call themselves a parliament. No parliament can there be without the king's consent!' Despite her efforts Lady Phillipon was white in the face, tears streaming down her cheeks.

' Look at her, John, weeping for her whelp. She will weep more bitter tears when his head rolls on Tower Hill. Keep her here while I search the house. I'll roust him out at the point of my sword.'

'No need,' growled Walter grimly, driving two abject figures before him into the room. 'Our bird has flown some hours since. This ball of lard here has set him off in her second best shift. While we were purging the devil's den in the village young Phillipon has taken his fastest horse and fled. Our piety has allowed the villain to escape; we have been most remiss.'

'Nay, brother Walter, the spirit moved us to purge the church of its devilry. All has proceeded as God ordained. Clearly the Lord wished his house to be cleansed so the souls of the villagers would once again be pure, alive to their sins and to the hope of salvation in a further life, free from backsliding and evil images. Where is the capture of one royalist captain against the souls of a whole village? Now their souls will be free; with Phillipon gone their bodies, too, will be freed from servitude, freed from forced labour, rent and tithes; to till the land as they see fit. God has shown us the true path. Let us depart now for London, to vent the people's wrath upon that man of blood, Charles Stuart, the principal author and prime instrument of our late wars, that he may account for all the blood he has shed.' Gabriel waved his gloved fist in the air, as if concluding a peroration before a crowd of thousands on Goodman's Fields instead of two soldiers, a pair of snivelling servants and a terrified woman in a country manor house.

Unembarrassed by his enthusiasm he swept from the room, followed by his two companions, pulling down paintings and wall hangings as he went. Lady Phillipon trailed behind, struggling to keep to her feet in her apprehension.

Gabriel was still in prophetic mood as the trio rode first towards the city before continuing their journey south. 'I know my soul to be sanctified,' he declaimed as if preaching to the rabbits and badgers hiding in the hedgerows like a clip-eared Saint Francis. 'This world will end in fire and destruction to burn away the false; only the righteous will survive it.'

By the manor gates an old woman stood shivering in her

fashionable gown, gazing into the distance as if to peer as far as the coast of France and her hopes for the future.

Behind, the manor house itself blazed in a glorious conflagration: wall hangings, furniture, books, clothing and expensive linen alike contributed to the howling flames, shattering the window glass, devouring the roof beams. All collapsed into an amorphous heap of fire and destruction.

1757

Memorial

Madam

I have the pleasure to inform you of my imminent departure from these shores on the first of the proximate month. This missive, being despatched by His Majesty's man-of-war, should reach you well in advance of my arrival in the Company vessel 'Gloriana'. I adjure you to prepare the manor house fully, with all furniture and chattels in good order. Should you wish, you may purchase for yourself a new gown, and clothes for the children also. Thanks to the patronage of General Clive and my good friend Hastings I am now well provided for, as I will divulge to you on my return.

Take care most to stop all draughts within the fabric of the house. Have Gedge sweep the chimneys and lay in a bounteous supply of dry wood. He may cut some more of the box from the copse for laying down in the coming year should he require. The captain informs me we may dock within some days of the beginning of April or end of March should winds prove favourable, though weather in the Channel at this time of year is notoriously unpredictable. Recall, I leave India in the middle of summer to arrive in England at the close of winter! Even a stoic such as I must admit to the need for some extra care and coddling on first return; yet still do I desire the comforts of my house and above all the comfort of my own sweet lady.

I presage the boys will now be long out of skirts and my little Amanda, her who I have never seen, will be speaking and singing as sweetly as her mother. I commend the children to your care and command them to be obedient to you. Greatly am I desirous to see them once more and listen to their lisping sounds. Most of all I dream of your own sweet face from which I have been too long absent.

Hastings has much for me to arrange prior to my departure. He has gifts for the king as well as for others of influence, which he wishes me to convey. Pray that the messenger on this occasion will be rewarded for what he bears!

So I rest, your loving husband. Wish me 'God speed' and send me your blessing as I send my blessing to you.

William Hailwood Esq.

Dearest Hester

What joy it is to have my darling husband once more by my side! Since his arrival we have been like two young lovers, walking arm in arm along the country lanes, dancing together at the assemblies in the city, progressing to church of a Sunday with the children in our train. Our dear little church, which has felt so cold and lonely for so long, now feels the warmest place on earth since my prayers have been answered and William has been delivered to me safe and sound.

Before he arrived I was fearful he would take from me all I have won for myself over the years. Gedge, the steward, obeys all my orders without demure. Where I am unsure or ignorant he discusses the matter with me as if I were a man. When I make sound decisions I see the approval in his face. All too often I make poor ones, which he accepts, not reproaching me but doing what he can to ameliorate the harm I cause.

I was trembled lest I should lose all I had gained, that my husband would throw me aside, taking on all the management of the estate, treating me like a useless vessel fit only for the bearing of children. No! He sits there in his great armchair, swaddled in blankets against the cold and damp which he says pierce him to his bones, while I receive Gedge's reports and give him his instructions. The gardener he leaves to me also, alongside all the indoor and outdoor servants, the dry nurse and the governess. Do I make him sound lazy, uncaring? It is not so. Every evening we sit together after dinner once the servants have been dismissed and discuss the day's doings. Why have I done this or that? How is the estate faring? Which of the farms are productive and which are failing to produce? Is it determined by the quality of the land or the quality of the tenant? When we are silent I catch him watching me fiercely, like a hawk considering a tasty vole. Surely no vole can be as content as I to be so regarded!

But he is not completely happy here in this cold countryside. I tell by the way he moves, how his hands tremble when first he lifts his goblet of wine or port, how he is never satisfied when he returns from a day's shoot, no matter how many birds or coneys swing from his belt. Of an evening he sits huddled in the chimney twisting his hands like an old man, as if they were the icicles that only recently dangled from the eves of this ancient house. Oft-times I see his face, brown as oak from the fierce sun of India, turn grey and yellow as the east wind blows in from Russia, finding its way around the door jambs, rattling the windows in their frames.

Yet I am happy and determined to make him happy. We share such closeness and I well know how to warm his heart and body. I have become such a wanton! Perchance it is all of the tenderness I have stored up in the three years we have been apart. I fear it will lead the way all of our couplings have led since we made our acquaintances. One more will not make much difference, though I fear a fate like that of our late queen, Anne. 'Tis said she gave birth seventeen times, though none of them survived for long. We have both been lucky in our broods, dear Hester, and in our husbands. May we continue to live long in love and amity.

Your dearest friend and sister

Georgiana.

Your most gracious Majesty

I beg leave to attend Your Majesty at Your Majesty's pleasure to present to you letters of import from General Clive, subsequent upon his recent glorious victory at Plassey and from the Honourable East India Company's representative Mr Hastings on the governance of the Indian territories. Mr Hastings begs me to present to you the written submissions of various Nawabs and Rajahs alongside their gifts and representations.

I remain, sir, Your Majesty's most humble, loyal and obedient servant.

William Hailwood Esq.

Dear Hastings

His Majesty was pleased to grant me an audience at his palace of St. James to receive the letters and communications from yourself and General Clive. As you can imagine he was most pleased with the gifts, particularly the bronze elephant with the amethyst eyes and the ivory tusks wrapped in gold foil. My own bronze monkey wearing the coat studded with diamonds found more favour with the Duchess of Yarmouth than with the king.

Still, it has achieved its purpose, alongside Clive's recommendation. I am to be appointed quartermaster-general for the expeditions to North America and the Caribbean to eject the French from their holdings there next summer. It is said that Lord Pomeroy had previously secured the post for his son and is now most put out. General Wolfe tells me he was never happy with Pomeroy's appointment, he having no military or supply experience, being merely a salon popinjay. The king knows from his own experiences against the Scottish Jacobins how important it is to keep the army fed and supplied. "We starved them of shoes!" he said to me when I mentioned the matter. "They got as far as Derby then had to slink off back home in their bare feet.'

Wolfe has been a great friend and supporter, introducing me to many factors, ship-owners and merchants whose assistance I shall need. I suspect it was his word in the ear of the king that saw me raised to my current distinction. As you know, my estate at Boxwood comes to me through my dear wife Georgiana. Her father, Lord Phillipon who was, died leaving her the estate but could not bequeath his title to her. Thus the line of the Phillipons, which goes back to the Conquest, has died out and I had no title for me or for my sons. Wolfe conveyed this to the king, alongside the comment that it would be difficult for a mere gentleman, however well connected, to demand obedience from men in trade or to deal on an equal footing with officers and others who bore titles as well as holding His Majesty's commission. Hence I am now (or soon to be) Viscount Hailwood of Boxwood. Doesn't that sound grand! If the missions against the French prove successful I may yet grow to be a full baron!

I have petitioned the king to be allowed to accompany the expedition to Guadeloupe, to no avail. Even though spring is almost over and summer upon us, this poxy climate still chills me to the bone. I feel the damp melting my bones, the cold freezing my marrow until I shrivel like a sour and discarded ancient medlar. Here in London at least I have respite from the cold, which in Boxwood shrieks through every slit and crack in wood and stone. If it were not for the warmth and comfort of my darling Georgiana, who holds me so tight and fierce through the long cold nights, I would forever leave it for the squalor and sea coals of our foggy capital. Business forces me to stay in town and her advancing condition keeps her in the country. How sick I am of us being forever apart, even though now it be only a hundred miles.

Last week I took me to Woodstock and Marlborough's magnificent palace. It is built in the Italian style; in what they call Palladio. All is symmetrical, ornamented only in the severest of fashion. I have a mind to tear down the rotting corpse of the Phillipon mansion in Boxwood and replace it with another Blenheim. One not so grand, for they say the old Duchess bankrupted herself in its completion and never did pay the architect for his troubles. I shall cut the coat according to my cloth, not allow ambition to get the better of me, for the will of kings is fickle and we must all be prepared for royal patronage to crumble into royal displeasure at any moment.

You, too, should remember these words. Much is said against you in London: that you bear yourself too proudly, consider yourself a king in your own right among the maharajahs. Worst of all, they say you are corrupt, defrauding both the crown and the Company. Be kind wherever you can, take the sons of important men under your wing but most off all, hide your wealth from all, so you may appear a mere clerk and servant, underpaid and overworked.

Your dedicated friend

William, Viscount Hailwood of Boxwood

My dearest Hester

Are you not surprised to hear from me in town when I should be coddling myself among the cows and the sheep in the countryside? If I were not so delicate I would tell you of all the balls and entertainments that abound here but as yet I have attended none. William says that next week, if I am not so feeble, he will accompany me to a performance of a piece by Mr Handel. He says that Handel himself will be there, though he is much reduced by cause of his near blindness and his advanced age.

William is delighted to have me with him, as I am with him, but neither is happy with the cause of this connection. As I was descending the stairs, having prepared my soberest gown for church, I lost my footing, tumbling to the landing below. Fortunately, no limbs were broken but my body was much disturbed. The doctor ordered me to bed and rest at once. To no avail. The child had been shaken from me and I bled most prodigiously and was despaired of by the servants who insisted upon all sorts of village remedies, all of which the good doctor refused, prescribing only rest and drafts of hot brandy in milk. At last the child lost its grasp upon me and released itself. I was too shocked to look but Tabitha, my maid, told me it was no more than the merest kitten of a thing, which she could not believe would ever have survived even if I had gone my full term.

She is a foolish child but it is comforting to be told such things even it is the comfort of childish ignorance. So, I have left the children behind and taken lodgings with my husband here in London. Being with him once more is my heart's desire, though it will be long before I may be able to allow him to share my bed. The doctor insists I can bear many more children but my body tells me my mothering days are done. So much the better, that I may enjoy my sweet William for himself alone with no interruption to our daily felicity.

William is much exercised about the king's business, settling orders for the supply of ships and men for the continuing campaign. As if he were not so much occupied he has engaged an architect to assist him in new designs for changes to the house in Boxwood, which he says is too small and too damp for our thriving family. For me, I do not find it damp at all, or cold for that matter. But William feels it so! Even here, now it is summer, the fires blaze in the hearth day and night, especially in his office where he wraps himself yet in blankets as he goes about his work and negotiates with the king's tradesmen. I find this unbecoming but he says he must be comfortable or his mind goes awandering far from the business in hand.

Part of the business he conducts in a dangerous part of town, the haunt of low women and cut-throats called Covent Garden, though they say the only gardens there are the ones belonging to the prostitutes that the men water every night. I am not allowed to accompany him on his trips even though he is always attended by two stout chairmen with heavy cudgels. His object is a Jew from the Low Countries, a most unsavoury character of low repute even among his fellow religionists. I admit I am anxious to see this person and the whole of the garden. Maybe it is the way we wish always to look upon wickedness and become excited by it as long as it does not come too close to our persons. Do you remember clinging together as the governess read us the stories from the Arabian Nights with all the jinns and genii, witches and wizards and sultans cutting off peoples' heads?

There, I have made myself shiver! Write to me when you can and I will tell of all the sins and wickedness that I discover in this city of dirt and smoke.

Your devoted sister

Georgiana, Viscountess of Boxwood.

Is that not grand!

(first page missing, believed lost or burned)
and you should see the state of her shoes, no better than a common tart's.

To the Duchess of Yarmouth yester eve for a large supper. Warm champagne and a tenor who cold not hit the higher notes, not like the sophisticated entertainments we used to see when Suffolk was the *maitresse en titre.* Having a crude German royal house is bad enough but they will import their own German mistresses instead of sticking to our home grown variety, who have so much more taste and sophistication.

Talking of which, the belle was once more the delectable Countess Boxwood, in the lowest cut bodice you have ever seen on a public forum. Perhaps her husband bought it from one of the doxies he visits in Covent Garden. For a woman from the backwoods who has had three children she has worn pretty well, even if she has recourse to yards of muslin to hide the stretch marks on her bosom, which she hoists up on layers of the best whalebone. The gentlemen spent much time trying to penetrate the mysteries of the muslin, whilst we women had our eyes upon the sumptuous necklace which she wore. Quite barbaric in its design, there is no denying the beauty and value of the stones. Stolen by her husband from some harem in the east, I expect.

Her complexion is that of a summer apple, unless her paint has been applied by an expert in the art. Her colour, though, is too dark, typical of those country women not content to leave the real work around their estates to their husbands or their stewards. Fine ladies may sneer but the young men, and some of the old ones, cannot tear their eyes away from her. Lucky for her the Viscount is black as any negro, for she appears pale by comparison. He stands by all night watching her, like some beached whale. Have you seen the old beggar women in the streets who even in summer are bundled up in rags, carrying upon their persons every scrap they own for lack of a safe resting place for them? My Lord is exactly the same. He pretends to be a fat man but all know he is a mere stick bundled up in four or five layers, to pretend he is in Calcutta still. My cook says he demands meals of such fiery heat none but he can touch them, hoping to stoke the fires within to compensate for their lack without.

As for his wife, he will need to stoke her fires. Others would be all too delighted to take the task upon themselves. Philip, Lord Pomeroy's eldest, dances with her every chance he gets. I have heard him extolling the grace of her ankles, the charm of her conversation, the sharpness of her wit. Whenever they visit concert hall or theatre Sir Philip contrives to be of the party, willing to share his father's box with the happy couple.

Quite how happy they are we may well doubt. The husband's regular visits to the stews of Covent Garden suggest he may not find his home comforts completely to his liking. That, or he prefers the perverse practices of the doxies there, more in keeping with what he has discovered in his foreign travels than delicate and refined couplings with his own wife. Old Pomeroy is another such to be found in the dens of that quarter, though it is not girls he is after. Like Boxwood he funds his visits by recourse to the old Jew who has his squalid quarters in the gardens. Pomeroy is busy selling his wife's jewellery. Boxwood doles out diamonds from time to time. Once the necklace fails to shine upon the Duchess's neck we will discover to where it is all this foreign wealth flows. They say he is the most honest of all the king's servants; not a penny within his care but is diverted to the procurement of goods and men. Such probity cannot long survive in this wicked world. One only needs to study Lord M. to know that the king's service is a road to riches and advancement. I have invited the good lord to my soirée this evening. I believe him to be a man much in need of some entertaining female company.

Your affectionate friend

Cecilia.

Dear Hastings

When will this damn country ever get warm? I sit every day shrouded in blankets. Then last night I could not sleep for the sweats, soaking the linen so it needed to be changed. Yet here I am once more huddled before a roaring fire, the only one in any drawing room in the whole of London. Georgiana fusses over me like a mother hen. To be honest I enjoy it greatly, the attentions of her who is of such a tender and sweet disposition. She is not just admired at home but all abroad dote upon her beauty and tenderness of understanding. I am indeed a fortunate man to have such a wife. Many say to marry for love is a recipe for disaster, whilst for me it has been a recipe for constant joy and delight.

Work upon the new expedition moves on apace. Many of the dealers try to exact my trade by offering bribes and other inducements, just as the maharajahs in India have offered you all manner of things to retain power in their principalities. I trust you are resisting and refusing them as I am refusing these villains at home. It is not yet time for cargoes to go aboard but I shall be sure to be on deck, ready to inspect each delivery as it is loaded. Any but the best quality will be rejected without payment. No rotten pork or spoiled beef on my watch. The 1759 will be the best supplied expedition of any of the whole war.

Some continually seek to profit from it, knowing I cannot hold all in my hands or resolve all matters in my head alone. Aristocrats vie for places for their sons and nephews, incompetents and grasping nonentities all. Most pressing is Lord Pomeroy who throws his eldest son upon my attention at every step. We cannot visit theatre, concert or ball but he is there, seeking to gain his suit through constant conversations with my Georgiana. I remember Wolfe's warning and give him no credence. If he is so anxious to enter the king's service, he should ask his father to purchase him a commission in the Guards.

My architect, Macready, is a serious, morose young man in love with the buildings of the ancients. He travelled widely through France and Germany in his youth and before the recent wars visited King Louis's new palace in Versailles. Which new palace instructs us, he says, that to design a building in isolation is insufficient. Any dwelling of consequence must be planned together with its gardens. To which end he insists that the old red brick and stone building must be demolished completely as it is unsightly, even as a ruin. Of that I am fully glad for I find it the most banal and unsightly as ever was, with its bow windows and twisted chimneys, as well as being a colander through which the winds blow incessantly at all seasons.

Dear Georgiana will be furious once she learns what I and Macready contemplate. Now is the time for dissimulation. We maintain we are merely repairing and extending the old building. I intend to appease her by requesting she designs the grounds. In his zeal Macready already has his initial ideas on paper, which I shall present to her alongside a new box of pencils and watercolours.

For now, I have ceased my visits to the Jew. The more frequently I visit him the lower the price he offers me, claiming the market is flooded with raw stones from Amsterdam which no-one wishes to purchase on cause of the war. He is deceived; not I. My absence will squeeze a better price from him, for I know he has made promises of supply to his jeweller friends. Building and the services of a man such as Macready do not come cheap and I am determined the house will be finished entire without leading me into bankruptcy and the children into poverty and want. Once the jewels are gone I have but the rent from my tenants or a descent into peculation.

Enough for now, dear fellow. You are ever in my thoughts. Much as the king and the Company have need of your undoubted talents in India I cannot wait to see you in this windswept isle once more.

Boxwood.

My loveliest Aurora

For such you are, my dawn risen in the east, the light of my life. Lovelier than Ophelia. Wiser than Portia. More virtuous than Lucretia. How my heart leaps upon the barest glimpse of your features, how it languishes in your absence from my sight, becomes a veritable necropolis of love, darker even than that of the fair Juliet and her love-lorn Romeo

Every day I drive my valet to distraction. 'Will I see her again today?' I ask him. 'Will she like me in this waistcoat, approve of the buckles on my shoes?' Three or more times I change my mind, daring to aspire to Aurora's rays, ready to melt beneath the heat of her gaze. Last evening, I dressed and re-dressed so many times, knowing you would be at Lady M's reception, fearful I should not find favour in your sight. And there you were, shimmering in gold, the jewels at you throat surpassed only by the jewels of your eyes.

And what joy when you graced me as my partner in the quadrille! Surely not often enough. And I held your hand in mine as we progressed, the graceful embodiment of all my sleeping and waking fancies. Do not tell me that you did not feel the heat of my love, my longing, my sincere and abiding passion surging like the larva from some re-awakened volcano, besotted as I was by your beauty and your delicate touch upon my fingers. Could you have been, madam, impervious to my longing, engulfed as I am by your charms which have caused me unspeakable agony of mind?

Long have I endeavoured to smother my passion, but how may I endure if Aurora be not mine? I beg you to have mercy upon your servant, your lover for all eternity, your slave. Grant me but a few moments alone for me to tell you of my passion, so you may see I am no dissimulator but constant in my ardour. How may I say all this to you in the midst of the madness of ball or assembly? My heart has had no rest since I saw you last and I confess I never was so full of sorrow as I am this time, removed from the vision of your loveliness. Revive the light in my life, o glorious Aurora! One word from you suffices to spark the fires of my ecstasy; I burn beneath your glance, struck dumb by the sight of you across a room.

Be merciful, I pray you, to one so true of heart. No! For heart I have no longer, now it is stolen away by you, leaving me desirous at your feet. I die your eternal slave, for how may I endure if Aurora be not mine?

P.

Dear Hester

What a wicked city this is! Seduction and adultery are the pastime of most of those in the best society. A wife who has borne her husband an heir is assumed to be ready to take a lover. A man of any age knows all of the stews as well as keeping a mistress even into his dotage. As long as marriage continues as a market such things will continue. A man takes a wife to sustain his family name, a woman takes a husband to maintain her in luxury and satisfy her desire for children. Love is not a question, except with oddities such as me and William. He had no name and little money. I had property but no name or money. We should both have been seeking safety. Instead we found one another. Only now, after living apart for so long, are we as comfortable in our pockets as we are in our hearts. But more of that later. For now, I have much gossip to impart.

Lady M has taken another lover. Not unusual, you may say, except she has kept the old one as well. Her husband frequents one of the stews in Covent Gardens but not one where there are members of our sex. Lady M must feel slighted in the extreme! Others are trying to supplant the boys in her lord's affections, to little effect.

The fashion in polite society is a competition to see who dare the lowest décolleté. A competition I have entered into with the greatest enthusiasm. You know how proud I have always been of my bosoms, a pride which William shares with me. Despite the three children they are still quite firm and smooth, especially when reinforced by my new stays. Perhaps this is what has brought me so many admirers, young men who crowd me like bees around a honey pot. Sadly, I cannot recall their faces for I spend much of our conversations staring at the tops of their heads! They are very flirtatious and to avoid their solicitations I spend as much time as I may either on my husband's arm or dancing with as many as I choose, to avoid any scandal should I show particularity.

And I have a lover!

Not that his love is reciprocated. Yesterday, as you know, was my thirtieth birthday, signalling my youth is gone and done with. I am now a middle aged matron, though that seems to add to my attraction to the young men who suppose I am no longer an object of affection to my husband. My lover is a callow youth of some twenty years, the son of Lord Pomeroy. He is handsome enough in all honesty: tall, well featured with an upright and stately bearing. His conversation is easy and witty, if lacking in real substance. From it I gather he has been schooled in Shakespeare and the classics and has read much of the current spate of what is called 'novels'. As for serious matter and holy works he is totally deficient, which may account for his lightness of mind.

From him I have received several declarations of undying love. Incoherent nonsense worthy only of a village schoolboy. He reveals himself as a mere empty fop, a would-be Lothario intent upon filling his bed in the interval before his marriage. Which is imminently expected. The bride to be is a little dark thing, the eldest daughter of the Duke of T. She has a settlement of some five thousand a year from her father, who is one of the largest landowners in the county of Lancashire. Lord Pomeroy, my lover's father, is said to have wasted his fortune at the gaming tables and has little but a name to pass on to his son, a name which the Duke of T is anxious to attach to his waspish daughter.

I know she suspects young Pomeroy's attentions to me by the way she stares at me with her sharp little black eyes as if they would bore a hole in my skull, pierce my brain, leaving me lying dead upon the ground amongst a flurry of excited onlookers. I allow Pomeroy to dance with me no more than twice of an evening and encourage William to believe he attaches himself to our party purely as a way of achieving appointment to an office of profit under the crown. To succumb to his blandishments would be evil and disastrous to my peace of mind. At the same time, the flirtation is exciting and attractive enough to keep me dangling the boy upon my string, if only as a distraction while we are forced to remain in town as the new extension rises from the ground.

It is the grounds with which I am concerned. Macready has sent me his ideas of a possible design, to which I have added an ornamental lake or canal leading out from the new building, which will be reflected in it. Not as grand as Marlborough's lake and river at Woodstock, of course, but still one of the finest in the county. What a joy to wake of a summer's morning to see the sun glinting on the waters, view the regularity of the box hedges, the brilliance of the flowers in their beds. I am sure the children will love it as I will. With this letter you will find a rough plan Macready and I have determined upon. I trust you approve! If you do, perhaps we could re-plan your own curtilage in a more modern manner?

Now I must rush to dress, or rather undress since I will again be showing my bosoms to their best advantage. At their best they are sufficient to make William's eyes sparkle and make him forget the cold for a moment.

Your loving sister

Georgiana.

My Lord

Her ladyship insists that I should report all matters relating to the management of the estate directly to you as well as to her. As she says, all that is done is done in your name and reflects to your Honour. I also have tidings anent Mr. Macready's activities which he wishes me to convey.

To agricultural events first. Harvest has begun and is well advanced. Crops are good this year. Corn is ample and will fetch an excellent price on the market as the war continues. The turnips have proved a success for a change and the sheep will be let upon them to graze on the tops in the coming weeks before they are lifted for winter feed.

The geese have been gathered into their temporary enclosure and the tar cauldron set up. Betts, the smith, will assist with the tarring of their feet from tomorrow and the drive to London will begin the moment all are ready. Her ladyship has engaged with the Duke of Argyll to fatten his herds in the southwest meadow over the winter. His Grace writes to say the drovers have already set out from his lands. They are expected to arrive in the first week of next month when the harvest will be complete and the geese will be gone.

Her ladyship is most insistent upon detailing to you the terms of the arrangement with His Grace. He will pay an agreed fee for the accommodation of his herd, plus a bonus for the general increase in size of the cattle, to be determined in discussions between his head drover and myself and with the agreement of the two principals. In spring the cattle will be sold to the king's quarter-master general, yourself, for supply of the North America expedition. Her ladyship is adamant that the sale is solely between His Grace and the crown, the Boxwood estate having no part in it. Hence you have no conflict of interest and your Honour and Reputation are preserved intact.

As for Mr. Macready, he has completed the demolition of the old house and has stored such tiles, timber and stone as he deems appropriate for use in the new building. More will be required for the new foundations than was at first thought. The clay is only a foot and a half deep. Beneath is sand, forcing us to dig further in order to provide a solid base. Once the harvest is complete and the cattle settled in, our men will start work upon digging the foundations and upon the excavation of the ornamental canal which her ladyship has planned. Mr Macready says that the clay taken from the foundations can be used to line the canal in the same manner that the common folk use it to line their ponds.

At your instruction I have not informed her ladyship of the demolition of the ancient building, although she has been informed that Boxwood will not be suitable for a family Christmas celebration or for the harvest festival. The Rector has agreed to host both the harvest dinner and the Christmas celebrations in the church, it being large enough to hold the whole population of the village. I have kept back four geese for him to have cooked and disbursed to the congregation as has been the tradition at Boxwood for many years. Often have I been asked whether the tenants will be welcome for festive celebrations in the new manor once it is completed and have conveyed your assurances to them that such will continue during your lordship's lifetime.

I leave you, sir, as your humble servant

Isaiah Gedge.

December 1758
St. James

Dear Hester

Pomeroy has become most tiresome. Although he praises my virtue he is determined to maintain his assault upon it. Consequently, I do all I may to avoid him, dance with him only when it would create a scandal to refuse him in public. His behaviour is a matter of most annoyance to me, for I have to forgo many amusements which I would otherwise enjoy because of his insistent presence. Nor do I relish the eyes of his intended upon me at all times. It is like facing a firing squad of king's grenadiers.

Not that these troubles lessen my pleasure in our residence in London. Each week we have concerts by the finest singers and musicians as well as operas in full costume. Mr. Handel's oratorios are moving and conducive to one's finest religious feelings, which I find to cement me firmly into my faith. But there is nothing as exciting as a full blown opera! Once the new extension is completed my duties on the estate entail my presence in Boxwood, where the children will once more run wild, free of the dirt and dangers of the city. Much as I look forward to those days the winters here are delightful, especially as we are now together as a family. And it is so much simpler to find tutors for them, men of distinction from the universities of Oxford and Cambridge versed in Latin, Greek and the new continental philosophers as well as all the tenets of the Christian faith. Where will I find such paragons in the wilds of Boxwood?

The geese have arrived and are selling for excellent prices. Only a few were lost upon the road, most of which we are able to sell for enough to keep the drovers in ale! The Duke's cattle are fat and strong, so I anticipate a good bonus when they arrive in Smith-field in March. He is responsible for any losses on the road and for supplying the ale to his own drovers. A not inconsiderable expense, for these wild Scots have unquenchable thirsts.

As does Mr. Macready! Not for ale, but for money and materials. Every letter from him contains requests for more of both. The foundations need to be deeper, he says; more cement and lime are necessary; our farm workers cannot dig fast enough and other labourers have to be brought in from the surrounding villages. William visits the Jew increasingly often, each time returning with a lighter bag. It will not be long before we have to rely upon rents and bonuses from the Duke, a precariousness I do not welcome. There promises a short respite. All have returned to their homes for the Christmas celebrations, which is good news since there is no work for them to do. With the winter frosts the ground is frozen solid, impervious to pick and shovel. No-one may dig and the foundations have filled with water above the level of the broken brick. No cement may be added until the water seeps away. Even my lovely canal is only half dug, a danger in the dark to humans and animals alike.

William freezes even harder than the ground. His body grows smaller as his public silhouette grows larger. Now he is no longer brown but yellow as a Chinaman and frequently too ill to venture out of doors, lying wrapped in his bed under as many blankets as we can command. Yet his brain is as sharp as ever. When we discuss projects in the estate, such as using new crops like lucerne or introducing beans and peas into our rotation, he gives me such excellent advice, having read all the new thinking of Young, Tull and Coke. Once back in Boxwood, what a team we shall make! How lucky I am to have such an intelligent, honest and diligent husband who appreciates my good qualities and forgives my bad ones. What need have I for fops and popinjays like that idiot Pomeroy? The sooner he is married or shipped off to the Americas to fight the French the better.

Your loving sister

Georgiana

Sir

Much to my displeasure I have received yet another importunate missive from you.

I inform you once more that your attentions are disagreeable to me. All you say of my qualities is mere hyperbole, except in one regard. My virtue is highly praised and so it will remain.

No doubt you are accustomed to women who prate of their virtues whilst cunningly deceiving their husbands, cuckolding them with a string of lovers. I am, sir, a resolute Christian woman who has preserved her Modesty against all temptations of rank, fortune and appearance. I refuse to have any more social intercourse with you, be it at ball, theatre or place of worship. Should you present yourself at my abode you will be informed that I not at home to you.

My relations enquire why I have not informed my husband of your conduct. They fear many may impugn my honour and constancy, but I take this action merely to defend the life of the man I love and respect so dearly, my beloved husband. I reply that, should I inform him of your unwelcome pursuit despite my protestations that you desist, he will surely call you out. All know that such meetings end badly for all parties, especially ones where one of the principals is racked with illness.

I reiterate: your attentions to me dishonour both yourself and your family. They are insulting to me, impugning as they do my Virtue and my Constancy.

Georgiana Hailwood, Vicomtesse Boxwood.

Dear Hastings

Tidings reach us of great doings in Murshidabad. By the end of the year the French will have been ejected from India for ever. Company officers here are delighted, having their eyes on Danish and Portuguese holdings to boot. My expedition has departed for North America despite the recent severe weather. With God's grace we will see the end of French pretensions north of the Great Lakes and in Guadeloupe.

I have urged you in the past to beware of jealous and wicked people who will seek to do you harm. I, too, have had recent experience of such underhand practices seeking to undermine me and impute my Honour. His Majesty is not well, leaving much of everyday business in the safe hands of Mr. Pitt and the Prince of Wales. It was the Prince who approached me, having been told I had made large amounts from selling my own cattle to the Expedition for grossly inflated prices. 'Not what he would have expected from a servant of the Crown with such a reputation for honesty as my own.' Never was I so grateful for my good Georgiana's care and dedication to my well being.

I required the Prince to visit me in private at our lodgings in Jermyn Street where I keep my private papers. Or, rather, where the excellent Georgiana keeps our papers. There I was able to show to him the notarised agreement with the Duke of Argyll for the fattening of his cattle on our land, the agreement 'solely for foraging, all weight increase to be subject to an agreed bonus to be paid to the Boxwood estate. Any further sales of the animals to be purely an arrangement between the Duke's representatives and the purchaser from which the Boxwood estate will not receive a pecuniary benefit.'

Naturally the Prince was most apologetic that he had entertained thoughts of my misbehaviour. I intimated to him that I felt his secret informant was connected to a person who I supplanted in the King's favour and who I had subsequently refused to employ. His Highness was most gracious, assuring me of his continued favour and patronage, which was most welcome given the current poor health of the King, his father. I have given orders to the servants that the person in question be not admitted to our residence. They inform me my wife has issued a similar fiat concerning the son, which may account for his lack of persistence in our presence recently.

Work on the new building progresses rapidly at last. The sharp weather over Christmas did not last long and the east winds have dried out the land rapidly, allowing Macready to finish the foundations and start work on erecting the walls. God willing, most should be complete by the autumn, though the harvest will draw the majority of the workers away to the land. As for the workers themselves, they have been a great expense, even over the winter when there is normally little work to be had on the land and wages are normally lower. The war has made much for clothiers, metal workers and others to do, supplying uniforms, arms, horses and other necessities for the army and navy which has forced up wages, even for the least skilled and least able. My last jewels are jingling at the bottom of my bag but I expect them to last at least until I have put a roof over the head of my family come October.

Georgiana is delighted with the news, though she was hoping we might finish earlier. As well as looking forward to returning to Boxwood she is also looking forward to another season in town, where there is so much to do. Her dedication to the dance has abated in favour of Italian opera and the theatre. Many of the plays are scandalous, tales of adultery and misdeeds which I would not wish my children to witness. Georgiana quotes the Greek theatre to me, saying that we witness scenes of vice and wickedness so they are burned out of our desires, leaving us free and pure within. I am not wholly convinced and only attend such entertainments at her insistence, for she requires my escort at all times in public. Given our financial situation I have no choice but to remain in this dirty town, when I would much prefer to spend time in my new residence, which Macready assures me will be free of draughts and be the warmest country house that ever was. With the Prince's patronage and, one hopes, the success of the North American expedition I am assured of a lucrative position at court or in the administration.

My health is not good, which I ascribe to this filthy weather and dirty city. You are well advised to linger in the friendlier climate of India as long as you may.

Your intimate friend

William

Sir

The little plays of Fidelity that you see enacted in your drawing room are far from the truth, a farrago of Nonsense which far exceeds the twisted imagination even of Mr. Congreve.

You live, sir, with a woman famous for her loose and immoral behaviour far exceeding the licentiousness of the strumpets of Covent Garden or the stews of Poplar and the docks. A woman who displays her ageing charms to all and sundry in public, a spider spinning its web to entrap unwary young men into her snares. And some older men, too, it is said. A woman who regularly receives missives of undying affection from all and sundry, placing their hearts and their bodies at her feet. 'My life is bound up with yours' they say to her. 'My good heart, my dear heart' no doubt she replies.

Why do you suppose she pines so to remain in town when your lordship's heart and health yearns to return to the country? Is it not to fulfil the Assignations she has made with her numerous lovers, counting upon your impending presence at the harvest celebrations to free her from all constraints? There is one young man in partic-ular, one who is about to marry, she has ensnared, playing with like a cat with a tasty mouse, refusing access to her presence, avoiding in public, all the while trifling with him at secret meetings, enticing him away from his betrothed.

I counsel you, sir, to remove your wife from the temptations of the flesh and yourself from the Sorrow and Contempt of all those who know you and revere your excellent qualities. If I esteemed you less I could say more of the misbehaviour of one whom you mistakenly believe to be a paragon of Piety, Loyalty and Virtue!

Please forgive my importunity in so addressing you, which I do only out of respect for your Honour and Constancy.

Mercury

Gedge

I may no longer endure the noise and dirt of London. Despite the warm commendations of His Majesty and the offer of the post of Equerry to His Highness the Prince of Wales I must return to Boxwood to oversee its continued prosperity, for the good both of my heirs and the people of the village.

Mr. Macready informs me that much of the new house is complete and the whole of the living space made safe from wind and weather. Whichever new parts are fully habitable you are to prepare for our arrival today sennight. At the very least we require a dining room, two bedrooms for the children, a bedroom for myself with the largest fireplace and another for her ladyship. For now, the nursemaid must share a bedroom with the children and her ladyship's maid will sleep with her.

Pay careful attention to the cooking arrangements. If the roofing for the kitchen is incomplete obtain canvas from the shipyards in Lowestoft to provide a cover. It is imperative that there is an adequate supply of wood laid in both for the kitchens and to heat the house. Coppice the willows, supplementing them with further amounts of box and yew if necessary. Leave the two old oaks for now. They have been sold to the king's shipwrights, who will fell and trim them in due course. We will retain all trimmings for our own use once they have had time to dry.

As for household servants, you must make do with such as we bring back with us from London. Under cooks and scullery maids bring in from the village. None are to live in until all of the servants' quarters are finished; proper arrangements must await the completion of the building. Mr Macready has been directed to make all haste, to which end he is to employ as much labour as can be found in the vicinity now harvest is ended.

Even with his best efforts I do not expect all to be ready before Christmas. Kindly inform the Rector that the celebrations for the village people will once again be held in the church, for which we will supply candles and various comestibles. Once over, I expect all able bodied men not required on estate work to be directed to whatever activities as Mr. Macready requires on the building. If he is in agreement, the people may now remove such of the old stones from the ancient manor as they please. Reserve old wood for burning to heat the house in the coming winter. Most of it is oak which in its matured state should burn slow and hot. Mr Macready assure me this is the warmest and driest house in existence, but I fear I shall continue to suffer from this accursed English climate.

Over the past weeks, with her ladyship's assistance, I have prepared a list of our tenants with a statement of their holdings and their rent, which I enclose with this missive. Alongside the list I require you to prepare a statement of the efficiency of each tenant, his accuracy in meeting rental payments, his income and a calculation of earnings against the acreage he holds. Should this calculation prove trying to you, you may consult Mr. Macready who is well versed in the arithmetical arts.

William Hailwood, Viscount Boxwood.

My dear Hester

Never would I have imagined I would ever come to hate my lovely Boxwood so! The old house with its memories of our childhood and our dear mama and papa is no more. Without telling me, William has caused it to be destroyed. The very stones are gone, used as rubble for foundations or carted away by the people to line their meagre plots or provide a flooring over the beaten earth of their cottages. Every day sees another beam sawn into lengths to heat this already over-heated Italian box.

And it is so ugly! Absolutely square and mathematical; not a curve or an elegant alignment anywhere. Every window is exactly the same, all at exactly the same distance from one another, all right angles like some school lesson in trigonometry. How I miss the odd smoke blackened corners we used to hide in, the sudden discovery of a secret room, the curve of a turret or winding staircase, stones cracked or exfoliating from the great fire a hundred years since. All of our decorative twisted chimneys have gone, the new ones hidden behind extended walls. The decorative canal I designed is a huge disappointment. Macready has had it lined with the local clay but this is so impregnated with sand and impurities it allows the water steadily to drain away. There is so little rain in this part of the country it is only ever half full although now is the wettest part of the year. All the fish have died. Come the summer all we will be left with will be a stinking streak of slime and stinging insects.

William has spent much money on decorative plaster work, even before completing the kitchens. No doubt he has done so to please me, imagining that swags, putti and plaster leaves are to my taste. I would rather he had spent the money on extra tulip bulbs or decorative shrubs and bushes as I had in my design. I suspect Macready eliminated them in favour of his manicured lawns and geometrical walks, now so badly out of fashion.

Nor is the house complete, even yet. Labourers bang and crash at all times of the day, laughing and cursing, singing their vulgar songs.

Henry is away at school, which allows James to have his own room, with the nursemaid and the governess sharing the room between his and Amanda's. The governess is a treasure I discovered among the nonconformists in the city. Quiet and restrained in demeanour, dull in her dress, she is well read in literature, including the great poets Pope and Dryden, and even has passable Latin. She has agreed any religious instruction is to be purely from the Bible with nothing from any sectarian texts of any description. Each Sunday she spends in the city with her co-religionists, many of whom I have met and found to be both eminently well behaved and properly deferential.

No longer do I have to sleep with my maid, who has taken up quarters in a commodious room at the top of the house. She even has a fireplace and William has her supplied with a monthly allowance of sea coal, which is shipped in to the city along the river from Yarmouth. Yet am I displeased. William and I both have our own bedrooms, so there is no discord of a morning as to who is to dress when or how much room is taken up by my hairbrushes and unguents. His bedroom has a huge fireplace but is much smaller than mine. I am sad he never offers to share my bed, much as I entreat him. He says he is tired from supervising the builders or visiting the farms, that his illness bothers him so. His illness never bothered or constrained him in London!

London I perceive to be the cause of my resentment and discontent. There I was able to taste the culture of the great metropolis; here I am buried away in the country far from music and entertainments of all kinds. Nor do I understand why William has forgone the opportunities offered to him by the Prince of Wales and the King himself. I fear I may be the cause, that he has listened to gossip and slander from those who hate me. Tis true I have flirted outrageously with many gallants and have endeavoured to show my figure to its best advantage but I have never exceeded the bounds of propriety or forgotten my marriage vows.

One in particular I suspect of having whispered poison in my dear William's ear. Lord T's daughter, her of the gimlet eyes and minute waist, owner of a mendacious turn of mind, affianced companion to Lord Pomeroy's son Philip, he of whom I have complained much of to you in the past. She has finally achieved all she has sought. I am well out of the way, a hundred miles distant from the court. Philip and she have married; they wait only for the old man to breathe his last before she becomes Lady Pomeroy in her own right. Evil has its own reward. Old Pomeroy is said to have lavished all his fortune upon the boys and girls of Covent Garden, the son further consuming his fortune at the gaming tables. Their land is much mortgaged; more than its rents can sustain. The bankers lie in wait for the crash, which will come when the current war is ended and wheat prices return to normal, for even her settlement of five thousand a year will not be sufficient to save them. Those few who still write to me from London tell me that the marriage does not go well. Despite her condition she is seen about heavily painted to hide the bruises on her face and scrawny shoulders and he is to be seen more in the company of the Duchess of D than in the company of his wife.

Am I wicked for wishing ill to those who have done me disservice? If William were to admit to me the real reason for our hasty departure hence and his unwillingness to share my bed perhaps I could behave in a more Christian manner. I declare I should be a better example to the children and the servants. I know my dear Hester will chide me for my discontent and will give me good counsel. Once the roads have dried sufficiently I will inflict my discontent and my noisy children upon your good will and good sense.

In the mean time I remain your loving sister

Georgiana.

My darling William

How do I miss you! My heart was never so full of sorrow as at this moment when we have laid you to rest for ever in the earth. You are gone, you who was full of such wonderful Civility, a man of prodigious Charm and Generosity. You were always part of my existence, part of myself. To the last hour of my life you are fated to be the one I long for, the one who has stolen my heart and keeps it waiting for me in the tomb alongside your own.

Why could I not say this to you when you were alive? What has driven us apart over these past two years? Not only your advancing illness but some evil and malignant and malevolent force has been at work, casting aspersions upon my character. Would that you had told me of your suspicions, opened to me the poison that has been slowly dripped into your ear. I can brush away all, find an antidote to restore me to your good opinion, for I was ever much obliged to you for your good opinion of me.

Have I not always been a good wife, exulted in your company, a companion in your conversation, your nurse, advisor, person of business? Wherefore do you thus desert me for a second time, first with your heart, now with your body, your very presence. Oh, my love, how I yearn to have you by me once more. A thousand times I would forgo the pleasures of London, the stairs and chimneys of my old red house, the attentions of gay young men, if only I could feel and touch you one more time.

I know you might say in London I was too free, too audacious, too forward in my manners. But I was like so, as a child newly released from school running and skipping among the meadow, taking pleasure in the sun and light but always ready to return to its house when recalled to duty, indifferent to the lures and snares that surrounded me. For I swear that never did I stray from that course upon which I first embarked when dashing Will Hailwood took my hand sixteen years since. That Will Hailwood who, as the vicar said only yesterday, is now cut down like a flower, leaving me but a short time left to live, a time full of misery now his shade has departed.

But I shall not repine. Your children shall be the sweetest tempered, best beloved and cherished of all of the kingdom, for part of you lingers still in them. Your estate will grow in size and wealth, your name shall be honoured throughout the country, your Honour, Benevolence and Faithfulness recorded for all time, or as long as Boxwood exists.

My darling, the love I have for you will ever increase, it shall never decay.

I remain yours for ever, your faithful, grieving and obedient wife.

Georgiana

"The Norfolk Mercury"
July 1761

In the presence of Lady Georgina Hailwood and her children was yesterday erected in the parish church in Boxwood a memoriam to her late husband, William. A service of thanksgiving and remembrance was conducted by the incumbent Rev. Charles Betts in which he praised the late Lord for his Probity, Sanctity and Generosity. A letter of condolence from His Majesty King George iii was read, in which the king praised Lord Boxwood's part in the success of the late expedition to the Americas which gained the lands of Canada and Guadeloupe for the Crown. 'No man more Efficient nor more Honest could be found in all of the king's realms,' the letter concluded. Lord Boxwood leaves a sole male heir, Henry (14 years) a second son: James (10 years) and daughter Amanda (7 years).

The plaque is a large classical monument in grey marble. An heraldic shield sits on top of the central inscription which is flanked by columns. Three cherubs representing his Probity stand at the base, an open arched pediment on top. The memorial is the work of Joseph Lyle of Norwich, being inscribed as follows:

Sacred to the Memory
of Ld. William Hailwood of Boxwood
(Son of EDWARD and SUSAN his Wife) Who in An Age exposd to Temptation and prone to vice In Spite of the Contagion of corrupt Examples, blushed at every Vice, practised every Virtue
every generous Principle
was implanted in his Soul by Nature
Improved by Education matured by Practice:
a large and diffusive Benevolence distinguished Him to the World:
to his Friends, Faith & Constancy inviolable,
to his Relations the purest Affection
and to his Mother, Piety & Tenderness beyond Example. At the University of Cambridge
for the Space of three Years He pursued his Studies with Diligence

and Success,
And being ready to enter into
The publick & busy Scene of Life,
Fully prepared to Satisfy
The Expectation of his Country, the Hopes of his Friends, And the
fondest Wishes of a Parent;
A malignant Fever put an end to his Life,
In the 41st Year of his Age.
He died Ap: 7th. 1761.

1803

Desertion

'Gentlemen, turn. And fire.'

A single shot swifts away across the river, melts into the trees on either bank. A figure in red stands. A figure in blue stands. Slowly the figure in red sinks to his knees, crumples to the ground like the umpire's fallen handkerchief. The red seconds rush across, the doctor more slowly.

The blue figure bends, places his pistol on the ground. Takes his second's arm. Walks rapidly to the bank. The pair unfasten a small boat which the principal rows diagonally with the current to the far bank. 'Take horse now. Go to the country,' whispers the second, as if all around had not already been roused by the sound of the shot. 'If he lives or if he dies there will be a hue and cry. Best you are in the country until the fuss dies down. The peace will break soon. Collingwood will require you in Brest roads. No-one will care about one redcoat more or less.'

'My Honour forbids me to run.'

'You have vindicated your Honour this morning. There is nothing to be gained by remaining in London to be arrested; nothing to be lost by returning to Norfolk. Your friends will assert they know nought of your whereabouts.'

The journey was long and tedious once they had left the turnpike behind at Ipswich. February rain had turned the country roads to

140

mud, the horses sinking to their fetlocks, passengers forced to quit the shelter of the coach to lend their weight and strength to the beasts' efforts. Long after nightfall, covered in mud, coach and passengers arrived at the Coach and Horses inn, close to the centre of Framlingham, in the shadow of its crumbling castle. As the youngest and most agile, the man in the blue jacket was first to alight, accosting an inn servant making his way across the courtyard.

'A room, with a good fire. A fowl, some roast mutton and the best wine this hovel can afford.'

'Yes, sir. Straight away sir. At your service, Lieutenant Hailwood, sir.'

'Captain Hailwood, if you please, fellow. And tip your cap when you speak to me. Have my luggage sent up. And a jug of hot water. I suppose even a place like this runs to a towel in every room?'

'Only in the best rooms, Captain. You may be assured there will be one in your room.'

The servant scurried away. Captain Hailwood paused in the inn vestibule to tug off his boots, thumping them against the wall to shake from them the worst of the mud. 'Here, fellow,' he cried to the pot-boy, 'take these away. Have them cleaned ready for me in the morning. There's a penny here and another tomorrow if they are to my satisfaction. Don't stand about, boy. Get on with it.'

A noise of huffing and puffing behind him; his fellow passengers hauling their luggage across the courtyard, endeavouring to find someone willing to help or to engage a room on their behalf. William shrugged, wandered into the bar to escape the encroaching hubbub, ignoring the wet beer soaking into his stockings. Wet feet were nothing for one who had endured months at sea in raging gales off the French coast, tossed about in a frigate like a cork caught in a whirlpool. He scowled at a red faced farmer hunched up in a massive high backed chair, a bare inch of ale in the glass before him. The farmer caught his eye, looked away, twisted uncomfortably in his seat; in one motion, drained his glass, eased himself to his feet, drifted slowly towards the door.

Captain Hailwood smiled grimly, unbuttoned his dark blue jacket, settled himself into the farmer's chair. The pot-boy reappeared with a flagon of ale. 'Your meal will be ready soon, sir. I trust you will take it in your room?'

'Yes, of course. Tell them to hurry. I am starved after a long day on the road.'

Groups of men huddled round tables looked at the newcomer from the corner of their eyes. Word had gone around of the arrival of the hero, William Hailwood, second lieutenant of the frigate 'Astraea' which had captured the 'Gloire' off Brest in ninety-five despite being outgunned and dismasted. None had seen him before but all knew of his reputation as a hard and valiant sailor, not one to suffer fools gladly. They agreed he looked the part, his features hawk like above a protruding under lip, eyebrows thick and black as the thatch upon an old cottage roof, a complexion weather-beaten into a sheet of tanned leather, despite his bare twenty-two years. A captain now, the youngest in the service. 'On the beach' like so many others as this peace limped on, derided by all on both sides of the Channel.

'Your meal is ready in your room, sir. Would you care for more ale?'

The Captain shook his shaggy head, his short pigtail resolutely standing firm despite the fury surrounding it. He was glad to be rid of the fug of the bar, its tobacco smoke and odour of drying wool mixed with caked cattle shit on the boots of the herders and drovers. His room was no better than he expected. A single bed piled high with blankets, unwashed through the rain sodden winter, a dark grained washstand complete with bowl and steaming copper jug, a dry towel hung over the rail on the stand still showing streaks of dirt from a previous occupant. Hailwood threw it down in disgust, poured the contents of the jug into the bowl, splashing water over face and hands to remove the worst of the dirt from his journey. He untied his neckcloth, turned it inside out and used it as a towel with which to dry himself.

Ablutions over he tried the mutton, from which rose a heady smell of dead animal, blood flooding the greasy plate on which it stood. By contrast the chicken had been long alive and long cooking, dried out to pale strings as thin and strong as whipping twine. He had eaten worse after a ninety-day voyage with no chance of renewing provisions, weevils crawling out of the hard tack, a bright green slime around what water was left in the barrel. But this was dry land, a supposedly high class coaching inn. One thing his captains had always insisted upon, a decent drop of smuggled Bordeaux on hand in which to soak the hard tack or drown the weevils. Not like this piss! Not even fit for vinegar. He had pissed out better wine than this after a long night's drinking.

'Landlord!' he shouted from his door. 'Where is the landlord? Get the wastrel up here.'

The landlord, a short barrel of a man, much taken with sampling his own wares, rolled up the stairs, wringing his hands on a filthy cloth.

'What do you mean, serving this muck to a gentleman? If you were on my ship, I'd have you flogged with a cat o' nine tails till your blood filled your disgusting boots. Get away from me, man and fetch me something to eat. And something palatable to drink.'

'But, sir, the blockade. No wine has arrived from France in years.'

'Don't tell me about the blockade, you old fraud, it has been cleared these last eighteen months. Why else am I sitting here in this pit staring at your grasping features? Be off with you and thank your lucky stars the navy is here to protect you from Napoleon and his armies.' With that he caught the innkeeper an enormous buffet around his ears, sending the man tumbling down the stairs, leaving him screaming in pain at the bottom, clutching his arm to his side.

A nervous pot boy quickly reappeared, bearing a bottle covered in dust. 'A 1780, sir,' he whispered. 'One of the landlord's own specials. Don't tell him I gave it you, sir.'

Captain Hailwood fished in his pocket for a sixpence, settled down to taste the wine, savouring its vintage flavours, while waiting for a meal he could tackle with pleasure.

Next morning the landlord was nowhere to be seen, still in his bed nursing a broken arm and bruised shoulder. To the passengers' relief the pale sun shone through the clouds. The pot-boy grasped the extra penny he had hard earned in bringing the Captain's boots to a high shine. 'Might I do well at sea, sir?' he asked piteously.

'Once this damned peace is over I will need volunteers, even ones as youthful as you. Catch me on my return. Have you bag packed.'

'I have no bag sir, nothing bar what I stand up in. But I will be ready on your return, sir.'

The twenty miles to the city was slow and tedious but less muddy than the previous day's. By mid day the spire of the cathedral was in sight, the roads solid and well kept. Hailwood lost no time in hiring a horse at the Dun Cow for the five miles out to Boxwood. 'And your luggage, Captain?' asked the ostler. 'Shall I engage Barkiss, the carrier, to deliver it to you on the morrow?'

'Certainly. You know where I shall be. Old Gedge will pay him when he delivers and arrange for your horse to be returned. I shan't need it; my father has animals enough.'

A blustery wind was blowing from the east, enough to keep the fleet clear of the dangerous sandbanks off the Brest coast, enough to clear the travel cobwebs from a sailor's brain. Odd hedgerows were coming cautiously into blossom, autumn wheat carpeting the fields. Lambs clung pitiably close to their mothers, shivering in the wind. Unexpectedly, Hailwood's face burst into a smile. This was what he was fighting for, the beautiful English countryside, its free yeoman farmers, the unquestioned social hierarchy undisturbed by uprisings and republicans. No guillotine here, no marching peasants, scythes in hand. A government of free men by free men.

The road turned slightly south-east, in the direction of Bungay and the coast, bordered now by fields he recognised. He hailed Mother Goss, returning from delivering a sheep of twins; old George, digging over his vegetable patch. 'How goes it, George?' Hailwood demanded. 'You are as hale and hearty as ever.'

'The year has been mighty hard, Master Hailwood. Rain, rain, rain. All the cabbages eten up by dodmans. Narry enough to feed the bairns. You know this soil, right clarty it be, falls like putty, sets like concrete. Over your knees one minute, cutting the soles of your feet the next. The world be a dreadful hard place, what with rents going up and rain a coming down. All right for some what sell for war prices, not for the likes of we who have to pay' em.'

'Never you mind, George. Gedge will bring a trifle something down from the house to tide you over for a while. How's your lad? He must be full grown by now?'

'Full grown and far away. Gone to the city. Dreadful unhealthy place, he's always full of cold and disease. Good job, though, working in the counting house. A relative of yourn, no doubt. A sort of banker. Work for him all hours, all year. Us on the land, we work when it's light, sleeps when the sun go down. He ruins his eyes by candles. Paid well, must say that. Not that I see none on it. A little near, that son of mine. Don't even spend it on the girls. 'I'm saving to move to London, pa,' he say. 'Move up, get a better job in a real bank, be a manager one day.' Why you want to be a manager, I ses to him. A roof over your head and enough bread to fill your belly, that's all a man needs. But he don't listen to I. All the young ones want to do nowadays is rush off to the bright lights of the city. Hardly none of them left round here. If it's not the city, it's the army. Gone off to Spain and the like.'

Hailwood smiled at the old man's rant, one he had been hearing as long as he could remember, though perhaps more often since the war began ten years ago. He shook George's hand, pressing a sixpence into it as he did so. A sixpence was enough to keep him indoors for a couple of weeks instead of out poaching the lord's game. Once he inherited his father's land and title he would need to be more severe with poachers like George. Their lives were hard but they must become more efficient. He will force them to it. All renewed leases will have a clause in them forcing the tenants to farm under the direction of the agent, whether they liked it or not.

Grandmother would not have approved but she was two years gone now. Even she had been hard on the bad tenants, refused to renew leases to bad payers, threatened the inefficient ones, put up their rents. Life had been hard for her, he knew, managing the estate on her own with all of the money spent on the new mansion, which she cordially hated. The farm and the tenants had to be squeezed to keep the family in their proper station, to send the boys to school, provide aunt Amanda with a decent dowry, enough to attract a rich merchant's son, a rich merchant who had bought William a naval commission, to his eternal delight.

And here was the mansion. Grand beyond was an alley of lime trees, clearly visible from the road. What had changed since his last visit? The canal had been filled in, now replaced by vegetable beds within hedges of decorative box to hide their practical and agricultural function. 'A sensible idea,' Hailwood thought. The canal had always been a disaster, never full enough to swim in even if they had thought to brave its scummy waters, a breeding ground for stinging insects and choruses of noisy frogs. And a portico had been added to the facade, breaking down its severe lines. Another improvement, he thought, allowing visitors to shelter from the rain whilst waiting to hear if the master was 'at home'. He would keep it so, as well as re-rendering the facade itself, perhaps with a pale blue surface, or whatever his wife preferred.

As yet he had no wife. Once he returned with prize money in his purse and the prospects of a title after his father died there would be no end of fathers anxious to introduce him to their daughters. He had no further demands. Blonde, brunette, short, tall. A pleasant malleable disposition and a charming smile will be sufficient, alongside a sizeable dowry in her own right. His brother was more susceptible, making cows eyes at every lithe figure or flattering glance that passed him by. But a second son must make do with what he can get, for he has little to offer.

Here he is, the second son, Charles, bright eyed, bright haired, jumpy as the rabbits that ruin the flowers beds every March. Together with father, Henry Hailwood, Viscount Boxwood, hale and hearty as George and just as brown and weather beaten. The product of shoot and ride; George of dig and harvest. The returning son was welcomed with merriment, enquiries after Admirals Colpoys and Collingwood, rumours of Nelson's amours in the Mediterranean. William decried the peace as putting an end to any chance of prize money. Father winked, hinted underhand plans were afoot for a surprise attack which would put an end to the peace and send William to sea once more.

There were no women left in the family. Grandmother Georgiana was two years dead. The boys did not remember their mother, killed by an incompetent surgeon while giving birth to Charles. Their lack showed in the unbridled conversation and over-indulgence in wine and port.

'We have lived well since ninety-two,' said Henry. 'Prices are high and harvest respectable. But these last two years we have seen how the world will be once Napoleon is defeated. The price of wheat has fallen each year of the peace but costs have continued to rise. It is imperative that we improve our methods and our organisation.'

'Papa has already bought a seed drill,' interjected Charles. 'Instead of sewing broadcast, casting our seed upon stony ground and wasting it, the seeds are sewn in a regular manner. Where we used to get two stalks for every five grains, now we get five.'

'Not only that, we have increased the yields because the stalks don't crowd one another and can be harvested in straight rows, without any waste.' Father leant back in his chair, gulped at his port.

'But that means there are no gleanings for the women afterwards,' objected William. 'Many of them rely on the gleanings for their winter loaves.'

'I can't help that. I pay them to harvest, not to scrounge pickings from the fields. Sir Timothy and Sir Peter Truscott are joining with me to fund an enclosure bill in the next parliament. We aim to move the old road down to the south so all of my land is on one side of it and all of Sir Peter's on the other. We will be able to walk to the church without having to cross the road, and herd our cattle as we will.'

'That will leave the village over a hundred yards from the road, father. How will they get their goods to market?'

'Never mind about that. Our solicitor, Evershed, has it in hand. Between us we will build five new roads, one to each of the existing villages. Once it is complete we can drive your new bride to the church in our dogcart instead of her having to walk across the fields and get her dress all wet and dirty. Sir Timothy's girl is a pretty little thing. Tomorrow we may go there for the shoot so you can pay your respects.'

The conversation continued, growing ever more technical and disjointed. Charles condemned the use of turnips in the rotation. William declared his grandmother swore by them. Outdated rubbish opined Charles. Grandmother was just a senile old woman. William jumped to her defence. Words were said, violence offered, wine spilled. Father played the peacemaker, packed the boys off to bed, reflected on what a hundred years later will be referred to as sibling rivalry, wondered when the three of them would ever be able to assemble in the same room without it ending in an argument.

William woke next morning with a splitting headache, which he put down to the stuffiness of his room. He armed himself with a gun from the gunroom downstairs and allowed one of the pointers to trail him into the largest of the copses. A light drizzle collected on the naked branches of the trees, dripped off the brim of his hat. Birds and rabbits burst out of hedgerow and undergrowth at his approach, causing excitement in the pointer but little reaction in the man. By lunch time he had traversed the whole of his father's land, across Sir Peter's and into the depths of Sir Timothy's. Rain and exercise had cleared his head, brought on a thirst.

Earlsford boasted a fine array of cottages and an inn famous in the locality for the quality of its ale. "The Royal Oak" proclaimed itself with a swinging placard of the eponymous oak surmounted by a shining gold crown, putting William once more in mind of his brother Charles and of their argument the previous evening. The hubbub of voices died as he entered, loudly demanding a flagon of the best ale, but resumed once he had taken his place in a high backed settle in the snug far from the blazing log fire. Voices rose in anger from the public bar.

'You are wrong, Alfred Wenn, the enclosure will be the best thing what ever happened to us in Earlsford. All our land will be in one place, not spread out all over the estate. No more time wasted walking from one field to another, lugging our spades and forks with us. Fields large enough to keep a good number of sheep or cows on. I can breed up some proper sheep, not some scabby old runts like those on the common.'

'Of course you could.' Alfred had a low, hard voice of one not expecting to be contradicted. 'And where do you expect to find the twenty guineas to hire a prize ram to service your sheep. Or are you going to do it yourself?' Ribald laughter ensued.

Not to be put off the first speaker continued. 'With the enclosure we'll all get a parcel of land equal to our share in the common. We can farm it as we like without Jake Howell's cows trampling all over it.'

'And where will Jake Howell graze his cows?' roared a voice.

"In everyone else's fields like they do now, Jake Howell,' chimed in another.

'You mark my words,' Alfred gruffed on, 'no good will come of this to any of us. By the time we've paid for hedging and ditching there'll be no money left for seed corn or fodder for the winter. The lords don't care; they have more money than they know what to do with. Turn all the fields over to sheep and cows so they don't need to pay the likes of us to harvest. Maybe it won't be so bad for we over here in Earlsford, but there won't be nothing left of Boxwood once old Hailwood gets his bill through parliament. All for 'improvement', he be. His ma, she were all right and that young 'un over there, he's stern but fair, they say; but the old man will hang on for a good twenty year yet.'

'Boxwood's a dead hole anywheres,' broke in Jake Howell. 'Nothing but hansas and mavishes, narry a good fowl to be found for love nor money. Now Mathew Graver's closed his brew house no-one will go there for nothing.'

'All the better,' chipped in the landlord, arms full of tankards for his customers, 'they can come here instead and make me rich.'

'The amount of water in this ale, you must be half way there already.' A muffled voice from someone anxious not to be shown the door too early.

William slipped away out of the back door, leaving a couple of coppers behind on the table to pay for his drink. 'There is much amiss here,' he thought. 'These Norfolk folk are a miserable lot at the best of times, but I've rarely heard them in such a pessimistic temper. Alfred Wenn never has any good to say about a change, even if he makes money out of it, but there is much in what he says.' He pointed his gun in the general direction of a pair of rabbits roused from the undergrowth by the noise of the man and the smell of his dog. Thought better of it, pursued his way homeward across fields of rough pasture grazed by the Duke of Argyll's herds, being fattened up for sale to the army drilled for war in Spain.

So engrossed was he, his gun remained unused as he rounded the large copse to come upon a shiny carriage, its empty traces dragging on the ground, the horses having been led away to be fed and watered in the stables. A rich visitor and one who intended to stay for some time. No opportunity, then, to discuss the lot of the village labourers with his father and brother. Sir Timothy by the looks of it, his coat of arms painted on the carriage door, wrapped around by the family motto: 'aut nunquam ten tes aut perfice'. William shrugged cynically. The old fraud did everything he could thoroughly, whether it was perfect was a completely different question. A good job the Latin was ambiguous.

'Sir Timothy and Miss Phyllida, sir,' observed the butler. 'His lordship has ordered supper served once you are home.'

'Kindly inform his lordship and Sir Timothy I wish to clean up and change before dinner. If you could arrange for hot water to my room.'

'Of course, Captain. Might I inform his lordship that supper will be ready in an hour? That will give you plenty of time for your ablutions.'

'Excellent. Get young Gedge to see to the dog for me.'

Supper tonight was a much more formal and decorous affair than the night before. Purple faced Sir Timothy was not one to relax his dignity or the formality of his conversation, oracular as one unaccustomed to being contradicted. Rarely would anyone as much as interrupt a Justice of the Peace who also sat upon the government benches in the House of Lords. Though William thought of him as old he was only a trifle over fifty; in the prime of life he would tell his drinking companions, ones who egged him ever closer to obesity and an early death.

His daughter, Phyllida, milky of complexion and demure of manner, had inherited her father's figure if not yet his habit of consuming copious amounts of wine and spirits. A generation later she would have been delighted to adopt the bustle to hide the roundness of her figure. In these more permissive Georgian times she adopted a fashionable low décolleté to show off her ample bosom. 'A Norfolk dumpling' was the judgement of Alfred Wenn and his companions in the 'Royal Oak' in Earlsford.

Nevertheless, at sixteen she had youth on her side, unspoiled as yet by flirtatious city mannerisms and fake coyness, as well as employing the best dressmaker in Norfolk. While Viscount Boxwood and her father discoursed loudly on important matters such as the carcass weight of cattle, the price of chalk for marling the fields and the merits of horse hoes and horse rakes, she carried on a quiet conversation with William, expatiating on the delights of Mrs. Radcliffe's novels and Mr. Wordsworth's poetry. William in his turn warned her to be less promiscuous with her reading, to avoid the atheist Godwin and his immoral consort Madame Wollstonecraft, both bidding to overthrow the existing social order and turn England into a French style republican autocracy. Phyllida objected that 'Republican autocracy' was an oxymoron, a contradiction in terms, leading on to an animated discussion of the rights and responsibilities of lords and peasants alike, during which discussion the young people found much to admire in one another.

Supper in those days ended early when guests had an hour's journey home on unlighted country roads, troubled by wandering discharged soldiers. Candles were lighted, port decanters replenished, the three Hailwood men settled themselves by the fire. 'You seemed much taken by Timothy's gal,' observed the father. 'She would be a good match for you once you finish in the service. Her brother will inherit, of course, but Timothy would give her a fair portion. I'll speak to him about it, see how he feels.'

'Father, you are over-hasty as usual. I exchange a sentence or two with the girl and you have us wed already.'

'Far more than a sentence or two, dear boy. You had her ear for the whole of the meal and I swear if they had stayed you would be monopolizing her still.'

'While Sir Timothy monopolizes everyone within earshot, there is no choice.'

'We shall see. I meet him in the city tomorrow to go over the details of the Enclosure Bill with Evershed and I'll put it to him then.'

'Father, do you really think enclosure is the right way to go? Most of the villagers will have so little land they won't be able to survive. They'll become mere labourers or vagrants.'

Viscount Hailwood stayed unmoved. 'We must think in terms of improvement and efficiency. New machinery demands bigger fields. And what do I care if the villagers are labourers? That will stop them demanding higher wages or slouching off to look after their own fields and cattle when they should be tending mine.'

William remained unconvinced, especially when Charles joined in on his father's side. Once more the discussion grew heated, only subsiding when the father ordered his two sons off to bed.

It would be pleasant and romantic to report that William spent the night dreaming of Miss Phyllida. Instead his sleep was broken by the lack of wind in the sails or creaking of spars, by Alfred Wenn's voice declaring he was now a pauper, by Jake Howell whining he had nowhere to graze his cattle. But he did take the opportunity next day to take gun and dog off in the direction of Sir Timothy's mansion, to encounter Miss Phyllida pruning her roses, rather too late in the season.

On into April he continued his walks and much unnecessary pruning decimated the incipient rose buds. As the weather grew warmer William frequently broke off his return journey in the snug of the 'Royal Oak', listening unobserved to the conversation of the villagers in the bar. It had rained steadily all that day and Phyllida had not been able to frequent the garden or to appear at all out of doors. The villagers, too, had been kept in by the downpour, their spirits lifted by noisy games of dominoes and large quantities of the landlord's latest brew. Jake Howell was worried his youngest daughter had been sporting with the vicar's son behind the church in Boxwood, on the pretence of gathering hard yew branches to reinforce Jake's ageing cart shafts.

'Tis all the same with young maids nowadays,' grumbled Jake. 'They be always putting on parts. No respect, not like when we were their age.'

'That's right, that is,' agreed another. 'We kids got out of line, our old man would be something savage, there'd be a right old barney, he'd larrup the lot on us. Then off to bed with no supper.'

'An it's not just us little folks, neither,' Alfred Wenn agreed,' there's that titty-totty lass of Sir Timothy's what is carrying on something rotten with the sailor boy. Can't blame her much, good looking feller such as he be, and she nothing but puppy fat. He's a gret catch for such a lummox as her, that fine house and all the Boxwood estate. She'll have to hurry up, though, if the rumours be true and we'll be back at war with the French within a month. Get herself on her back in them stables, make sure he leaves her a present when he go sail the ocean main.'

A chorus of ribald laughter.

William erupted from the snug, gun in hand, buffeted Alfred Wenn around the head so hard he fell to the floor, kicked him as hard and as often as he could, aiming at the softest, most vulnerable parts. The drinkers leapt to their feet, stood around in awe as William's face grew redder and redder, his blows harder and harder. 'He'll kill the man,' cried Jake Howell. 'Someone do something.'

No one dared, until the landlord arrived with his wife, pot-boy and ostler. At the price of several buffets on their own account they managed to pull William away, held him as he struggled. 'You should go home, sir,' advised the landlord. 'A long walk will do you the world of good. Maybe not come back here for a week or two in case of any nastiness. They be a funny crowd here in Earlsford.'

Released, William grabbed his hat and gun, ran out of the bar, dog at his heels.

'Alfred Wenn, you stop your blaren, its getting on my wick. If you're going to blow off a load of old squit about your betters, a thrashing is all you deserve. Now you get out of here yoursen, go roll in the nettles, it'll make you forget your bruises. The rest on you, 'bout time you went home, too, now the jollifications is over. Go and look after your own bairns instead of mouthing off about other people's. The sun will be out tomorrow, you'll have plenty to keep you occupied, and if you haven't, I've a stable what needs mucking out.'

William did not return to Earlsford the next day, nor the one after that. The third day an invitation came from Sir Timothy to the

Hailwood family for a formal supper together with some of his other acquaintances.

It was not a jolly party which set off from Boxwood that April evening, despite the unseasonably fine weather which was busy drying out marsh and meadow. Charles had been forced to abandon an assignation with a dairymaid from Allington. His father was still smarting from being accused of unchristian avarice by his eldest son, who in turn was mulling over the tone of a letter he intended to send to solicitor Evershed demanding he put an end to the preparation of the Boxwood Enclosure Bill, on the grounds that it would seriously endanger his patrimony. Solicitor Evershed felt these were insufficient grounds but had nevertheless stopped work on the Bill until his clerks had thoroughly disinterred all precedents and statutes since the Conquest. Additional searches and delays could only mean additional fees.

Dinners at Sir Timothy's could always be relied upon for substantial fare, thanks to Sir Timothy's efficient wife, scion of an extremely rich northern family used to entertaining members of the royal family on their periodic progresses to the provinces. Both William and Charles feared for a night of unmitigated boredom when confronted with the other guests: Sir Peter Truscott and his family. Sir Peter's conversation was limited to shooting and the hunt. Less of the latter now that his dedication had caused the virtual extinction of the fox in this part of East Anglia which had led in turn to an explosion of the rabbit population, a connection Sir Peter completely failed to understand. His wife, a vapid creature, spent much of the evening complaining of her health in lurid detail, to the discomfort of her listeners, much exacerbated by the arrival of a hugely underdone joint of beef, at which point she hastily moved to a description of the latest London fashions.

Relief came in the form of Sir Peter's eldest son, John, about to return to Cambridge for his final term. John and Charles had conceived a liking for one another over a bowl of rum punch whilst roistering one evening in the city, where John had introduced Charles to some underdressed and compliant young ladies. The two conversed animatedly across the table while William tried in vain to discuss the poetry of George Crabbe with Phyllida across the ample bosom and silent disapproval of her mother.

Giving up the forlorn attempt, William returned to the conversation of the two younger men, deep in the details of agricultural mechanisation. 'We have seen how manufacture has been expanded fourfold by the introduction of new machinery,' proclaimed John. "Within ten years the same will be so with agriculture. When you are lord of your estate, William, you and your wife will own more steam engines than you employ labourers. All small farms will have disappeared; your children will inherit from you a farm that will run itself with no human intervention.'

'I'm not sure that is such a good thing. Change is not always for the best. Humans are better at inventing for destruction than inventing for peace. The French have a ship that will run under the water to plant bombs under other ships.'

'Fie, man! Are you afraid you will be out of a command, blown sky high by a French plot? Come now, have some optimism. We have peace, the world is full of pretty girls. You must take your chances while you may.'

"I feel my brother has already taken his chance,' murmured Charles, careful to keep his voice below Sir Timothy's droning bellow at the far end of the table. 'He visits much in certain houses of late when the elders be far from home.'

'Oho!' John was in his element, his particular area of expertise. 'And has he declared himself? Or is he merely passing the time before his meeting with Mistress Josephine? Tickling someone's fancy, perhaps?'

'I'm not sure I care for your tone, sir.' William addressed himself to the carcass of a pheasant on the plate before him.'

'Come, man, be jolly. There be plenty of buds ready for the plucking if one knows where to look. Our host's eldest might do at a pinch. For pinch you must do to find something firm to hold. Round enough to roll in the hay of an autumn eve, I'll be bound. Not a beauty, but she would do to pass the time. Young enough to know what she has got, too young to know how to defend it. Might even have a crack at her myself.'

Holding fast to the seat of his chair, William leant across the table. 'You demean yourself, sir, much as you demean others. Such language is not for polite company, sir.'

'Surely you have heard worse on the deck of a man of war or in the stews of Portsmouth or London? A man of the world such as you must be immune to it, more than a dull stay at home such as I? Where are your wits?'

'I may have forgotten my wits but Mr. Shakespeare has a hold upon yours. 'Home keeping youth have ever homely wits.' Though he may have struggled to find yours.'

Phyllida giggled nervously. Her mother stared in blank amazement.

Infuriated by being insulted before the women, John Truscott shot to his feet, banging his fists upon the table. 'Thank God we have an army to keep us safe when the navy is populated by such witless fools as you.'

Without rising, William flung his wine glass full in John's face, cutting his cheek, spattering wine and blood down his silk waistcoat, like tears from a saint's eye.

Servants rushed forward to prevent the two coming to blows. Sir Timothy stood and roared from the top of the table. 'I will not have this in my house, in front of my wife and daughter. John Truscott, this is not Rose Lane nor the Cardinal's Hat that you should bluster and roister here. William Hailwood, is it not enough you cause riot in country inns, beat inoffensive ploughmen that you should bring your anger to my house and table? Save your aggression for the French, let them bear the brunt of your fierceness. Begone, the pair of you. I forbid you both entry to this house until you have made a full and unconditional apology to all here gathered, shaken hands before the priest and sworn to eternal amity.'

Charles caught William by the arm and marched him to the door, neither staying long enough to collect their hats. In the dark of the drive William stood firm, refusing to move further, despite his brother's protestations. For which he had little time, as John Truscott hurried towards them, chest thrown out, waving a pistol.

'This is neither the time nor the place,' urged Charles.

'You will both be cooler in the morning and all may be made well.'

'You are right, brother,' declared William icily. 'The time is dawn tomorrow. The place is the level ground by the river behind the willow stand. You know where I mean? You have a second? I have pistols; you may prefer to bring your own.'

A silent dawn. The birds have not yet risen. Two heron stand watchfully waiting for the stream to bring them their breakfast. Five men arrive from different directions. Three huddle together. The other two stand back to back, march twenty paces apart.

Fire.

The two shots sound as one, rolling away across the meadow, disturbing sleepy birds and the last remaining fox slinking home, baby rabbit in her jaws. The figure in grey shrinks to his knees, helped to lie down by his second. A doctor follows.

The figure in blue stands, his right arm extended, smoke still rising from his pistol. Charles moves towards him. William stares back at him. Crashes to the floor, stone dead among the orchids and marigolds of the marsh.

In May 1803 the British broke the peace by impounding every French and Dutch ship in British waters. Sir Henry Hailwood brought his Boxwood (Enclosure) Bill before parliament.

In October 1805 Nelson and Collingwood caused national celebration by their convincing defeat of the combined French and Spanish fleets at Trafalgar. The same month the Boxwood (Enclosure) Act became law.

Nobody noticed.

1863

Reconstruction

'A quaint setting, do you not find? The artist has caught the romantic feel of a much loved but ancient building in the twilight of her years.' The art dealer lifted the drawing from the wall, surreptitiously wiping the cobwebs from the frame with his white gloved hands. 'See how every tile has its own prefect line and individual shade, the flints glistening with the early morning dew. See how the building fades into the foliage, blends with the landscape beyond.'

Edgar Hailwood shook his head dubiously. Old Crome had certainly caught the spirit of St. Wandrede's church in Boxwood as it had been thirty years ago but had exercised immense artistic licence on depicting it as an imminent ruin. Even now the roof did not sag quite as badly, the eaves were not as tattered, the foliage more kempt. Inside, the chairs were kept in perfect order by the churchwarden even if the vicar had refused to mount the crumbling pulpit, delivering his sermons from a raised box covered with baize, reading from a lectern he brought with him from All Saints in Earlsford for the purpose.

'Of course, it would need reframing,' added the dealer. 'These simple wood frames are merely for exhibition purposes. Your good lady would no doubt wish to choose a frame that blends in with the décor of wherever she decides to hang it.' He rubbed his hand down the side of his trousers to remove the last of the cobwebs.

'It is not for my wife but for my daughter. She has a love of these things and has conceived a passion for Old Crome and Mr. Cotman. I wish to present it to her for her tenth birthday.'

'And a very fitting gift for an artistic young lady it is, too, sir. I do have another by the same artist, a view of the river and the water mill, if you would be interested. As you can see, we have several larger works by Mr. Cotman as well as a selection of pieces by Mr. Stannard, which are in store at the moment. I could arrange to have them brought up if you are at all interested.'

'No, no. Children may be indulged on occasions but not spoiled. This will be sufficient for now. That elegant little gold painted frame you have on your display will do nicely. Kindly arrange to have it delivered to me before the twenty-third of this month.'

'Of course, sir. I think a cream passe-partout will set it off nicely, with the title of the drawing and the artist's name etched upon it in gold ink. That will be twenty guineas for the drawing and another two guineas for the framing. To what address should it be delivered?'

Hailwood brushed aside the sombre black of his coat, reached into the pocket of his flowered waistcoat to discover a visiting card to the astonished dealer. 'Lord Hailwood! I am sorry, your lordship, I had no idea. Of course your daughter would be delighted with such an exquisite depiction of St. Wandrede. I apologise for not recognising you immediately, your lordship, especially with your appreciation of the visual arts.'

'No reason why you should. I am much in London where there is more modern work to be seen. My wife and daughters pester me to patronise the paintings of Burne-Jones and Rossetti, though I consider their moral tone questionable. I find Mr. Egg far more to my taste, though some of his scenes are also questionable he clearly points out the evil which lurks within them. A man of sound principles. Sadly, I fear we shall hear of him no more.'

The dealer made a mental note to purchase as many paintings by Augustus Egg as he could find. Nothing shows a profit like a dead artist, especially if one can corner the market.

His lordship proffered a finger for the dealer to shake, which he did with much bowing and scraping. A good day's work, getting rid of that tearing from Old Crome's scrapbook. Been hanging around the gallery for years. No-one wants a sloppy drawing of a broken down church now the fad for romantic countryside scenes is over. Religious scenes are all that sell locally nowadays: high moral tone for the non-conformists, bleeding Christs and tearful Marys for the high churchmen. He has a couple of artists tucked away in garrets on the other side of the city churning them out by the dozen. It does him good to live in times when beauty and religion are equally rewarded and evil and poverty shunned by all right thinking people.

Josiah Gedge also was buying a present, proud to be doing so. His gang master had paid him an extra shilling as overseer of the gang working gathering potatoes on the Truscott land, in addition to his contractual eight shillings for the week. The shilling he had spent on a pig's head as present for his mother to go with the dozen potatoes he had smuggled off the field hidden under his blouse. She would cook the pig with an infusion of wild garlic, parsley and marjoram before laying the pig fat down to solidify and be spread on bread for his breakfasts in the coming week.

His mother would have no use for pictures. She already had one, a portrait of the young queen (now no longer young) surrounded by her various children, which she had torn from a copy of the 'Norfolk Mercury' the week before. One day she will be like the queen, she thought, surrounded by Josiah's children. A pity Obadiah would not be there to see them. Taken from her so young, a mere fifty-five, killed when the new steam engine for the mill broke its chains and crushed him to death. What a waste of a good man, and all for a mill the nobody wanted any more. But Josiah was big and strong like his father. Soon he would be the lord's agent, the fourth in an unbroken line of Gedges to hold the post. This Scottish interloper, this McIntyre, would not last the distance. He understood neither the land nor the people. A man short in his temper and long in his drink, zealous in religion, sour in conversation.

She shivered. A mist was rising across the marsh, bringing with it miasmas and the first indications of winter. Too early in the day and too early in the year to light a fire. She would wait until Josiah came home and complained of the cold before eating into her precious stores of firewood. Her father had told her of the good days when there were stands of box and ash across the landscape before the present lord's grandfather had enclosed them all, had them dug up for pasture and grazing, denying the poor people even a stray bough or broken branch to augment their meagre fires. Still, it was all for the best. There were more sheep and cattle here now than ever, not that she ever tasted either unless the lord were to donate a carcass to the church at harvest festival.

Josiah breezed in, bearing a hempen sack and followed by a whiff of marsh air. 'We eat well tomorrow, mother. See what I have here, potatoes and carrots to go with it. Tonight is bread and cheese, tomorrow we feast like royalty.'

'You are a good boy, Jos. When you are the lord's agent we will eat like royalty every eve.'

'You don't listen to me, ma. I shall never be the lord's agent if I stay here until I die. He has Macintyre who he brought specially to clear us all out, make way for cattle and the machines. There will be no room for the likes of us. Nor would I wish to stay. How many of us are there left? Four, five families? None of us grow enough to feed ourselves. Even you at your age have to hire yourself out to harvest, sickle in hand, to avoid the workhouse. There is no life here any more. The road itself has passed us by! Have you heard about Clare?'

No, she had heard nothing. Clare was a superior being, a man who owned the tallest building in the county, taller even than the spire on the cathedral, taller than the dome of St. Paul's in London, some said. 'What of him? Who has he robbed of his grain this time?'

'Mother, you should not say such things. Charles Clare is an honest man, at least until a court finds him otherwise. Mainwaring the miller has defaulted on his rent and fled the country. Clare cannot find another miller and has put the mill up for sale.'

'There are six men employed at that mill. What are they going to do, where are they to go? I remember it being built, floors and floors of it. We lasses went every Sunday after church to see how high it was grown.'

'And to see which boys had told their mothers they had to see how the new mill had grown and how beautiful the village girls had grown in the meantime, I'll be bound. Didn't you tell me my father first kissed you behind the mill of a Sunday?'

His mother laughed. What a bright day it had been, the cowslips in full flower, a gentle breeze through the hawthorn; a boy, eyes as bright as the day, lips as full and soft as summer fruit, first whiskers tickling her upper lip as they embraced.

'You are blushing mother!'

'Not for shame, I assure you. For pleasure at such wonderful times, when the world was so young and I was but a slip of a girl. Your father was a handsome man, strong, too. You should have seen him throw a sheep for the shearing, pitch hay into a stook. Both of you took after him, brave as Indians.'

'Would that Ham had been less brave. He would be with us now, not mouldering in some Russian field. Fancy going all that way and not to fire a shot. Killed by the idiots who sent him there. No food, no tent, no medicine. Our betters, they call them. In what way are they our betters? Because they have more money? What money they have is sweated off the backs of us labouring men.'

'Hush, child. You speak like those of the combinations. Carry on as you do and you will find your way to van Diemen's land with the others. We are comfortable here. The lord looks after us. We have goose at Christmastide, mutton at harvest festival.'

Josiah was silent. He knew better than to argue with is mother. If he told her what was in his mind she would only burst into tears, beg him to stay, waste his life carting manure and digging potatoes. Boxwood is dead. Dead bodies carry contagion. He had no wish to be infected with the plague of apathy.

'I do find the Reverend Betts exceptionally dull, mama. Does that mean I am very wicked? Am I in a state of irremediable sin?'

'My dear, I cannot conceive of any sin you may possibly have committed. The Reverend Betts is a learned man but, I must confess, he does not wear his learning well. I believe he could quote the whole of the Bible by heart, in Latin and Greek as well as in English. Despite that, I find myself falling to sleep in his sermons. It is only Mrs. Gedge's snoring that keeps me awake.'

'Mama, that is naughty of you. If you are not good, I shall tell papa. Reverend Betts was trying to tell us last week why we should have stained glass windows and decorated altar cloths even though the Bible says not to worship graven images.'

'That is simple, Henrietta. Those images, like the stations of the cross, are there to remind us of the life of Christ and how he suffered for us and delivered us from sin. We don't worship them; they are reminders to us of our faith.'

'And original sin, and trans, transub, sub..''

'Transubstantiation, my child. A wicked Papist belief, a gross error.' Mama folded her napkin, edged her chair backwards. 'Breakfast is not a happy time at which to elucidate such matters.'

'And it is so cold in the church, mama. The wind whistles in round the windows and under the tiles. Old Crome's drawing, which papa gave me for my birthday, shows the church in better condition than it is in at present. I am constantly afraid the roof will fall on my head, pigeon nests, rats and all. The only part of it I trust is the tower.'

'You must always trust in the church, my dear.' Her mother giggled. 'It is our firm foundation. As for this particular church, I fear neither Reverend Betts nor Bardell the churchwarden nor even your papa has done their duty by it. Tithes are supposed to pay for its upkeep but I suspect most of them go towards the upkeep of the vicar's huge brood. About time he reminded himself of what St. Paul had to say about lust.'

'What's lust, mama?'

Mama rose from her seat. 'Reverend Betts will explain that to you during your confirmation classes. I am far too much of a weak minded woman to be able to keep all these theological definitions in my head, especially at this time of the morning. Why don't you take your nice new sketch book and see if you can outdo your precious Mr. Crome; stop bothering about sins and heresies.' Mama drifted from the room, turning her crinoline aside to allow easy access through the half door.

Henrietta was delighted with the suggestion and with the amusement she had gained from the brief conversation with her parent, one which she was sure had led her into some kind of sin. Failing to honour her father and her mother, probably. Her mother was open and approachable on most things, far more so than the other mothers of her class, but theology and the difficult questions related to everyday life always threw her into a tizz. Henrietta was well aware of what lust was. She had heard the older boys in her confirmation class whispering and giggling together behind the church porch. As a country girl herself she had often seen the stray dogs coupling and the agitation around the farms when a prize ram arrived with its owner in late summer or the efforts of the farmhands in trying to aid the bull to heavily mount one of the breeding herd. What she failed to understand was why it was a sin and why anyone found such matters at all interesting or shaming. She was sure she would never bother with them herself.

Frost still lay on the ground as she hurried across the crisp fields towards the church, ignoring the longer way round by what was still termed the ' new road', though it had been there for nearly sixty years. By the south-east corner of the churchyard she paused. Could she incorporate the old village pond into her composition? Sighed. Her grasp of perspective was, she knew, too weak to manage the combination of church and pond. The result would be like one of those naïve paintings she had seen in village churches where one object seemed to sit on top of the other. Getting the church's proportions right was a large enough task. A simple tower, taken from one corner, yielded satisfying results, as did the addition of the west end of the nave and the base of the entrance porch. But how did the pitch of the porch interface with the right angled pitch of the nave?

Three times she started a new page and three times ended in failure. A wind had started in from the north, promising snow. To avoid both wind and failure Henrietta moved her position so she faced the south facade head on. From here the tricky intersection vanished behind the front of the entrance porch. Furiously she worked on, abandoning her initial careful attempts at architectural detail for a more impressionistic feel to bring wind and nature into the composition. Once she had a sketch she could transfer the main ideas on to watercolour paper at home and add in the details later. A light snow began to fall, whipped across the churchyard by the gathering wind. Henrietta closed her sketchbook, turned to leave. A browned tile, covered in lichen flew past, embedding itself in the ground where she had been standing only a few seconds before.

'God's will,' she muttered, turning rapidly for home in case God changed his mind.

Edgar Hailwood led his family down the north aisle of the cathedral to an unoccupied pew near the front. Regular attenders had their own pews, set well back to save them from the gaze of the unwashed and allow them to be as inattentive as they chose to the mundane sermons gleaned from George MacDonald's transcriptions. The family rarely made the tedious trip into the city to worship at the cathedral, but since the wind had ripped the roof off St. Wandrede's Edgar had decreed they could not be seen in All Saint's or even St. Dunstan's. Only a cathedral was sufficient for a Viscount. Where the servants and the farm labourers worshipped at present, he had no idea.

Family included nanny, for little Harry, at two years old and still in skirts, was not to be trusted to sit through a whole service without becoming fractious or soiling himself. Should the occasion arise nanny must spring into action and remove him. Today he managed the service itself but baulked at the sermon, setting up a piercing wail, echoed by several other infants in the pews behind. Glad not to have to sit through another two hours of exhortation the nannies exited as a group, to stand shivering and chattering in the commodious porch or sheltering from the wind in its lee.

Henrietta listened attentively for the first hour before opening a set of reproductions of church buildings her mama had found for her. Crome's drawings were there, of course, alongside the equally romantic versions by the late Mr. Turner and some dull pieces by the Mr. Egg who papa admired so much. Claribel had long since plaited and unplaited the hair on her doll and began experimenting with the fastenings of its underskirts before planning how to persuade papa into buying her a pony. Mama's delicate face stared attentively at the preacher, apparently drinking in every word, while she considered how to convert at least part of her lawns into a woodland garden. Rhododendrons and camellias were a foregone conclusion. Photinia would provide interest in spring with its early red foliage, while wisteria might be induced to climb one of the trees, perhaps a silver birch. Acanthus worried her. Too florid, perhaps? Too many classical connotations and it did take up such a large amount of space with all those floppy leaves.

Papa nodded attentively, especially when references were made to specific Biblical events, his mind attuned to the regular 'as St. Paul tells us' or references to Leviticus and Genesis. Nodding was a tactic he had developed since being thrashed by his father for falling to sleep during one particularly long and abstruse sermon. Not having to engage his intellect he was considering what he would do at the next sowing season now that the government had withdrawn the potato subsidy which had been in place since the repeal of the corn laws. Corn was out of the question, given the price of imported American wheat. On the other hand, their civil war had reduced supplies and was steadily pushing the price up. But who could know how long the war would last? What certainly would not last was the agreement with the Duke of Argyll, who was shipping his cattle directly to the London market on the railway without need to drive them down to Norfolk for fattening first.

'Thank heavens for the railway,' he thought. Only two hours to London, stay at his club over night and return the next evening. For now, that was sufficient, but cousin Bignold was already pushing for him to turn two days into three or even four. Certainly Macintyre could handle the estate on his own with only minimal guidance from his principal but he did not relish four days every week away from his wife and children, especially now they had grown so interesting. Claribel loved to sit on his knee while he read to her and Henrietta was a treasure trove of interesting questions about artists and their techniques. How could he forgo such delights for the confusions of setting up a new insurance company for cousin Bignold in the smog and dirt of London?

'In the name of the Father, and of the Son, and of the Holy Ghosts. Amen.'

'Amen.'

Sermon and service over, the family rose, lingering in the porch to exchange greetings with others of their circle and to compliment the preacher upon 'another excellent and inspiring sermon.' Neither the nurse nor young Harry were in prospect, much to mama's dismay. And here is the coachman, ready to take them back to Boxwood, a roaring wood fire and an excellent lunch, which would be spoiled if nanny did not appear soon. Here she comes, all hot and flustered, a screaming Harry tucked under her arm.

'I'm so sorry, Ma'am. He would not keep still, insisted he must go for a walk, lay down outside the church and screamed until the Beadle came and moved us on. We didn't go far, just down Magdalen Street and along the Colegate. Then outside St. Andrews on the way back he declared he was tired and would go no further, just sat down in the road, yelled and yelled. What could I do? I picked him up as you saw me, and here he is.' She put the scarlet faced child down in front of his mama and sisters, both of whom immediately rushed up to him and started petting him, brushing his downy hair with their fingers, wiping tears from his face, straightening his skirts.

Without a sound the boy allowed himself to be led into the carriage, where he lay smiling across the laps of his indulgent sisters. Desperate to avoid any word of blame for her conduct, nanny rattled on about the sights she had seen, how high the river was, the number of carriages obstructing the narrow streets. 'And you'll never guess who I saw in the Colegate,' she continued, not leaving anyone time for recollection or speech. 'Josiah Gedge from the village. Coming out of that funny chapel. What do they call themselves? Unitarians, whatever that is. Not proper church, anyways. He shouldn't be there, should he? By rights he should be at All Saints in Earlsford while ours is out of order.'

At that moment Josiah Gedge was heading for a place of worship even lower in nanny's esteem: the Friends' Meeting House in Goat Lane. He hurried, fearful he would be late, dreading the length of the wait he might endure. Friends did not have fixed hours for services. Sometimes they sat for hours analysing their lives and how they might serve man and God. At others the spirit would descend upon a member of the congregation who would be moved to testify. Or upon several members, in which case the meeting could amble along even unto the evening.

Today he was lucky. Soberly clad men began to emerge from the Meeting House, each accompanying wife dressed almost funereally in greys and black. No-one, not even the children, raised their voice or moved at any more than a gentle amble. Yet they were not sad and dreary but earnest and quietly emphatic, smiling mostly as if they had been newly blest. Josiah found their peace and certainty irresistible; it was not like the mechanical observance he had endured for so long at St. Wandrede and All Saints, even stronger than the feeling that stroked his soul in the congregation of the Unitarians.

Lofty his thoughts may be they were lifted still higher by the sight of Esther Durrant in her dark bonnet and full grey skirt floating towards him as if on a cloud.

'Josiah Gedge, it is a cold morning for you to be wandering the streets.'

'Miss Durrant, it is not like you to play the coquette. You know very well that I do not wander the streets but linger in this draughty alley for you to finish communing with your soul.'

'If you wait for me to finish communing with my soul you will wait a good many years. My soul has much to say.'

'Does it say anything about marriage to you, good lady?'

'My soul is silent on the subject but my father, and more so my mother, preach longer sermons on the subject than any you have had the happiness to hear in church this morning.'

'We had an excellent preacher,' replied Josiah earnestly, 'who was full of fire and enthusiasm, raising us to a pitch of holy excitement which echoed the excitement in my own heart on encountering your delightful face.'

'My parents do not approve of enthusiasm, especially misplaced enthusiasm. Allow me to disclose to you the pith of their matter, the text upon which their sermon is based. We are a respectable family. Not noble, but good solid stock, tradesmen and brokers, bankers and lawyers. We live simply but comfortably. I can bake, at a push, and manage servants but I do not cook nor clean nor hang out the linen. I am what you may call a gentlewoman.'

'And I am nought but a labouring man, one with dirt under his fingernails, with a mother who does all those things which you tell me you cannot do.' Josiah turned away, playing with a loose button on his jacket.

'But you are a God fearing man, Josiah Gedge. A yeoman who tills the soil, brings forth fine crops as one day you will bring forth a fine crop of children. You are worthy, but your life is not my life. I could not be a helpmeet to you; I could not manage your life and your house. Nor could I be poor. I have seen how the poor live.'

'None more so. You are beloved in the alleys and back ways of this town for your generosity and kind words.'

'I thank you for that. I have, I say, seen how the poor live. Together we might survive but with only a straw between us and destitution. My family would not help if I were to go against their wishes; they would tell me I have brought misfortune upon myself by breaking the sixth commandment, failing to honour my father and my mother.'

'Then there is no hope for me?'

Esther sighed. 'Josiah, I will wait for you as long as you wish, but as long as you remain a mere labourer my parents will not give me permission to marry. There are openings in our businesses here for a willing young man anxious to make his way in the world, one who could prove himself over the course of a year or two to be in a sound position to support a wife and a family.'

Josiah felt the anger and resentment rising inside him. 'You give me no hope. My mother is old and needs the help of her only surviving son. I cannot leave her to till her land on her own, friendless and dependent on the good will of the lord and his agent. All I can hope for is the grant of the tenancy of a farm in my own right, where I can earn a living by the toil of my own hands.'

Esther's face brightened. 'Should you be able to obtain a lease on a substantial farm my parents may relax their prohibition. Better still, your father was the lord's agent and steward, as was his father before him.'

'And his father before that.'

'If, as I say, you were the lord's agent you would have a cottage of your own, a goodly income and status within the community. My father would surely see you as a fitting consort for his daughter.'

The couple shook hands and parted, Jos to a five mile walk back to his mother's cottage, pondering the alternatives of managing the estate, becoming a tenant farmer in his own right or living a landless, hopeless bachelor.

Months later Edgar Hailwood was interrupted by the manservant, somewhat disturbed from his usual urbane manner. 'Two gentlemen from the Dean, sir, wishing conference with you. Rather unusual for churchmen, if I might say, sir.'

Unusual they were, dressed in the height of cosmopolitan fashion with neither neck cloth nor roman collar to distinguish them as clergy. Edgar was used to such dandies with their decorated paisley waistcoats ambling along the Strand but felt the incongruity of such a vision here in rural Boxwood as emissaries of the Dean and Chapter.

It being early in the day the gentlemen declined both spirits and wine but were happy to accept tea with both milk and sugar. 'My lord,' began the taller of the two, a young man, ascetic of face if not of dress, who introduced himself as Underhill, 'I regret to have to state that the Dean and Chapter have received reports that no steps are being taken for the repair of St. Wandrede church, which is under your care. Since your father purchased the tithes of the parish as part of the enclosure of these lands, it devolves upon you to maintain both the building and the vicar of the church.'

Edgar stared into his cup, wondering whether to have these dogs beaten from the house or to put them off with honeyed words.

'I confess I have been remiss in the matter. Before the unfortunate act of God, which made the church unsuitable for worship, the congregation consisted merely of ten other persons beside my own family and our house servants. We could all be accommodated in All Saints or St. Dunstan's. Perhaps it would be for the best to allow the church fabric to collapse and for us to make our devotions elsewhere, using the money to help the poor or support missions oversees.'

'Your lordship's intentions do you much credit,' broke in the second man, already florid and rotund though only in his mid twenties. 'The movement of populations from the land to the cities, particularly the industrial ones in the north and the midlands, have had a deleterious effect upon the mission in rural counties. I admit, we have failed in the cities, where Methodists and other non-conformists have established themselves among the working people. Let us not by inaction allow the same to occur with the rural population. Already we have seen chapels in villages and hamlets where the local priest has failed to keep the Word alive among the people, and lords and squires have not maintained their benefices or enforced regulations against non-attendance. Surely, you do not wish to be numbered among such, my lord?'

'The question still remains,' responded Edgar, sweating uncomfortably under the gaze of his two earnest visitors, 'as to where the money for repair is to come from and where we will find a congregation.'

'Your lordship is right to pose the questions.' Underhill leant forward in his chair, staring directly into Edgar's eyes. 'We have seen St. Wandrede's church. It is a poor thing, a mere shed with a tower. Uncomfortable for worshippers and divine alike. We represent a group of like minded people, supported by senior clergy, willing to finance the reconstruction of village churches such as yours. We do not intend repair or renovation. We wish to remove the existing nave completely and rebuild it in the modern manner, complete with heating and a proper vestry.'

'And my family monuments?'

'They will naturally be preserved. My friend Mr. Wilkins here, will draw up plans for the new nave.'

'And transepts!' interjected Wilkins. 'St. Wandrede is too small for side chapels but transepts would do nicely. Your family monuments could all be placed in the north transept, almost like a family chapel in its own right.'

The idea of a new church at no expense to himself, complete with a family side chapel, moved Edgar to allow a modicum of enthusiasm in his voice. 'A new church would, of course be welcome, but what of the congregation? What of the people?'

'The people will come,' affirmed Underhill, rising from his chair. 'The Lord will provide. I bid your lordship good day. Perhaps your lordship would be so good as to meet us at the Dean's residence this day month, when we can discuss Mr. Wilkins' preliminary designs?'

Henrietta settled herself on the divan, prayer book in hand. The Reverend Betts had been even more confused and confusing during confirmation class that afternoon. Betts was not a natural teacher, better suited to writing learned tomes among the spires of Oxford than attempting to express the mysteries of the Christian religion to a group of unruly and uneducated country bumpkins. Henrietta's presence had further complicated his task, she being neither unruly nor uneducated and given to penetrating questions. Henrietta was genuine in her search for knowledge. Religious observance was universal throughout the local villages, and the town, too, as far as she knew. A practice of such significance needed thorough investigation if one was to grow to be a competent adult and caring mother, a destiny she knew to be inevitable.

'Mama.' she began, 'does God look like us?'

Mama looked up from her catalogue of varicoloured camellias, her mind still wandering through her half complete woodland plantation. 'Of course he does, child,' she muttered, absently.

'Then, is he a man or a woman, mama?'

'Why, a man, of course, my dear.'

'Don't we have a man God for men and a woman God for women?'

'That's absurd, my dear. Then we would have to have a boy God for boys and a girl God for girls. We would be no better than the heathens or the Hindus with their outdated beliefs. There is only one God. Remember the words of the hymn we sang in church this morning: 'immortal, invisible.... hid from our eyes.' So, there is only one God.'

'But if we can't see him, mama, how do we know he is there?'

'We know him by his goodness, my dear, by his wonderful creation. Have faith, my dear and he will manifest himself to you.'

'How can I have faith if I don't? '

'That's quite enough, Henrietta. These are questions for the Reverend Betts, who is far better versed in theology than I am. All I can say is that everyone believes in God, except for some crazy Darwinians.'

'What's a Darwinian, mama?'

'That's all from you, young lady. Time for us to dress for dinner. Papa has visitors and we must look our best.'

Papa's visitors stood smoking in the drawing room, much to mama's annoyance. Tobacco smoke made her feel ill and dulled both her thinking and her appetite. She was minded to make her dissatisfaction known but the presence of the Dean impeded her natural impulses, rendering her silent for most of the ensuing meal, dominated by the rolling tones of Mr. Wilkins, enthusing over the progress that had been made on Boxwood church and telling the company at large of the magnificent furnishings which were to be bestowed upon it at its completion.

'The ladies of Reading are sewing a huge tapestry of Christ in Majesty to hang behind the altar, with portraits of Viscount Hailwood and St. Wandrede on either side. Despite his reservations, the Dean has approved the gift of a pair of magnificent candlesticks from the Duke of Norfolk and Mr Rudd here has persuaded his brother's company to carve and install ten rows of pews to match the family pew that our host has graciously donated. Again, with the approval of the Dean, the monks of St. Wandrene in Rançon have sent us an altar cloth they have designed and woven themselves.'

'I confess to being disturbed by the source of some of these donations,' put in Edgar nervously. 'The Duke is a notorious papist who is constantly talking of his plans to build another Catholic cathedral to rival our own, while the monks of Rançon are recognised as extremists even by the Catholic church itself.'

An extended silence ensued, broken at last by Underhill. 'We are all Christians, whatever small differences in doctrine we may have. Our object should be to repair the schisms in the church, to return us to the unity and purity of the early fathers before secular forces drove us apart. Whilst one cannot approve the desertion of the Archbishop of Westminster one might see in his actions a way of bringing all the sheep back into one fold.'

'Having all sheep in one fold results in disease and cross-breeding,' commented Edgar, the countryman. 'Personally, I fully subscribe to the thirty-nine articles of the Church of England, whatever Cardinal Manning might say or do.'

'Christian unity is a goal to which we must all aspire. On our way along the path we should retain the friendliest relations to those closest to us.' The Dean fingered his crucifix lovingly. 'At the same time we will strive to convince others of the error of their ways, particularly the schismatic non-conformists and Darwinists who deny even the divine creation.'

All murmured in agreement, especially Henrietta who found such a profound conversation far more exciting then the Reverend Betts' ponderous and lengthy explanations. By the time her father proposed a toast to 'the ladies' and she and her mother retired she was beginning to yawn under the weight of analyses of the policies of Lord Palmerston and fulminations at his unsuitability for the post of Prime Minister.

Submissive to the influence of the abstemious Dean, who would take only one glass of brandy, the church representatives retired, leaving Edgar alone with Mr. Rudd, who had been largely silent throughout the meal. 'My lord,' began Mr. Rudd, drawing contentedly on his cigar, 'Mr. Bignold your cousin is a distant connection of my wife. He tells me he is anxious for you to take full control of his new business in London. A man of probity and energy is required, a man of your lordship's calibre. I might be in a position to aid both Bignold and yourself, simultaneously expanding my own business. Currently my factory produces a small range of bottled condiments. While the market for them is expanding, much to my satisfaction, it is expanding slowly and, I fear, will soon reach its peak. While I could continue at this level until I die without any financial detriment to myself or my family such a situation would not be satisfactory. I am a man of energy, sir. I must be doing, expanding, progressing.' Another strong draw on the cigar.

'Agriculture has made great strides over the last hundred years, feeding our ever growing population. But it is a stagnant industry, sir. There is no more land. As yet there are no new crops which have a lucrative market. But the condiment market can and will expand. To do that requires men like myself, entrepreneurs, masters of the retail trade, to tempt the palates of the great British public, to provide them with ready foods they can consume in the houses and tenements of Birmingham and Sheffield with little expenditure of time and effort. To provide those is my aim. To do it I need land where I can produce my own raw materials: malt, milk, mustard and others.

'Consider, sir, what a great advantage it would be to yourself and your family if you were to leave the stagnant agricultural sector and devote yourself to building a mighty business in London in partnership with your cousin. You would have access to the finest entertainments, your children would listen to the greatest musicians of the age, browse the refined artistic productions in the halls of the Royal Academy, see the finest architecture of the world: St. Pauls, Mr. Barry's wonderful palace at Westminster and its abbey. Would you deny them these advantages, sir?'

Edgar had long considered the question of expanding Bignold's empire in London and his own stake in it beyond two days a week as a mere employee, if a well remunerated one. However, there were others to consider. 'While we have not discussed terms, I would find any offer you might make difficult to accept. My wife is most devoted to this estate and her plans for the gardens. Little Claribel has her pony, which she rides in every season and every weather. Henrietta takes artistic inspiration from the countryside and the church. Harry runs across the lawns all days pretending to be a wild indian. None of these things could we do in London.'

'To the contrary, sir. The countryside around London, in Hampstead or Islington, say, gives much opportunity for a clean and healthy life such as you enjoy here, without the added responsibility concomitant upon the duties of a lord of the manor.'

'Nevertheless, Mr. Rudd, I am forced to reject your offer, if only for the time being. There is yet another harvest to be brought in, new leases to be considered and the church rebuilding to be completed before I could even begin to consider a possible sale.' He did not mention the investigation of his own precarious finances or the repairs required to the manor house, built so hurriedly by his ancestor.

The two conversed for some while longer, discussing local politics and the increase of labourers' unions as a danger leading to republicanism and a rise in agricultural prices. Mr. Rudd was reasonably content. He knew how difficult it was to prise land away from the aristocracy despite the low financial returns, less than investing their money in the funds and many times less stable.

Josiah Gedge had no money to invest in anything. 'If we moved into the city, mother, I have the offer of steady employment with a kind master.'

'And what would I do all day? No garden to look after, no chickens to feed or cow to milk. We might starve to death relying on others to pay us. You had better take yourself off to some other village or hire yourself out to the gangs again.'

'The gangs pay nothing, mother. And all the villages here are closed parishes; I would have to walk miles to work every day and still not earn enough for a new pair of boots. We could starve here just as well as in the city.'

'Then I'd rather starve here than live in the workhouse. I'll stay here with the chickens; you do what you want. Go off to Australia or Canada if you must. Leave me behind on my own.'

She pulled out a decayed handkerchief to wipe the tears from her face, dreading the thought of maybe another fifty years of poverty ahead of her. Josiah knew better than to try and continue a conversation with his mother when she was in this mood. All he would get would be repeated accusations that he was looking for excuses to run off and leave her behind, to waste away in poverty. Instead, he did what men have always done in such situations: he took himself to the alehouse.

Where there was scarcely more cheer. The ancient Alfred Wenn, said to be over ninety, slumped in one corner, an inch of ale going stale in his glass. Two others played a silent game of cards, not even bothering to score, neglecting to take turns or count the number of cards in their hands.

'Not seen you much around here, Josiah Gedge,' boomed the landlord. 'Next time you come in I might not be here myself, what with trade being so bad.'

'If I had a shilling for every time a publican has told me how bad trade is, I'd be a rich man by now.'

'Just look around you. How much do you think I make from this lot? And you, coming in once a month, sitting over a pint for two for three hours? Even my brewer has given up. Gone to the city. Got himself a job with Steward and Patteson. Now I have to get my beer from them, who charge me a fortune for it, though it costs them less to brew than I paid my brewer. Country's going to the dogs. All down to them there foreigners.'

Josiah had never seen any foreigners in Boxwood or in the city either, though some folks there had funny names, to be sure. 'Never argue with the landlord,' he thought. 'Or with your mother.'

That day he confounded the landlord's expectations, drinking more than his usual ration, allowing the ale to add to his resolution, leading him to Viscount Hailwood's front door. He paused for what seemed an age before knocking firmly on the varnished wood, too afraid to use the brass lion's head knocker. Another age passed during which his decision faded. Before it could disappear completely a manservant opened the door and stared down at him along his aquiline nose.

'I wish to speak to his lordship.'

'Wait.'

The door was closed firmly. Again he waited. The door was opened. 'His lordship will see you at eight tomorrow morning. Come to the kitchen door. Make sure your clothes and your boots are clean. Good day.'

Josiah turned away. At least he had accomplished something. Enough to keep him awake most of the night trying to compose his application the next morning. The manor house kitchen was warm and welcoming, the cook a friend of his mother's, the skivvy a girl he had been at school with when she was a pert little thing with her hair in braids. Now she scurried about, her hair lank and dripping with sweat, her hands red and chapped. Still she had time to smile at him, lift an interrogatory eyebrow and wish him 'good luck'. By contrast the drawing room was chill and forbidding with its dark wallpaper and shelves of leather bound books which nobody ever read but which were still dusted every day before the master of the house descended for his breakfast.

Today the master sat behind a mobile desk covered in papers, its cubby holes overflowing with old bills and letters awaiting a reply. Josiah stood before it, hat held tightly in both hands in front of him.

'Excuse me, your honour. I come before you today to remind your honour of the service my forebears have rendered your honour in the past and to crave a boon.' Edgar Hailwood nodded.

'As your honour knows, my great grandfather served here as the estate steward, as did my grandfather and my father after him.' A gracious inclination of the head. 'Should he have survived the Russian war, Isaiah, my elder brother might have been appointed to that post upon my father's death.'

'Indeed,' agreed Edgar, leaning forward slightly. 'His unfortunate death in the Queen's service was a great loss to us all. Should you have been old enough when your father died you would have been the first person I would have considered for the post. However, that was not the case and I engaged Mr. Macintyre on a trial basis. Mr Macintyre has proved more than satisfactory and I have confirmed him as my agent and steward for as long as he wishes to stay and performs his duties in the outstanding manner to which I have been accustomed. Only the other day I was pleased to grant him permission to marry. A local girl, you know, from Earlsford, one of the Wenn girls, perhaps slightly older than yourself.'

'Yes, sir. Even the youngest is two years older than me.' Josiah turned his hat between his hands, wondering how to proceed now that his first approach had been so neatly turned aside. 'My mother, sir, is getting on in years and I feel the need to settle myself into a secure establishment in life in order to care for her so she does not descend into being a cost upon the parish.'

'That is very proper of you. Any advice I can give you on how that might be accomplished I am happy to tender.'

'I have heard, sir, that two of the farms will become vacant following this year's harvest. I am a hard worker, sir, and know much of sheep and cattle. My mother may be old but she has a way with hens and all manner of growing things. Clever modern ideas she learned from my father. We thought, sir, that you might see your way to granting me the lease on one or other of those two farms. A lease of ten or fifteen years.'

'Gedge. Normally I ask an applicant if he has ready money with which to purchase the lease. I know very well you have none. As one whose family has served this house so well in the past I could overlook the lack of a purchase price and spread the amount over the length of the lease.'

Josiah gripped his hat tightly.

'Unfortunately, I have one overwhelming objection to your tenancy. All tenants of this estate must be communicating members of the Church of England, fully conversant with the thirty-nine articles and prepared to accept them in full. They must also attend the nearest church on a regular basis. Whereas you, Gedge, have not attended any of the local churches for nearly a year. Instead your regular attendance at the Unitarian chapel in the city has been noted. I can tolerate such behaviour in a labourer, but not in a tenant. I am afraid I cannot grant you a lease on any of my properties. I wish you a good day. Cook will let you have a little something for you to take home to your mother.'

Too distracted to speak, Josiah turned away, followed the manservant to the kitchen steps. Taking their cue from his face neither cook nor skivvy spoke a word, combining to load as much of yesterday's evening meal into a basket for him to take away as they could find.

Home was even worse. His mother had not yet risen, rare in someone who lived by the sun. Her face was blotched and pale, sweat standing out on her brow despite her protestations of being icy cold. Josiah wrapped her in his own blankets, then set out again to fetch old Joan, known to have a knowledge of fevers and all manners of illnesses.

'A few days,' declared Joan. 'She will be well in a few days. Keep her warm, feed her on broth whether she wants any or no. No ale. Ale is not good in these cases. When she is better feed her whatever meat you can. Chicken be good. You have several chickens, kill the oldest one and boil her up with dandelion leaves and nettles. The meat will give her strength; the leaves will settle her stomach. Do not fear; all will be well. All manner of things shall be well. Amen.'

'Amen,' responded Josiah automatically.

'I admit I do not feel I have treated that young man fairly,' said Edgar Hailwood to his wife that evening after dinner. 'His family have served mine for four generations and I turned him away with no hope and no future.'

'That is not like you, papa,' piped up Henrietta. 'You are a man of much faith and given to charity. Why would you not shower your charity on such a worthy man?'

'My dear, I am not as strong in my faith as I should be. Look how long I left our church in disrepair. Only now is it completed because the Dean, aided by Mr. Underhill, has poked and pestered me along the right path. Moreover, the Dean has frequently pointed out how lax I am in the question of non-attenders, a matter which is dear to his heart. How could I extend a favour to one who has been a non-attender for over a year?'

'Papa, you are right to defend the faith. Maybe you could change your mind a little? Request that Mr. Gedge attend All Saints regularly for a period of time, a month or three, perhaps? After which you reconsider his request for the lease on Elm Farm?'

'From out of the mouths of babes and sucklings!' cried mama. 'You are indeed a wise child. Is she not, my dear?'

'How can I resist?' Edgar was all smiles. His problem was solved and his child had proved to be one of the highest worth. 'After your confirmation this week I will call upon Josiah Gedge and put to him your proposition.'

'Yes, nanny. Do you have a problem?'

The question was superfluous. Nanny clung to the door frame, panting and shaking, her hair writhing down from under her mob cap.

'Master Harry, your lordship. He be took proper poorly. Sweating and blotching and cold and all. I can do nothing for un, sir.'

'I will go.' Mama burst from the room, accompanied by Henrietta.

'Nanny. Go to the stables and order the carriage made ready. Tell them to harness the best horses. And for God's sake hurry.'

His lathered horses returned with the doctor, having covered the ten-mile round trip in under an hour. The journey had done little for the doctor's digestion, the port in particular repeating itself along his oesophagus. Nor was he any happier being confronted by a simple case of childish fever. Only the thought of a fat fee kept him calm and amenable. 'There is no danger,' he pontificated. 'Keep him warm, feed him on broth whether he wants any or no. When he begins to recover feed him whatever light meat you can. Chicken is good, boiled up with carrot and turnip. Some light herbs such as thyme or parsley. The meat will give him strength; the herbs will settle his stomach. Have someone sit by the bed to keep the child company, perhaps read to him while he is awake. Children become so fretful when confined to bed.'

Edgar led the doctor downstairs for a restorative glass of brandy, which merely exacerbated his already deranged digestion, and to arrange for a horse and a servant to see him safely home. Henrietta and mama sat by Harry's bed, each arranging the blankets at any sign of their becoming dislodged. 'Read something,' said mama. 'I do not care what.'

'The sermon on the mount, mama. It will revive our spirits. Then we will pray.'

They sat there all night, fitfully dozing, and in the morning Harry was calmer, his face pale but with fewer blotches. Nanny sat with him during the day, repeatedly swabbing his sweating brow.

Edgar spent the day shooting and walking the bounds of his

estate, taking out his worry on pheasants and lazy tenants alike. Henrietta failed to appear at dinner. 'She is sitting at Harry's bedside,' said mama. 'I will relieve her at midnight, so we may both get some sleep. Nanny says there are signs of recovery, for which we must thank God and the good advice of the doctor. I have taken the liberty of cancelling Henrietta's confirmation tomorrow. The vicar will understand.'

'And he will receive his fee twice over,' replied her husband. 'He will be relieved. The builders have only just quitted the church and he has had much to do to make it ready for the ceremony. The confirmation may wait another week.'

At midnight mama quietly entered the nursery. Nanny snored gently in her chair. Henrietta lay fast asleep, her head on Harry's lap, her Bible open on the cot beside her. She thought of picking up her daughter and carrying her to bed, if it could be done without disturbing Harry. Nothing would wake Harry. He was dead.

All curtains were drawn. Cook lit two candles to work by. Two other candles burned in the nursery. Mama sat in nanny's chair staring at Harry's inert body. Neither nanny nor Henrietta had yet appeared, too distraught to move from their beds. Edgar had ridden out to fetch the Reverend Betts. Anything that would stop him thinking.

Funeral arrangements made, Edgar, tired of the priest's oleaginous attempts at sympathy, ushered him from the door, attempting to compose himself before his reincarnation as a tower of strength and comfort. Nothing he could say was sufficient for the grieving mother, insistent they could both have done more for their child, alternately weeping and accusing him of all manner of faults and omissions.

Henrietta lay abed, silent; her face to the wall. Edgar leaned over to kiss her goodnight, as he had done most nights since she was born. Her face was cold, wet with sweat, covered in ugly red blotches. He recoiled, aghast. Took her in his arms, held her to his chest, thought of calling the doctor, his wife, anybody. The child's breathing slowed, hesitated. 'Goodbye, dear papa,' she whispered. And died.

'The children may not be buried inside the church itself,' insisted

Reverend Betts. 'The Dean will not allow it. A new floor has been laid, pews put in place. Both of them have been christened but neither have yet been confirmed. Even without the Dean's practical objections there are theological difficulties in an interior burial for the unconfirmed. A memorial plaque in the north transept is acceptable, of course, perhaps one which has space for your own details and those of your good lady in time?'

'This is inhuman.' Lady Hailwood, normally the kindest and most quietly spoken of women, had become adamantine in her antipathy to the ineffectual vicar. 'My children are worth more than any stupid flooring or oak furniture. Poor Henrietta was fully prepared for her confirmation. Only her devotion to her poor sick brother postponed the actual ceremony. In the eyes of God, she was a full member of the church.'

Betts did not agree, beginning a long explication of the views of saints Augustine and Aquinas, the admission of supplicants to the early Church and the nature of original sin. Both parents talked over him, oblivious to subtle points of theology and Biblical allusions alike.

Viscount Hailwood settled the matter. 'You hold this living directly from me. If you cannot find a solution to the problem, you should search for another in Birmingham or Manchester. The funeral is in three days. Consult with the Dean. Go now, I have business to attend to.'

The vicar left post haste for the city. Lady Hailwood retired to the dining room, where two small coffins stood starkly on trestles, white velvet rising incongruously from within. Edgar Hailwood confronted Mr. Rudd in the drawing room.

'Rudd, some time ago you made me an offer.'

'I did, indeed, your lordship. That offer is still open, as I believe is Mr. Bignold's offer to you of further employment in London. Though I can understand it if you and her ladyship wish to remain here in Boxwood beside your late departed children.'

'I thank you for your understanding. Her ladyship has taken a complete aversion to the place, as have I. She regards it as unhealthy and unlucky, not fit for either ourselves or for Claribel. We shall return from time to time, on particular sad anniversaries but we can no longer live here. I am pleased to accept your original offer. The only extra stipulation I make is that the church be maintained at all times and in good condition, however small the congregation.'

'I would do no other, sir. As you know, I am a non-conformist myself but we Unitarians respect the beliefs of others and I will do as you wish. If your lordship would like to retain a burial plot?'

'Not at all. We will cut off all contact with this place except for the visits I mentioned earlier. A local man will be engaged to tend the children's graves at our expense and a memorial plaque will be commissioned for the north transept. If you would be so kind as to arrange matters with Mr. Evershed all will be concluded as soon as my agent in London has found us suitable accommodation.' The two men shook hands properly, as gentlemen equals, though one was titled and the other a tradesman. Edgar Hailwood returned to the dining room and a perusal of his Bible in a vain attempt to find some consolation.

Reverend Betts returned the next day, full of deferential apology. 'The Dean remains intransigent,' he explained to the parents. 'He feels an interior burial of the unconfirmed would set an unfortunate precedent. However, he has a suggestion which I trust will meet with your approval. Between the vestry and the north transept, right against the church wall, is a good sized space which has not been used for previous burials. The Dean suggests the children might be buried there.'

'Together,' put in Lady Hailwood. 'Side by side as they lived.'

'Of course, your ladyship. Most fitting. The Dean points out that the rain water from the roof falls from the eaves directly upon this area, anointing the children, so to speak, christening them in perpetuity, welcoming them into the community of the blessed.'

Lady Hailwood dissolved in tears. Edgar nodded. Motioned to the priest to leave. Two days later the double burial took place. Mr. Rudd gained possession of the house and land. No more leases were ever granted on the estate.

The Hailwoods took a small house in Hampstead suburb, perfect for a family of three, complete with a cottage garden and a paddock for the pony. Mama wore black. Claribel wondered what had happened to her sister and her brother and why they had been sent away. Every day Edgar took the new railway into the City where he laboured on the intricacies of insurance and investment, becoming ever richer despite the poverty in his heart.

Again the single bell of St Wandrede tolled mournfully as the eight mourners left the church. 'There is nothing left for me here,' said Josiah as Esther took his arm. 'My mother's cottage reverts with its patch of land to the lord or Mr. Rudd. I am thrown upon the parish or to the mercy of the gang-masters.'

'Or upon mine,' Esther interrupted. 'My uncle Caley has an opening for a steady young man as foreman in his factory. He will be paid one hundred pounds a year for the first year, rising by five pounds each year as long as his performance proves satisfactory. However, there is one condition.'

'And what might that be?'

'You note I said one of the requirements was for a *steady* young man? My uncle does not regard bachelors as being steady. He therefore requires a respectable married man for the post.'

'And where would he find such a person?'

'I was hoping there was someone in Boxwood who suited his requirements. No, Josiah Gedge, one does not kiss in public. Only if one were engaged to be married.'

'Please consider yourself so engaged. May I kiss you now?' The merest peck, they being a respectable couple. 'Reverend Betts can publish the banns this afternoon and we could be married here within the month.'

'No.' Josiah's face turned from elation into disappointment. 'I cannot be married here,' continued Esther firmly. 'This papist edifice is not one for the likes of you and me. Do you feel the Spirit descending upon you as you enter it, among all the flummery of candles and incense? No, it is a harlot dressed in her finest gown hiding all manner of sickness and sin. By all means let our banns be read for the first time today, but let it be in that Unitarian chapel you favour so fervently. At least there I feel wrapped in a holy mist, if not one as fervent as among Friends.'

'Then we must step out and urge your father's driver to make haste to the Colegate. Once done I need to find us lodgings suitable for our station and within our budget.'

Esther smiled. 'I forgot to tell you. Mr Caley has had erected in Victoria Street a row of excellent detached houses for his senior workers, which they may rent for twenty-five pounds a year. I have engaged the one nearest the factory and furthest from the coal yard. Unless you prefer to rent two rooms above an inn like Mr. Micawber?'

Josiah had not had the honour of Mr. Micawber's acquaintance and felt that Victoria Street would do very well, despite the inevitable dust from the coal yard beyond.

'And Mr. Caley and Mr. Bignold have had a school built opposite the factory for the children of his employees, so we are well provided for.'

'I believe, Mrs. Gedge as will be, that you are getting a little previous.'

1942

Enlistment

Bright lights hurt my eyes. Soon the orderly will come, turn me over, change the dressing, disturb dreams and memories. How was it I got here, lying in this narrow cot, awaiting my death? The orderly has arrived, turns me over, is fiddling with my lower limbs. A pin prick. More morphine. Soon I will float away. He wraps bandages around my leg. Is it my leg or where my leg used to be? I cannot tell. At this stage in my death it is useless to bother with such mundane matters. He does his work efficiently and quietly. I am grateful for his silence.

Here it comes, I am slipping away. To where? Ah, to the market. Unloading carts and vans full of swedes, potatoes, great stalks of sprouts, the dead smell of cabbages. Already I am disenchanted, desperate to leave, to make a mark on a wider world, away from here and away from him, who also smells of death and cabbages. Old Simpson shouts at me to hurry up. Customers will arrive soon, he has his stall to lay out, make it more attractive than the others around him, others that sell exactly the same produce for exactly the same price. No-one dare undercut their competitors for fear of ambush on the way home, an ambush that I, now grown strong and muscular, delight in for the power and freedom it offers me.

Then I am home. A Saturday. He is already drunk, though there is light yet in the sky. He shouts at me, demands to know where I am going. 'To grandmother's,' I reply.

'Why visit that old witch. Off to church tomorrow when you should be here helping me tidy the house. What a waste. Give me some money for the housekeeping.'

The money is not for the housekeeping; we both know that. It is for the ale he will swill down his throat. Tomorrow there will be no house cleaning. He will lie abed groaning and swearing, wishing he had a few coppers left to wash down a hair of the dog. We do not want for dirt or food. Both we bring home from the market, the half rotten leftovers that no-one wants and nobody can sell. We are well fed. I am malnourished. Only my body is fed.

I dream along the five miles to Boxwood. Morphine makes those five miles perpetually sunny summer; there are no snows or howling gales in morphine country. I float along, feet barely touching the tarmac on the road, tarmac my grandmother remembers having been laid in her childhood. There is no ale in her house, only water from the well, which only she uses. She feeds me eggs from her chickens mixed with herbs from garden and hedgerow. I give her potatoes, beetroot, kale, turnips. We sit and eat. She tells me stories of the olden days, of the sailor lord at the mansion who fought at Trafalgar with Nelson, of fierce uprisings when the militia were called in to deal with the labourers' combination, of men turned off the land for nothing more than refusing to sell food at market, reserving it all for their growing family.

I believe some of it. Today in my comfort I believe everything. Tomorrow we will go to church. The church is new and large. Fifty or more could easily fit inside. Too large for the congregation of five; no, six, for I must include myself. Five old women and me, clustered around the candles, huddled into our coats. It is summer, but still cold in this interior of brick and flint. The responses come readily, automatically; hymns stutter along, half remembered by those who cannot read, followed slowly by those going blind. Only the enthusiasm of the young vicar steers the service to a close. He shakes hands with each of his parishioners as they leave for farm houses a mile or two away. Does he reflect on how long it will be before none of these are left alive for him to preach to of a Sunday morning?

I take my grandmother's arm, lead her gently home, the last house left in what was once the village. She wants me to come and live with her. What would I do here? I ask her. Raise chickens, dig the garden like some widowed old man. I am seventeen. I want to see life, do exciting things. One day marry, raise my own family free from want and poverty. She sighs, knows I am right. There is no life left here. I sit with her in the garden, play a game we have played many times before. She is a queen getting ready for her marriage to a handsome prince. From the garden I bring flowers, bright red roses, pluck the petals, cut each one into tiny oblongs which I lick and stick on her gnarled old fingernails. The remnants I squeeze, hard as I may until juice runs out. I ladle it gently upon her lips, turning them from an ashen grey to flamboyant red. She laughs and giggles as she must have done when she was a girl.

The scene fades. No, it does not fade, it shifts of a sudden like a badly cut cinema picture, and I am six or seven, again in my grand-mother's kitchen. I am crying. My mother has just died. She holds me, strokes my hair until I am calm. In the distance is father's voice. My mother is laid in the churchyard; he is already drunk, lurching off to drown his wits in one of the town's many taverns. He has forgotten all about me. I will remain forgotten for months, until the school inspector demands to be shown where I am. By then my grandmother will have taught me my letters. School teaches me my figures and some history. My grandmother teaches me about Nelson and Collingwood, how labourers were shipped off to the colonies for demanding a decent wage. Arithmetic I have at school but grandmother knows clever things, about how you cannot sail a ship directly at its destination but must allow for wind and tide. Her husband, my grandfather, had shown her how this was done, using a ruler and a protractor. She sets me problems beset with sandbanks, howling gales and only the tiniest of coves into which to navigate. One day I will use this. One day, when I am free of the market and free of him.

Is it my grandmother who is with me the night of the music hall?

Or is it a girl? The girl with the long black hair, who lets me hold her hand after the interval. The comedians have been and gone, now we are in for patriotic songs, for a recruiting sergeant on the stage. The audience singing:

We don't want to lose you
but we think you ought to go

The girl, or is it my grandmother, is urging me to get up on the stage, to take the sergeant's shilling. I will not go, I tell her. I will not be cannon fodder. She shouts at me. Those around turn and boo. Some threaten violence. I fight my way out, pushing past flushed faces and waving umbrellas. One woman spits at me. The girl, or my grandmother, shouts at me to return, to get myself up on stage. Fiercely I stumble out onto the street. On the Gentleman's Walk the ladies are going about their business. They do not bother with me, a youngster apparently already half drunk with less than a shilling in his pocket. I have no eyes for them. It is the recruiting station I seek. Not the recruiting station where all are brown with shiny belts and holsters. My destination is the tiny shop which does little business in this inland town, the navy recruiting station, where I present myself, sign on for twenty-two years or the duration of the war, which all tell me will be over in twenty-two days.

That is why I am here.

The nurse has returned. Surely too soon for more morphine. I have no watch but the pain tells me the time, counting down the minutes and seconds, just as we watched the bombers droning over from the Norwegian shore, praying for clouds or mist to come to our rescue. I have it now, a sea fog over my brain, clouding the few hours I have left. It is the bombers again! I hear them, rush to my oerlikon, pull off the cover, check the mechanism has not frozen over with ice from the sea spray. This cannot be right, only a white canopy above me. The bombers are not meant for me, they cruise overhead, on their way to Liverpool to flatten the docks or the home of some poor unsuspecting sod, too late to reach the shelter.

The first show was so simple, bobbing about in the waters off Zeebrugge, daring the Huns to come out and fight. Nothing to do but play cards all day long, curse the officers for uncaring martinets, swab and paint, swab and paint. See the fat bosun, Owens his name was, see how he shat himself when we hit that mine! Standing there, trying to decide if he ran for the heads or for the lifeboat, shit trickling down his leg. We couldn't move. Stood there and laughed at him 'till the second lieutenant descended on us. 'Get the bulkheads shut, check the bilges, signal men on deck, engineers below. Get a move on.'

Us signallers scooted away like frightened mice. At least we would be on deck if the ship went down, first ones to the lifeboats. The engineers and stokers stood around; the lieutenant virtually had to strong-arm them below, called them mutineers and lots of other words even worse. They'd seen what happens when a ship goes down, the boilers exploding, the stokers trapped in scalding steam before the water floods in and finishes them off. Never did find out where Owens took himself off to. We limped into port like a footballer crocked on one leg.

What port? More engines. Fighters this time. Must be ours, the Jerries don't have the range. Just like ours beyond Scotland and Iceland. Or the RAF weren't going to risk their precious Spitfires for an outgoing convoy, too struck on what was coming in from the States. Never so much as saw a fighter first time. Just Zeppelins floating over like huge grey clouds. No gardeners praying for them to drop their loads!

End of the war for us, that mine. Sitting in Portsmouth waiting for the welders to fit a new bow, drinking every night, flirting with the lasses. Home leave, too. Sneers from the men on the trains. 'What are the navy doing, eh? Sitting around all day drinking rum. Get round there, blast them to bits in Kiel like Nelson did in Copenhagen.'

No use telling them Nelson didn't have to deal with mines and submarines. Grandma was different. Now she had me home after three years she wasn't going to let me go again. Fed me up on eggs and pheasant. 'Froze on the tree in the frost,' she said. Hadn't been a frost in months. He was happy to see me. Fell over him one night, lying in the gutter down St. Stephens. Tried to touch me for half a crown. Just left him there, dirty old man, in his rags and vomit.

Never saw him again. Dead and buried long ago now, like I will be soon.

I could have kicked him where he lay. Would I regret it now? Confess it as a sin at the last rites as the Catholics do? Plenty of other sins to worry about beside that one. The girl from Earlsford, was she a sin? She was as willing as I was, ready to romp in field or barn. And romp we did. She wasn't there when I got back from the Med. Died after an appendix operation they said. Her parents never spoke to me or Grandma. Like I don't speak now. I groan. There are words in my head. My mouth moves. Water goes in. A signal disconnect. Messages from thoughts intercepted before they reach the brain. Lines from brain shattered. The medics think me a vegetable, a turnip.

I shift in my cot, as much as I am able. He comes, the nurse. Mutters some words, loads the syringe. I can drop into sleep, into dreams. Sailing from Scapa into a force nine. The corvette. "*Dahlia*". What a stupid name for a fighting ship. 'Flower class' they called them. 'Rose' I could endure, but 'Dahlia'? And stupid ships. No real guns, just ack-ack and depth charges. Planes and subs. Good job the '*Tirpitz*' never found us. And she buckets around. Bobs like a cork in a waterfall, plates burst at the seams. No armour, just tinplate buckling in the storm.

That young lad. Myhill. Vomiting his guts out all the way to Arkhangelsk. Left him there. Never saw him again. My wife, never see her again. Or the children. Will they miss me? A father they have hardly known. Married her on demob from Ceylon. What was I thinking? Settle down, raise a family, cushy job in an office. First year we fought like cat and dog. She screamed, scratched. I shouted, slapped her good and hard. And we made up. Like tigers we made up, having it everywhere: kitchen, living room carpet, behind the privies. What did the neighbours think? Nosey cows the lot of them.

Wedding in the old church where grandma was buried. December. No heating. Me just back from Ceylon shivering worse than I ever did in Russia. Vicar refused to let me keep my coat on. She with an off the shoulder dress, turning blue. 'No sermon,' I told him. 'Just get it over.' I shiver now. Banging, hammering. Deckies chiselling ice off the superstructure.

Remember the '*Astarta*'? Must have been sixty years old. A coal burner. Overcoats crated in the hold, tanks lashed on deck. Every wave froze solid as it hit. All hands on deck, chipping and chiselling. No use. Turned turtle in the end. We stopped, pulled as many out as we could. Ten, twenty degrees below zero the water. Few though we got aboard, even fewer lasted more than an hour. Pure shock, hearts gave out. No cushy sick bay for them.

No use swimming. The cold gets you. Remember swimming in Ceylon. Those Indian kids taught me. Called me names: jellyfish, tortoise, lard-belly. Told them 'sailors don't swim.' They laughed. Towed me out to the deep water and left me. God how I splashed and spluttered! Made it in the end. Never out of the water after that. Skin black and baked like any Tamil. Commander was furious. Was I going native? What Englishman looked like that! Letting the side down. Stupid old fart!

Talk of fart. All that curry. Never been so easy in my life. Blocked up for weeks when I came home. Potatoes and gristly meat. Couldn't pass a marble. And the girls, too. All very free and easy. Clean. Not like Pompey or Plymouth. Scrubbers with twenty kinds of diseases. All provided for: berth, food, grog. Hardly spent a shilling. Money in the bank when I got home. What did I do with it? Got married, that's what I did with it. Stupid fool. At my age, too.

Then went and volunteered again. How daft was that! Once bitten.... To get away from the house? Nappies all over. Kids crying, wife screaming, neighbours twitching their curtains, rent man always at the door. What to stay home for? After Dunkirk they'd take anybody. Especially the navy. 'Our last line of defence.' Not like the first show, keeping the Hun in, now keeping the Jerries out. And a commission, full lieutenant.

God, the ward room hated that! Upstart from the streets. Bad grammar. Drinks rum, not gin like us chaps. Can't keep a polite tongue in his head. I treated them like the lowest deckie. They knew less than deckies. Straight out of public school. Weekend yachtsmen. Never pulled a hawser, never fired a shot in anger. I hadn't until

Murmansk. Shell cases up to my knees. Junker 88s swarming like gnats. Buzzing in from every direction. Watch the torpedo train! Hard a starboard!

Exhausted. Attacks day and night. No. No night. June sun never goes down. Desperate. Signal officers on the guns. First lieutenant with his arm hanging off. Captain going crazy. Quoting poetry. In Latin! I'm on watch. Listen, he said. This is us, pulling into port:

> "With hoary frost begrimed, each hoary head
> strikes the astonished gazer's soul with dread."

That's us. Scare the kids in the street. And us, scared weeks at a time. Things going bang in the white night.

Grandma said never to be afraid of noises in the night. Foxes, she said. Hunting owls. What you can't see won't hurt you. True in Boxwood among the bluebells. Silent here is the U boat. Bangs in the night are torpedoes striking, the bomb's near miss, if we are lucky. A Polish ship, escaped from the Russians, now ferrying back ammunition to their old enemy. Never saw what hit them. Bomb or torpedo straight to the hold. She went up in an instant. Flames so high they disappeared into the cloud. Cloud? Must have been a sub. Cloud to low for flyers. We never found even a body. All blasted, all roasted, all drowned.

How did Williams go? I remember we met, late one night on the Clyde. A low drinking den grandma would have called it. He was from Yarmouth, he said. Recognised my accent immediately. Down the end of my street, I said. Thirty-mile street, he said. A pretty boy. What, nineteen, twenty? Been on trawlers since he was twelve. Less schooling than me, superb on deck. Got drunk together. Shipped out on the same convoy, PQ something or other. An early one. A milk run.

Hung around together on shore leave at Scapa. Can't let the Captain know. 'Associating with other ranks.' Enough to lose my commission. I don't care. Been 'other ranks' all my life. Who cares in the navy about a bit of bum now and again. He was sweet. Kinder, more gentle than my wife. Turtle doves we were.

'My turtle dove', that's what grandma used to call me, as if I could sing or had any feathers to preen. Tried to keep me in her cage, away from the old man. Williams and me, we had no cages. We lived in tenements in Glasgow. Rooms his friends left vacant when they were away at sea, escort duty from the States. Those old rattle-ships I used to laugh at back in '17, now saving us from starvation after the army let us down. Stay in bed all day. Out at night in civvies. Always the right sort of club in any city if you know where to look, have contacts.

'Ship out with me.' I said.

'No,' he said, 'you'd give the game away. Smile at me, give me easy duties. Call me darling like you do ashore. Subterfuge,' he said. 'Careless talk costs lives.' We laugh. We laugh all of the time.

I made sure we shipped out on the same convoy. PQ12. Mid winter. Ice, snow, gales. That's when the '*Astarta*' tipped over. Too much wind and cloud for planes. Too dark for U boats. No moon to silhouette us against. Rye bread and vodka in Murmansk watching the women unload the merchantmen. Underfed, covered in snow, working like Trojans. Where are the men, I asked? At the front, they said, fighting the fascists. Great Patriotic War, they called it. Patriotic they were. No war is great.

Back on the Clyde Williams and I got drunk on vodka. Laughed all day. Made love all night. The Commodore assigned him to a freighter. Signaller and gunner, firing a Lewis gun off one of the bulkheads. Couldn't hit a battleship at ten paces like that. Back of one of the lines. Chugged along as if its boilers would burst. We fussed around on the periphery. Close escort. Sub spotting. Keeping the chicks in order.

Grandma kept chicks. When they hatched she let me pick them up. Tiny bundles of fluff. Squeaking for their mother. Not that she cared. Or their father either. Like mine. Don't hold them too tight she would tell me. Stroke them. Gently. Speak to them soft. I spoke soft to Williams, stroked him. Smoothed his hair. Was mother, father to him. And lover.

His old tub didn't last long. Engine trouble. Dropped out of the line. Headed for safety in Iceland. Making all of three knots. No ship to spare from convoy escort. Left to her own devices. Never arrived in Iceland. A couple of empty lifeboats. We will know some day. After the war. I will never know.

The pain is back. Not the pain that disappears with morphine. The pain of loss. Losing the girl in Earlsford, losing grandma, maybe even losing the children. Not my wife. Losing Williams most of all. The pain of losing my legs, maybe. I still have not checked. What do I care, I shall never need them. I would give them gladly to have sweet Williams back again. He hated that: 'sweet Williams'. Worse even than '*Dahlia*', he said. Some simpering little girl.' He never simpered. Rough, some would call him. We both are. Both were.

Heard nothing of him until just before we left Arkhangelsk. Non arrival in Iceland. Five other ships sunk or missing. '*Edinburgh*' in dire straights. Destroyers and cruisers to her aid. '*Dahlia*' left with assorted trawlers to shepherd home the empty freighters. Caught in a storm of Stukas, whistling in like dervishes. Bomb straight down our funnel. I'm fifty feet up in the air, clothes in shreds. Hair burned down to the scalp. Landed on the forecastle. Land in the sea I'd be dead now. Dead soon in any case.

Eyes open. That ceiling was white. Grey now. A sea mist? Not in the sick bay. Not a grey mist. The flint walls of the church at Boxwood. Solid. Welcoming. Come home it says. Rest with me. Grandma is here, waiting for you. We all welcome you. Back where you belong. I am coming. I will be with you in a moment. I need the rest.

There lies a single stone memorial in the graveyard at St Wandrede. 'Died of his wounds. His name liveth for ever more.' The weeds and nettles have grown thick around the stone. Wind and water are beginning to erode the inscription. B52s fly in formation overhead on their way to enforce liberty and freedom.

YESTERDAY

Death

'Will your dad miss it?'

'No, of course he won't. It's mum's really. She needed some for a posh cake she made at Christmas. The off licence didn't have a miniature so she had to buy a full bottle, then only used a thimbleful. There's more or less the whole lot left. And I've got some plastic cups and a packet of wholemeal biscuits. We will need some food or we won't be able to crawl back.'

'You're lucky. My mum never cooks things like that. With Dad put away there's no money for cakes or little else. Pretty quiet at home, which is good. At least they are not screaming at one another of the time, her telling him to get a job and him yelling at her to get off his back 'cos he's bringing in more money than she is. And drinking and gambling most of it away.'

'How come he has any money at all? I thought he was on the dole?' The taller of the two lads swung his rucksack over his shoulder, the bottle inside clinking against the buckles on the straps.

His companion shrugged, his bony shoulders jagged inside a worn shirt. 'That's what he's in for, ain't it. TADA, taking and driving away they call it. He was lucky. Cops stopped him for speeding on that straight bit outside the village. Doing ninety he was. He could have made a run for it like they do in the movies but he stopped. Said he was out on a joy ride, took the car for fun. They couldn't

197

prove otherwise but I know what he was up to. He has a deal going with one of the mechanics at the scrap yard. Dad nicks the cars and his mate switches all the identification over from some old banger he's bought. Gives it a respray to make the colours match and sells it on; under the counter, like.'

'Don't the buyers get suspicious?'

'Of course they do, but they don't care. If you can get a Mercedes for fifteen grand when the list price is over thirty, why should you care where it came from? All the paperwork is in order and the engine numbers match, if a little bit scratched about. That's why he let the cops stop him. If they'd followed him to the garage they would have rumbled the whole thing and both him and his mate would be in for a fiver instead of the six months he's got now. He'll get his tag soon and be back shouting and screaming at home again and puking all over the front yard. He's disgusting my dad. No way I'm going to end up like him, in and out of the nick, in and out of the bookies, cops at the door all the time.'

'At least you get allowed out of the door without an inquest: where are you going, how are you going to get there, who are you going with, when will you be back, what are you doing while you're out? You'd think I was a spy.'

'Or a juvenile delinquent.' added his friend with a grin. ' What does your mum say about you hanging about with me?'

'She says you're a bad influence, The whole family nothing but criminals and diddicoys. Not that we are much better. Granddad was always ready with some pheasants, in season and out, until his leg got bad. They say his grandfather was shot for desertion in the great war. And what have my parents got to be snotty about, beavering away for the insurance company in some dreary office? That's not for me, either. I'm off to medical school when I leave. Bags of money in that. I'll qualify then scoot off to America. Doctors make millions over there. And all the pretty nurses fall over themselves for a handsome doctor.'

'No good for you then, if it's the handsome ones they go for.' The two boys pushed and shoved one another about, oblivious to the growing wheat they trampled underfoot. Responsible dog walkers had kept themselves and their charges severely to the edges of the field, the last before having to turn in the face of a herd of milking cows. Curious cattle had been known in the past to crowd and injure walkers, especially when aroused by prancing dogs. Now only the brave ventured across their grazing territory.

Jake, the aspiring doctor, held open the barbed wire to allow Duane to struggle through. Passing over the valuable bag he followed after, Duane doing the honours for him, Jake careful not to snag his new tee shirt on the wire. The shirt itself had gone unwashed since he had bought it at Glastonbury the previous year, signed by all four members of the band in what might be either feint ink or a home made stencil.

They stood together for a while, surveying the field. 'Look over there,' said Jake. 'See that line of earth? That's where the village main street used to be, off to the north of the church. Then those other lines are side roads leading off it.'

'Not much of a village, was it?' sneered Duane. 'Three streets and a church. These dips in the ground look like they might have been ponds at one time, but only the one towards the main road has any water in it. Not much fun living here. No wonder they pulled down the manor house. Who wants to live in a deserted village, miles from town? It's bad enough now, waiting hours for the bus, no cinema, no gigs except in pubs which won't let us in and no decent jobs. I'll come to America with you, even if I can't pick up a pretty nurse. Maybe you'll lend me one?'

'The Americans won't let you in unless you find a job first. They are desperate for doctors but I don't think there are many vacancies for scrumpers and poachers.'

'You sound like your old man,' Duane replied, 'preaching on about getting your exams and working hard at school, locking up your games player until you can show him you've finished your homework.'

'A good job I only let on to half the homework we have or we'd never get on it.'

'Must admit that's good of you.' Duane cursed as his foot slipped, picking up a dollop of manure from a wet cow pat. 'I just wish you wouldn't tell him I come over so you can help me with my school work. It makes me seem a right dumbo. A peasant or the village idiot. He'll be looking to see if I have six fingers next. You know it's a mutual arrangement. You have the words and the spelling but you'd be in the bottom set for maths if it weren't for me.'

'And I don't get the point of botany and you don't get the point of history.'

'Not the sort of history we do at school, all those boring kings and queens. This here is different. Our many-great grand-parents might have farmed these fields or be buried in the churchyard.'

'Little chance of us finding out about burials,' Jake said as they picked their way through another set of barbed wire into the churchyard. 'None of these tombstones have a date earlier than the late nineteenth century. Even they have been eroded into near invisibility. Our many-great grandparents lie there unmarked 'as if they had never been' as it says in the hymn. Can't see a Howell or a Wenn anywhere around. A couple of Hailwoods behind the railings and that's about it.'

Duane Wenn traced the lettering on a more modern stone. 'Died in defence of his country, 1943,' he said. 'Not much to say about a man once he's dead and gone. At least this one is well maintained.'

'A war grave,' explained Jake Howell, 'the war graves commission pays someone to clean it up twice a year, cut out the nettles and thistles. Wish they'd do the rest of the graves while they are at it. We can't sit out here, we'd get stung to death. Let's see if we can get into the church.'

Crushing nettles and tired daffodils beneath their feet they crossed the graveyard towards the church porch.

'Someone in there,' whispered Duane. 'What do you think: the vicar, a funeral or just some nosey parker?'

'We could nip round the back, wait until they go away. Don't want anyone seeing us here. You know what it's like in the village, make a move and all the lace curtains start twitching. If I farted in the street, my mum would know about it before I got home.'

'All right for you. Anyone sees me around after dark and there's a county wide police alert and a copper waiting on my doorstep.'

'No wonder,' joked Jake. 'If it's after dark you're probably up to no good anyway.'

'Not me, mate. Pure as the driven snow. You'll not find me in the Britannia prison alongside my old man. I'm off to America with you, remember. Quietly, now. Let's see what's going on. Leave your bag behind the yew tree; it makes a noise and will get in the way if we have to run for it. We can always come back for it later.'

The sound from inside the porch rose in volume, peculiarly regular in tone. Duane crept as near as he dared, squatted down to spy inside. With a grin on his face he beckoned Jake over, signalled him to squat beside him, pointed over to the church.

A girl leant over against the inner door, a silky skirt rolled up to her hips, black lace top pushed up to her shoulder blades. Behind her stood a man, skimpy grey hair, pinstripe suit trousers around his ankles, pumping away at her, puffing and panting like an ageing steam train. Now and again he paused, reaching out for her breasts as if to refresh himself at their touch for another bout of exercise.

Jake giggled, part in excitement, part in embarrassment.

'Shush,' whispered Duane, 'they'll hear you.'

'Why has she got her fists clenched?' demanded Jake. 'Is he hurting her?'

'I'll tell you later. Move back now, he's finishing.'

The boys retreated to the shelter of the old yew tree. The man appeared at the porch entrance, threw something to the ground, stooped to pull up his underpants and trousers, wiggling gently in an effort to fit in his still part-engorged penis beneath the elastic. Slowly, head down, he walked off towards the entrance gate and an expensive German car parked beyond.

The girl followed, pausing to wipe between her legs with a tissue, which she threw into the hedgerow. Without a word she let herself into the passenger seat next to the driver. Carefully the man manoeuvred the car along the overgrown loke, turning in the direction of the main road.

'That's not something you see every day,' said Jake, emerging from the shadow of the tree. 'At least not in real life and not in a church.'

'I've heard stories about this one,' said Duane. 'Something my mum let drop to Gran. I think she and my dad came up here from time to time when they were courting. A regular lovers' lane it used to be. Now you know where to come when you start pulling those pretty nurses.'

'Not me. I'm all for a comfortable bed, with tea and toast brought in the next morning. Now, tell me, what was the thing about the fists? I thought she was going to turn round and hit him, thought maybe that turned him on.'

'You've been reading the wrong sort of magazines. She had her hands closed because that's where she keeps her money. Nowhere else for it. Just wearing a skirt and a top, no underwear, no pockets anywhere. Couple of johnnies tucked in the waistband of her skirt is all. When she gets back to town she'll drop the money from this job at home or hand it over to her pimp, then back on the street again.'

'Oh.' The thought of a financial transaction had never entered Jake's mind. 'But did you see who it was? That's Stephie who was head girl last year.'

'And got kicked out at Easter,' continued Duane. 'We all thought she was in the club. Remember? Frankie says she was kicked out for selling stuff on school premises. The Head had it hushed up, refused to call the police for fear of worrying the parents and losing his job.'

'That makes sense.' Jake nodded. 'We got some ecstasy off her at Glastonbury last year. The real stuff, not the coloured aspirins other people were selling. A pity she left, I always fancied her.'

'Did you see her tits swinging?' Duane's eyes sparkled salaciously. 'Like long, soft lemons.'

'Melons,' corrected Jake. 'I need a drink after the floor show. Can we get inside, or do we have to sit on the benches in the porch.'

Duane winked. 'Stick by me, mate. I'll show you a thing or two. Watch out!'

Jake skidded, almost fell. Looked with disgust at the discarded condom beneath his feet. 'He must have had one hell of a prick on him, that guy. Look how long this thing is.'

'Don't be silly. They stretch; all that pushing about and hanging on to her fanny when he pulls it out. Probably only half that size. Watch. You might learn something.' Duane pulled a Swiss army knife from his pocket. 'Not just for taking boy scouts out of horse's hooves, you know.'

He opened the built-in screwdriver and set to work on the fastening which bolted shut the strong wooden door. 'The proper lock has been broken for years. No-one has bothered to have it replaced. Too difficult to renovate the original one, too expensive to take it off and replace it with a new one. Here we go.'

The padlock hung listlessly from its fastening, detached from the wooden frame. Jake gave the door a push, smiling as it swung back to reveal the shadowy church behind. 'Nice little place,' he said. 'Pity the door to the tower is locked. No silly padlock this time but the real thing. There's some more Hailwoods on the plaques up there. Children, those two. Surrounded by angels and putti.'

'What the hell are putti?' demanded Duane.

'Those silly little baby things. You see them all the time in old paintings, holding up the sky, carrying jewels or merely hanging about. Pure decoration. A waste of time.'

'I don't know,' said Duane, looking more carefully. 'They make the monument so much sadder, what with them being children and all. Have you seen this?' He indicated a stone at knee height set into the tower behind the font. 'William of Dunwich, 1272'. I wonder what the story is behind that? Do you know who the Phillipons were? There's at least three gravestones on the floor with their names on. Fifteen something this one.'

Duane ambled around the small church, carefully studying the monuments while Jake emptied his rucksack onto the front pew. A bottle of Budgen's best brandy and a pack of their own brand wholemeal biscuits. He half filled two plastic cups with brandy, taking a sip for himself as he did so.

'I've been thinking about Stephie Rudd,' he said. 'What's a lovely girl like that doing selling herself to all and sundry? It's not like her family is short of money, is it? Your lot don't have two pennies to rub together but your sister never ended up on the game.'

'She was lucky,' Duane confided. 'Got a few exams behind her, managed to land a supervisor's course at the supermarket where she worked at weekends. Did well, moved up. Most important, got away from my old man. Works hard, has fun of an evening, has her own flat. She says I can share it with her if the old man throws me out when he comes out the nick. Steph, she got into bad company, I suppose. If she was selling you ecstasy she must have got it from some supplier. Probably moved her on to harder stuff. Reckon she needs the money to keep up her habit. Won't be young and pretty for ever. See what happens to her then.'

'Come on. This is the most miserable conversation I've had all week. And I'm getting cold sitting here.'

'Don't fret.' The pensive Duane, still on his feet before one of the marble plaques, turned into the space beneath the tower. Vigorously he heaved out a metal construction even taller than him, like an overgrown sack barrow, the wheels squeaking in protest.

'Give me a hand,' he ordered, indicating a four foot tall gas canister. Together the two lads hoisted it onto its trolley, moved it into the space in front of the altar between the transepts. Deftly Duane connected the container to a giraffe-like mobile heater, checking all fastenings were tightly screwed down.

'Did this for a couple of times for old Gedge. He was trying to make his fortune rearing pheasants. Had a whole load of pheasant eggs in an old barn. Needed to keep them warn so they hatched out. He used a couple of these things, but he was so tight he wouldn't keep them on all the time. The moment they hatched out he turned the heating off. There was a sharp frost and the chicks froze to death. It's what my gran says: you only get out as much as you put in.'

'Like those roof beams,' said Jake. 'Should have been solid oak, not the pine they used. Another couple of years and they'll need replacing. Don't see anyone putting any money into them.'

'I wouldn't mind doing it,' said Duane thoughtfully. 'Maybe I could make a living repairing old churches, carving pew ends, restoring statues, replacing roof beams.'

'Hundreds of people can do that. Skilled, I don't deny, but where is the career progression? You are just as smart as me. Look how good you are at maths and physics. Pity about the history. You could really make something of yourself, be a teacher or a banker.'

'Pray god not a banker! And I don't feel like dealing with squalling brats for the rest of my days. Fancy having to but up with kids like Elvis Much all day long? Perhaps if I put a bit more effort into the history I could get an apprenticeship on a restoration course. I have to do something practical, not sit in an office in front of a computer screen.'

'If you went to university you could be an architect or an archaeologist.'

'What? Digging up old bones, like a grave digger? Bugger, the heater's gone off. Gas tank must have been almost empty.'

'Not sure about that,' said Jake. 'Look at the tube, it's rotted through. Can't you smell the gas? Best turn it off before it blows us to smithereens.'

The practical Duane was not happy to have missed an obvious defect. He took a strong gulp of the brandy in his cup, refilling it from the depleted bottle. 'It's bloody cold without it,' he muttered. 'What we need is a good fire.'

'In here? There's no chimney or anything.'

'Don't worry about it. There's no cloth or materials and the flooring is old clay tiles. Clear a big space so there's nothing to catch and we'll be as snug as a bug in a rug, as my Gran used to say.'

'Your Gran used to say a lot. Okay, I'll grab some twigs and fallen branches, then we can get nice and cosy. Don't drink all the brandy while I'm gone.'

Rather than address himself to the brandy Duane made a further tour of the church. It wasn't spectacular, but that was its charm. Large enough for a hundred people at a push it retained a domestic feel, like the corrugated church hall in Earlsford which still housed the village nursery. He shivered. Perhaps it was geese flying over his grave or the ghosts risen from the churchyard infiltrating through the walls. Maybe one day he would come back, excavate the past, find the Anglo-Saxon church that some said had been here, find where the two Hailwood children were buried, even locate his own ancestors, the bowls they cooked in, the plates they ate from.

'Tons of the stuff,' cried Jake, entering with arms full of dry branches. 'Should keep us warm for a while. Fancy a top up?' He poured a couple more inches into each cup.

Duane cleared a wide space, carefully building a pile of kindling which took immediately. He piled on larger and larger boughs until he had a substantial blaze, enough to keep them warm even on this chill early May evening.

For a while the pair chatted amiably about school and home, parents and teachers, the girls they fancied and speculation about who was 'doing it' with whom. Magically the bottle emptied itself. The fire died down to a few embers.

'I have to be getting home,' said Jake. 'Better be off before they send out a search party. Imagine if they found us here!'

'Fine for you. Your parents would just say you've been lured into bad habits by unruly elements that ought to be locked up. My mum won't send out a search party but she'd be worried I'm up to no good if I'm out too late. Nicking stuff from the chemists to sell at school like poor Stephie or finding an unattended Mercedes for my dad's mate. Suppose we'd better go.'

Unsteadily they got to their feet. Duane looked around for water to douse down the remains of the fire. No mains gas, no electricity, no water this far from the main road; what few church services there were, held by candle light. He shrugged, attended to the main door, screwing back the hinge as tight as he could in order to keep out undesirables and Stephie Rudd's clients.

A steady breeze had forced its way in from the coast. The boys walked closer together to shelter one another from its effects. 'Have you got any history books?' Duane asked. 'Not school books, interesting ones. How people lived in the past, what they ate, what their working lives were like. People from round here, not city folk or posh folk in castles. People like my Gran, you know? I fancy that archaeology lark, restoring old buildings, finding out where we all came from. Like my dad I could specialise in prisons, but from the outside, not the inside.'

They giggled drunkenly, arms round one another's shoulders.

Behind them light flickered in the church windows, fanned by the stiffening breeze. They staggered on to the outskirts of Earlsford, too far to hear the explosion as the fire reached the gas canister and blew the roof from the church tower. 'Wow, look at that! Awesome!' cried Jake and Duane together as two fire engines thundered through the sleeping village, lights flashing and klaxons blaring.

FUTURE

'Isn't it sad, all these old churches sitting about in the middle of fields, going to wrack and ruin. The ones in towns are not so bad; now they are arts centres and architects' offices but out here there's no congregation and no-one to look after them.'

'There are plenty of trusts and charities to do that, keep them in working order, make sure the grass is cut. Anyway, if we don't need them, why bother? Knock the lot down and build something useful on top, a housing development or an industrial estate. They will be more use to the locals than a pile of old stones or a crumbling chapel.'

'You don't really mean that.' She knew her husband was always ready to take an unpopular position, just for the sake of the argument. Her fault for marrying a man with a philosophy degree.

'Perhaps I don't, but how many derelict churches have we seen this week? Shouldn't they be put to better use? Remember what that vicar said to us yesterday, that the diocese was about to permanently close twenty churches, just leave them to rot and fester. Ridiculous.

'Now we are retired and the children have left home we should be thinking about where we are going to spend the rest of our days. I know you want to move to France but I don't speak the language and I'm not moving more than a day's drive from Addenbrooke's hospital. Staying on in a five bedroom Victorian pile which is difficult to heat and maintain is sheer waste. We can't afford it and there are plenty of people with growing families who would love it.'

'Yes,' he said warily, aware that an argument is likely to be lost once one agrees to one's opponent's first premise.

'Neither of us fancy a country cottage with miniature windows and restricted head height. We want somewhere small, easy to maintain and with a bit of distinction.'

'Yes.' He concluded all was now lost. Perhaps he should divert her into a discussion of what they were to have for dinner.

'I think we should take on one of those churches, turn it into a home. Put in solar panels and a wood burner, a bore hole for water and its own septic tank. Be off grid and completely self-sufficient. No more of those annoying bills.'

'We could stop off at the King's Head for supper instead of cooking at home.'

'Most of the churches here have stained glass and high windows you can't see out of. I'm sure Historic England would force us to repair them with traditional materials. Ruinously expensive.'

'Quite. The new chef has a fine line in roast venison and pheasant in a Muscat sauce. You loved it last time we were there.'

'So we need a church which has plain windows at a level we can see out of. And plenty of natural light, of course. St Wandrede is ideal. No-one can possibly object to us rescuing it from oblivion.'

'The one that burnt down! You can not be serious! Historic England will never agree. Even the nice man from the university we met there will object, not to mention the county planning committee. Besides, there is no roof, the north gable has collapsed, the driveway is a sea of mud and the churchyard is six feet high in nettles. You can't expect me to be clearing that at my age.'

'We'll get a man in, darling. Your nephew can draw up the plans. Open plan ground floor, a couple of bedrooms upstairs, massive double height glass door on the north transept leading out into the churchyard for the summer. Then, imagine how cosy it will be in the winter, curled up around the wood burner.'

'Blazing away fuelled by builders' bills and letters of objection to the local authority.'

'We'll talk about it over dinner. I think I will go for the venison this time and a nice bottle of Fleurie to help it down. What's your nephew's mobile number?'

BIBLIOGRAPHY

Given the scope of this book, around 1300 years, a full bibliography would be a large compendium in its own right. What follows is a selection which the general reader might find interesting.

Marc Morris: *'The Norman Conquest.'*
John Hatcher: *'The Black Death 1345-1350.'*
Blair Worden: *'The English Civil Wars 1640-1660.'*
Diane Purkiss: *'The English Civil War, a people's history.'*
Chambers and Mingay: *'The Agricultural Revolution 1750-1880.'*
Jose Harris: *'Private lives, public spirit: Britain 1870-1914.'*
B.B.Schofield: *'The Russian Convoys.'*
Michael G.Walling: *'Forgotten Sacrifice: The arctic convoys of World War ii.'*

Nun Macrina (trans.): *'The **Vita Prima** of Saint Wandregesilius.'*

ABOUT THE AUTHOR

Tony Warner has lived and worked in Norfolk for over forty years. Originally from Grimsby, he read Philosophy at Warwick University. He also has a degree in Art History from the University of East Anglia and was for many years the art critic for the 'Eastern Daily Press' as well as writing for many regional and national arts publications. His previous book 'Vincent and Pablo: the revised version' centres on the imaginary meeting of Vincent van Gogh and Pablo Picasso in Brixton in 1900.

He lists his favourite occupation as 'watching paint dry.'

THE ILLUSTRATIONS

The line drawings are by Zheni Maslarova Warner, after the roof bosses of Norwich Cathedral.